Charles Skinner

Myths and legends beyond our borders

Charles Skinner

Myths and legends beyond our borders

ISBN/EAN: 9783337198152

Printed in Europe, USA, Canada, Australia, Japan

Cover: Foto ©Andreas Hilbeck / pixelio.de

More available books at **www.hansebooks.com**

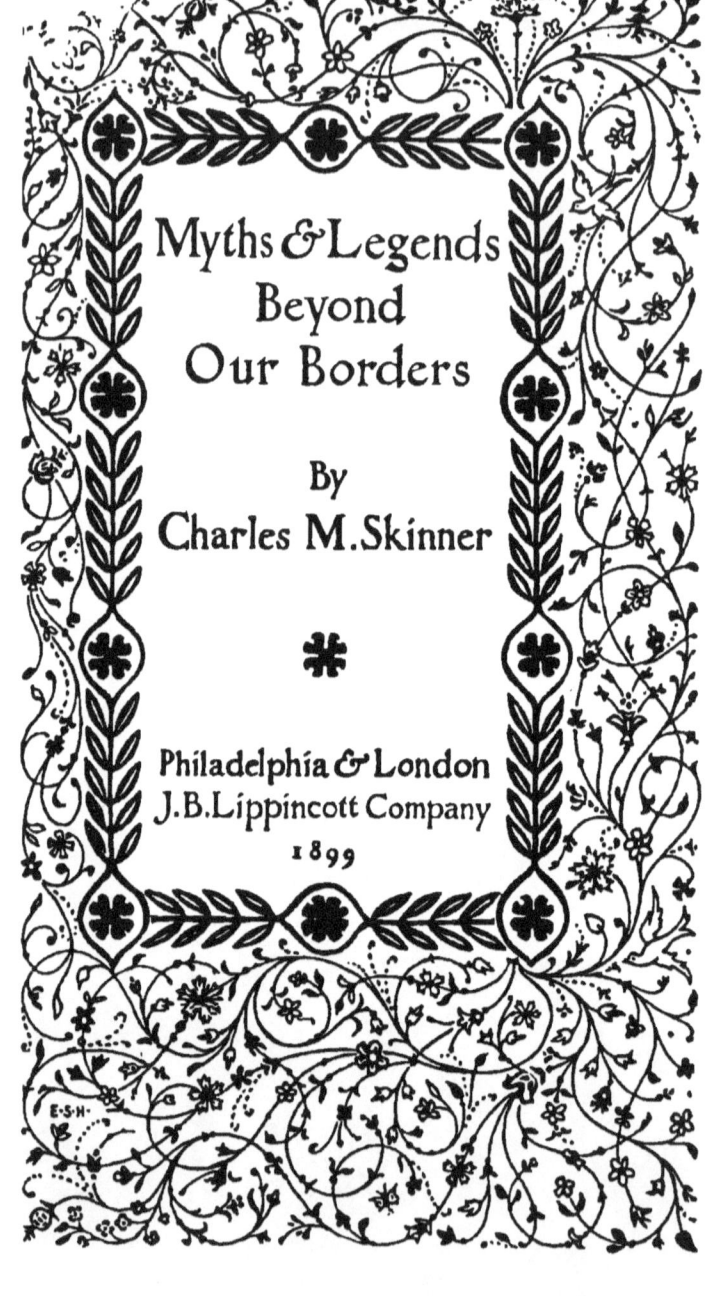

Myths & Legends Beyond Our Borders

By

Charles M. Skinner

Philadelphia & London
J.B. Lippincott Company
1899

SHE TO WHOM I OFFER THESE LEGENDS
IS IN HER ART SO CONVINCING, SO
POETIC, IN HER LIFE SO KIND, THAT I
HESITATE TO PRESENT A WORK THAT
MIGHT VEX HER BY ITS FAULTS. YET
IN HER CHARITY I KNOW SHE WILL
NOT LOOK FOR THEM. HENCE, I
DEDICATE THIS BOOK TO MAUD

Myths and Legends
Beyond Our Borders

Preface

THE kind reception given to the author's book of legends pertaining to the United States has been an incentive to continue the work in the same field, and herewith is offered a volume of tradition from Canada and Mexico, thus covering the North American continent. A need of brevity has made it advisable to keep to the method followed in " Myths and Legends of Our Own Land," of assembling traditions that attach to places, rather than attempting to set forth the almost exhaustless, always verbose, and sometimes childish folk-lore of the aborigines. Simple people, red people, and habitants, not readers, not logicians, not examiners, accept these tales from their old men and treasure them. Others may find amusement in them, and perhaps profit; for, ingenuous as they are, they sometimes symbolize high truths.

Table of Contents

Canada

9

Contents

Contents

Mexico

Contents

Illustrations

Canada

Myths and Legends Beyond
Our Borders

EXPLORERS AND ABORIGINES

CANADA, from its earliest settlement, has been
to most white Americans a dark, cool land
of mystery. Only since its railroads joined East
and West together, since the frontier settlements of
the last generation developed into cities, since the
farming districts of the prairie began to draw their
hardy populace from older lands, has it become
known to our southern millions that it is a country differing in little from their own, the same in
speech and spirit, akin in laws and faith and manners. The history of the republic and that of the
colony were the same down to the time of the Revolution, yet Canada's northern position, its settlement by the French, the individuality of its native
tribes, its exploration by missionaries, its imagined
remoteness, gave rise to tales that, while not verified, had reason for being. The history of the
province is full of romance. The legends that
have grown from it compel the attention no more
than the tales of conquest, diplomacy, daring, and
difficulty, and those new reports of wealth on the

Yukon. Many of the unwritten tales run counter to record, others so merge in it that it is impossible to separate them, but, as they have character, romance, humor, or quaintness, they deserve to be saved from the assaults of commercialism and commonplace.

Long before the time of Cabot, Cartier, Roberval, Champlain, and Hudson, Canada was known, in Norse tradition, and it is claimed that Basque and Breton fishermen caught cod on the Grand Banks a century before Columbus's day. Canada was the first part of America to be discovered, and Bjarne Herjulfsson, son of an Icelander who had moved to Greenland, reached Cape Breton in the year 986, while trying to join his father in his new home. Fourteen years later Leif Ericsson, son of the Icelandic jarl, Eric the Red, tried to find this new land. It is not known exactly where he went ashore, but Labrador was first sighted: Helluland, he called it; "a country of no advantages." Next he passed Markland, with its flat beaches and its woods: Nova Scotia? And Vinland, which is any place you please, was last explored. Somewhere, possibly on the Penobscot, was the city of crystal and silver, Norumbega, Norombega, Norumbeque, and maybe Aranbega, Arambek, and Lorembek. Newfoundland, oldest of the British colonies, was one of the first regions that seemed to promise wealth, for it did not take the explorers long to find that its waters swarmed with fish. Indeed, the

Beyond Our Borders

Portuguese name of Bacalhaos, long borne by New-foundland, means codfish. Nor was Labrador without its promise in the eyes of those same Portuguese, for the name, which is in their tongue, means laborer. (It is not Le Bras d'Or, the arm of gold, for Cape Breton has its Bras d'Or.) "King Emanuel, having heard of the high trees growing in the northern countries, and having seen the aborigines, who appeared so well qualified for labor, thought he had found a new slave-coast like that which he owned in Africa, and dreamed of the tall masts he would cut and the men-of-war he would build from the forests." Mistaken man! The power of the Latin races in North America was brief, and it left few marks in comparison with that of the Anglo Saxons who so soon possessed the land and who almost alone have made it what it is. Though racked by frequent wars in those dark times, the country advanced a little after every struggle, and the builders of air-castles, the founders of visionary empires, were jostled aside if they loitered in the way of progress.

The Indians themselves throw little light on their own history, and if facts were originally embodied in their fantastic myths, the forms of these parables have in almost every case concealed the meanings. That in the days of unwritten history there were great political and military movements there is no doubt,—movements that to the red dwellers in this land were as momentous as the wars and changes in Europe were to the Greeks and Romans. We have reason to believe that men existed here long before the last of the North American glaciers, and that they were driven toward the warm belt by its advance; that there are relations between the Alaskans and the Aztecs; that the Canadian Indians drove the mound-builders southward six hundred years ago. The "great horned snake" of Ontario, against which they battled, may have been the snake-shaped forts of these mound-makers, like those remaining in the Ohio Valley. Their man-god, Michabo, or Hiawatha, "drives the serpents to the south." On Moose Mountain, Assiniboia, are cairns with lines of stones radiating from them, the early work of mound-builders, or imitations of it by their conquerors, who relate that the stones were placed there by the spirit of the winds.

Various theories as to the origin of the Indians account for them (1) as autochthonous, or self-created: a legitimate theory, since the geologic age of this country qualifies it to have been not merely the original land of the Indians, but the cradle of the human race; (2) as members of the lost tribes of Israel; (3) as survivors of the sunken continent of Atlantis; (4) as Phœnicians; (5) as Carthaginians; (6) as Greeks; (7) as Chinese, who reached these shores in 458 A.D.; and (8) as Mongols, who arrived in the thirteenth century. The latter theory, which would have assumed the peopling of a vast continent in a couple of hundred years, is of course absurd, but an identity of certain Canadian and certain Asiatic tribes is at least suggested by likeness in their beliefs and customs, such as their tribal work and government, traditions, religious faiths, superstitions, way of regarding women, treatment of guests, sacrifices, burials, funerals, the wearing of feathers, use of bark utensils, form of weapons, dog feasts, games, emblems, pipe-smoking, serpent-worship, serpent-charming, sacred animals, dances, figures of oratory, and monosyllabic speech. In their free, sane life the physical adequacy of the Indians should have been maintained, and there is no reason to suppose that as a family they have deteriorated, in spite of the allegation that in the Ontario government park, at Rondeau, Lake Erie, the skeletons of well-proportioned men seven and one-half feet high have been unearthed. The later history of the red race is too familiar to recount, and it is most sad. When some royal commissioners in eastern Canada had the audacity to ask a native chief what claim his people had to the country, he replied only, "There lie our grandfathers; there lie our fathers; there lie our children." To the first settlers the idea that the savage could be a creature of sentiment was preposterous, and that he should wish to hold his ancestral woods and fields no less so. Bitter has been the strife that has driven him from his old estate. He is an outcast in his own land, a victim of wrongs uncounted and cruelties as dire as those with which he has retaliated on the aggressors.

But he is not what so many have painted him. In many of his traditions it will be seen that he has a moral sense as keen as any one's, and courage to live to it; that he is a man.

MYTHS OF CREATION, HEAVEN, AND HELL

BELIEFS touching death, the spirit-world, and the hereafter vary with the different tribes of Canada, and some of them have undergone change from contact with missionaries. Often the merging-point of the old and the new belief is impossible to descry, while in the case of the teacher who came across the Pacific in a copper canoe, preached morality to the shore tribes, was crucified, arose, resumed preaching, and was afterward obeyed, we find a blending of the Christ history and the Hiawatha legend.

The Nootkas in their version of this tale do not include either crucifixion or resurrection. On the contrary, they assume that the killing of the teacher was a good thing, because they secured his copper canoe and paddles, and the use of copper they learned at that time. Some of the great wooden images in their houses represent this teacher who promised a future life. Sheets of copper with eyes painted on them have been seen at Fort Rupert, and are thought to symbolize the sun. They are regarded with peculiar reverence.

Beyond Our Borders

In a Chippewayan legend the first country was that through which the Copper-Mine River flows, and the ground was strewn with copper. A bird created this country,—a vast bird whose glance was lightning, and thunder the shaking of his wings. He created the earth by touching the primal ocean. The first men wore out their feet with walking and their throats with eating.

Some pretty traditions have grown from the implanting of a new faith in imaginative soil. The loose quartz crystals found near Quebec are said to be Christ's tears, wept upon the earth for the sins of its people. The northern lights, which among ungospelled tribes are the spirits of dead friends dancing, the brighter the merrier, have turned to angels, throwing down snow to cool the parched in hell. An Indian who was discovered on all-fours in a wood near Wardsville, moving softly over the snow, was at first suspected of mischief; but he was only waiting to see the deer fall on their knees before the Great Spirit, as he had heard they did on Christmas night.

Biblical teaching and native myth are queerly mixed in the Ojibway tale of the beginning of the race, which they say occurred at Torch Lake, or Lac du Flambeau. The Great Spirit had made the vegetation about this water, and was surprised when he saw a creature wallowing through the reeds in the form since taken by men, but covered with shining scales like a fish. This object went mooning about in such a mournful fashion that the Manitou, taking pity on him, made a woman, also covered with scales, and breathed life into her. He told her to wander by the shore, and presently she would find something she would be sure to like. The man found her while she slept, and, rousing her, took her to walk, showing where roots and herbs grew that were good for food. Her name, she told him, was Mani (Mary?). He took her to his spacious lodge and went with her through his garden, warning her not to eat fruit from a certain tree that grew there. When she was alone, a handsome young Indian emerged mysteriously from the tree and urged her to pick and eat the fruit, adding that it made fine preserves. She ate, and persuaded her husband to do the same. The scales fell from their bodies, and they drew back among the bushes in shame. Then Gitche Manitou drove them away, so that they could no longer eat fruits, but had to live on meat. In his wandering the first man found a great book that began speaking to him. It told him to do so many things that he could not remember half of them, and he threw it away, whereupon he found on the earth a book in sign language that covered only two squares of bark. This sign-book gave no laws, but told much about foods and remedies, so that in a few years his children became not only hunters but medicine-men. Manitou repented his anger and restored the people to his

love again, ordering his own son, or agent, Manibozho, to make a paradise for them in the west,
where the world ended. It is a beautiful country,
and there, when they die, they battle and hunt no
more, but live on sweet, shining mushrooms, play
on the flute and drum, and dance all day. To
reach this land they travel the Milky Way, the
path of souls. They need bows or guns on the
journey, but none after they reach paradise. If on
the way they stop to eat a strawberry that a tempter
offers to them, they fall from the bright bridge and
become frogs as they touch the earth.

Among the Blackfeet the sand-hills of the plains,
near the United States boundary, were the shadow-
land, the ghost-place, the limbo of recently departed souls. Our shadows are held to be actual
souls. Dead persons sometimes live again as animals, and owls are the ghosts of medicine-men.
In the Red River country the dead hover about in
the form of eagles, but some of the Siwash believe
they take the forms of birds more foul of habit,
that lurk over the place of their demise for four
days. In order to keep them at a distance the survivors burn old moccasins that make a fetid smoke.
Some of the far northwestern Indians believed that
hell was in the ice, for it is natural that the cold of
the Arctic winter should, to them, stand for the
extremest suffering, but some of the Eskimos put
the place of future punishment beneath the sea,
and heaven above, with plenty of walrus. Their

hell is like Dante's: of successive cellars, and the deeper go the damned the colder it grows. The wickedest go to the bottom. The Eskimos, by the way, are advanced beyond certain primitive beliefs, and the new woman is no stranger to them. The Sun was a youth to whom the Great Spirit gave wings that he might chase the Moon,—a winged girl. Aoguta and her daughter Sedna are among their chief deities. The Hudson Bay Eskimos tell us that the first man sprang to being in a beautiful valley, and married the only girl on earth, after he had picked her as a flower. They were the parents of all mankind. The Assiniboins believed that hell was in the Great Selkirk glacier. The unspeakable majesty of this ice mass and its mountain setting to them was merely dreadful. The Chippewas held that the wicked were immersed to their chins in water, and that they could not leave it, although, to add to their discomfiture, the happy hunting-grounds were in their view.

Like the Greeks, many of the Indians peopled the woods, hills, and waters with gods and spirits, who were amiable or devilish according to their environment and according to the nature of the imagination that evoked them. They personified many of the stars and mountains; a comet was a winged creature breathing fire; the morning star was the Early Riser; the Dipper was the Seven Persons; the moon was the Night Red Light; the Milky Way was the Wolf Road. Spirits of places sometimes spoke to those who asked advice of them, and while La Salle's boat, the Griffin, was in process of building at Cayuga Creek, he went to Niagara to consult the oracle at Devil's Hole. A voice spoke from it warning him to abandon his voyage on pain of death by treachery. He met that fate. The Nipissings were stigmatized by the Jesuits as " the sorcerers," and Lake Nipissing was beset by devils and magicians.

The mountain in British Columbia, or Washington, on which life was preserved during the great flood is impossible of identification, but deluge legends pertain to several of the peaks. The Takullies say that the earth-builder was a muskrat, which, diving here and there in the universal ocean, brought up mud, and spat it out in one place until an island was formed, which grew to be the earth. After it had been peopled a fire swept over it, destroying all the surface save one mountain that held a deep cave, and in this hid one man and one woman until the earth was cool again, when they emerged and repeopled it. This myth is oddly repeated in Paraguay and Bolivia. Alaskan Kaiganees say that the big canoe in which a good man was saved in the time of a great flood rested on a mountain just back of Howkan, and one old fellow claimed, a dozen or two of years ago, that he had a piece of its bark anchor-rope. The crow that flew out of the ark still nests in the crater of Mount Edgecumbe, near Sitka, and catches whales. On Forester Island they say that towns were destroyed by pest and fire for their wickedness, and that a woman who looked back in the act of flight was turned to stone, her lodge and that of her brother being also changed to rock at the same moment, and you see them in the river to-day,—warnings to obey the Great Spirit when he speaks. A legend of a collision of the earth with a fiery dragon (a comet ?) is found among many of the Algonquins.

Among the Dog-Rib Indians of the Barren Grounds there is a belief in one Chapawee, a mis-chief-maker who plunged the earth into a long period of darkness by catching the sun in a noose and tying it fast, so that it could not rise above the horizon. Does this typify the Arctic winter? After a time he sent animals to gnaw the snare asunder, and they were burned to ashes. Does this clothe in parable the outbreak of a volcano, or the dissipation of the ice in the Arctic summer? Be-like it is neither, for many of the traditions are but old wives' tales, without a meaning. Men, meas-urably civilized, lived in North America twenty thousand years ago ; and some of the myths like the foregoing are thought to preserve the memory of the last great glacier, that covered the continent down to the fortieth parallel, burying beneath it the cities of this ancient people.

One of the traditionary characters among the western tribes, from the Blackfeet to the Aleuts of Alaska, was Old Man. He varies in power and importance in different parts of the country, but among the Aleuts he has many of the attributes of the Great Spirit, and is a secondary god. He played a Cadmus part, dropping stones on the earth, that presently sprang up in human form. Some that he flung into the air became birds, those that he cast to a distance were quadrupeds and serpents, and those that he tossed into the sea turned to fish. Thus was the world peopled. The Blackfeet say that Old Man acquired a wife, a daughter, and a son-in-law. The latter was not worth much. There arrived in the lodge a young man who had sprung from the blood of some game they were preparing for the pot, and this young one and Old Man attempted to stop the thieving and abuse of the son-in-law. They could not, and as this objectionable person had an especially violent tantrum on a certain occasion, the good ones shot him dead, and there were peace and plenty afterward. All of which has been construed as a day and night myth, a summer and winter myth, a sunshine and storm myth, a famine and plenty myth. Maybe.

While some ethnologists claim that the Micmacs are the Skraelings of the Northmen, the first known explorers of our eastern coast, others relate the western tribes to the Asiatics. There are Greek words in Central American tongues, likenesses to Greek, Indian, Assyrian, and Egyptian architecture in Mexico, Central America, and Peru, pictures there of animals more common to Asia than to this continent, round towers in the West like those of Ireland, and faiths and myths among the aborigines resembling those of the Old World.

The proud Abenakis, of eastern Canada, say that they are the original people; they acknowledge no ancestry; they built villages, and believe that "after making them and their land the Great Spirit made the rest carelessly." They were related in marriage to Pamola, the terrible One who lived in Ktaadn, and whose son killed game and men by pointing at them. On midsummer day, "the day of sparkling fire," they built a large fire and danced about it— a Phœnician custom, the fire representing the sun. This custom the Acadians modify in their "fire talk" on St. John's Eve, when the priest heaps fragrant boughs before his church and recites prayers as the flames crackle among them. So soon as this is seen the country glitters and the news goes round; for if a death has occurred the farmer dashes out his fire; if sickness, he lets it flicker and die; if all is well, it blazes jubilantly.

A theory that the northern Indians descended from Tyrians and Israelites who came over in 332 B.C. is based on the existence among those tribes of the deluge legend, that of the dove of discovery, and that of the ark of the covenant. The ark, which contains a shell that speaks oracles, understood only by the medicine-men, is never allowed to touch the earth, but is carried by the faithful into battle. When it is advanced among the enemy all rush to its safety, as the Scots pressed about the heart of Bruce when it was thrown among the foe, and as some tribes rallied about the heads of their chiefs when, after death, they were carried into the fight on poles, as standards. The exact whereabouts of this ark remains a mystery not to be revealed to the profane.

But most wide-spread of all beliefs among the red men of the north is that in Nanabush, Manabozho, Glooskap, or Hiawatha, who is buried beneath Thunder Cape, or " the sleeping giant," a basaltic uplift, thirteen hundred and fifty feet high, at the northwest corner of Lake Superior, and whose deeds of valor and charity are told in many tongues. Some say he was the statesman who federated the Six Nations and preached arbitration. He took on human form to benefit mankind, but often went away and dwelt with birds in a great space and great light. He came from the east in a granite boat, with a woman who was not his wife, for he never took one. When on a later voyage he gave room in his boat to a woman of evil character—as was proved by the storm that arose about him—he sprang ashore, leaving her to drift about until she became a shark. Hiawatha figures sometimes as creator, sometimes as Messiah, sometimes as a Noah who was saved from the deluge, and who sent forth the bird called the diver from his boat, to learn if the earth was emerging from the waters. On their subsidence he became the father of a new race, and walked over all America. In some legends he is the Hare, and the Hare was the sun. His foe, the snake prince, the god of evil, whom he destroyed, has been thought to be a comet. Another foe, the giant frog, vast and cold, squatting over miles of plain, was the great glacier of the ice age. Believing that his father had killed his mother, he chased him to the shores of the Arctic sea. His brother, the Flint, he killed in fight, and the boulders on the plains of Assiniboia, Alberta, and Saskatchewan were the missiles they hurled at each other. In the mission-yard at Victoria, on the North Saskatchewan, was a meteorite that Manitou—possibly Manabozho—had cast down, and the Indians believed that to move it would be to incur his hate, and bring upon them battle, disease, and scarcity of game. White men moved it, and, unhappily for those who had been inveighing against the superstition of the Indians, war, small-pox, politics, and famine quickly followed. In the east he was called Glooskap. Minas Basin, Nova Scotia, was his beaver-pond, dammed at Cape Blomidon, his throne; but when he saw that the pent waters were rising among the villages, to the alarm and distress of the people, he burst the rocks asunder, and swift tides now eddy through "the Gut." Here he fought and killed the Great Beaver, whose bones are the Five Islands, near Parrsboro', though this legend appears also at Sault Sainte Marie. Spencer's Island is his upset kettle.

Beyond Our Borders

On Partridge Island he held a great feast with Kit-pooseeagoono, and the pair of them ate a whale. Fragments of a great causeway of his building are seen in islands off the shore of the old maritime provinces. He was much in company with his uncle, Great Turtle, and shared many of his adventures. At one time, when he was not at hand, some hostiles caught the Turtle and condemned him to the stake. He rushed into the flames so eagerly that they pulled him out. Then they resolved to cut his throat, whereupon he seized a knife and hacked himself so fiercely that they disarmed him. Finally they agreed that he must be drowned, and this fate seemed to put him in terror, so that he caught at trees as they urged him on; but once at the water's edge the cunning fellow chuckled, dived out of sight, and so escaped. When the English came, Glooskap waded from Newfoundland to Nova Scotia, and either freed his hunting-dogs or turned them to stone, that their cries might not betray the lodges of his people to the strangers. But the red men became evil after they had known the English, and Glooskap, with Great Turtle, entered his white stone canoe and sailed away to the west, singing—some say up the St. Lawrence; others say across the Great Lakes. All nature mourns his return, and the owl, the loon, and other birds and beasts found new voices on the night when he went away.

GLOOSKAP AT MENAGWES

THE spirit of the river St. John having become noisy and audacious, damaging the banks and brawling defiance to the gods, the Great Spirit showed his anger by closing its mouth. The remains of his dam are overhung by the suspension bridge in the present city of St. John. When the tide runs out there is a fall toward the sea, and when the tide runs in the fall tumbles across the reef up-river. This is the only reversible fall in the world, they say, and the lumber barges in the whirl of it, going up or down with the tide, are a sight worth seeing. Were the rock at the foot of the gorge to be blasted, so as to afford free ingress to the salt water, some miles of the land now culti-vated and dwelt upon, back of the city, would be permanently flooded. One Indian legend has it that a giant beaver built a dam across the outlet, creating a flood behind it in which all the inland people were drowned. Glooskap visited this point and named it Menagwes. It once befell him to take a long journey for the good of the human race, for he went about teaching men how to build canoes, to smoke pipes, to raise crops, to use paint, to make maple sugar, and, as he left his house unprotected, this chance for injury was not neglected by the wizards and demons that always lurk in good men's shadows. Disguised in thunder-clouds, they wrecked and burned his lodge, slew his friends and

servants, and when he returned to find ashes and
tokens of strife where had been comfort and peace,
his tears fell so fast and free that they were like
rain. A few of the wizards he tracked to the site
of Pictou, where he slew them. A witch he caught
in her lodge, on the site of Liverpool, Nova Scotia,
and, after a fight that the stars stood still to see,
he tore her into pieces. Then, calling to the
whales, he mounted their backs and rode to Newfoundland, and appeared, so towering that his head
touched the sky, before other of his enemies, who
shrank into the fog in terrified silence. In vain
their cunning, for he searched out and destroyed
them. Returning to Menagwes, he wept afresh,
for his friends were ashes. He could not give
life.

THE DOGS OF CLOTE SCAURP

EARLY fishers on the Restigouche who had
Indian guides reported a disturbance at
night by unearthly noises that hurried through the
wood about them. The Indians would draw nearer
to the fire, listen to the uncanny laughter and wailing cries, making sure that they were not the
calls of owls and panthers, and remark, " Clote
Scaurp's hunting-dogs are out." Clote Scaurp,
who is only Glooskap under another spelling or
pronunciation, lived near the Restigouche, on the
narrow Waagan, for a time. In some myths of

this locality he is human, in others a demi-god, in more distant ones he appears to be the Old Man of the plains families. But he was a good-natured hero, who hunted more for company than for the joy of killing, and his dogs, though often heard, have never been seen. He talked with birds, beasts, and fishes, and only when he found that any one of them had become savage and cruel would he grow angry. The moon, for instance, was a huge and dangerous beast that went up and down the land devouring and killing, so that all things fled before it. Clote Scaurp set off with his dogs to check its devilish conduct, and, meeting it in the wood, he struck it such a terrific whack with his club that it nearly gave up its life. Not only did it cease to grow from that moment, but it peaked and pined to the thing we see at this day, or night, and clambered into the sky to be out of reach of his weapons. To nearly all other things Clote Scaurp was kind, and earth and his dogs have been sorry without him. As evil tendencies began to show themselves, not only among beasts but also among men—envy, avarice, dishonesty, ruffianism, laziness —he gathered all creatures about him and preached good manners. He helped them to be better by living better himself; but the more he did for them the less they would do for themselves, and they were full of evil will. Unable longer to endure this state, he resolved to say farewell to the creatures he had known; so he called them from woods and fields and waters ; but, though he spread a mighty feast, only the brutes attended. The men were wholly ungrateful, and they hated lectures. At the end of the banquet Clote Scaurp and Great Turtle entered their canoe and rowed away toward the setting sun. All the brutes watched sorrowing, and listened to the mournful singing that came fainter and fainter out of the west. When, at last, the beasts broke silence to express their grief, each, to the general astonishment, spoke a different tongue from all the rest, and all fled as in fear, never again to meet in general council. The white owl calls all night, "I am sorry ;" and Clote Scaurp's dogs still seek him, howling in the woods along the Restigouche. Two rocks at the foot of Blomidon are called his dogs, and he will awaken them when he returns, they say ; but those who have heard them know that they still enjoy their liberty.

THE MISSIONS

ALTHOUGH we concede the benefits given to new lands by commercial enterprise and their conquest by enlightened peoples, in the case of Canada it must be confessed that religious enthusiasm accomplished more, both for the explorers and for the natives, than any other cause. The first men to force a way to the inland lakes, to map the plains, rivers, and mountains, to effect a peace with the savages, were the missionaries, and but for

their eagerness for the conversion of the Indians
the safety and material development of the country
might have been long deferred. The Jesuits were
especially courageous. Their enthusiasm defied all
threats and survived all torture. One missionary,
Father Jogues, was shockingly maltreated, and his
hand was chopped off, yet he regarded these things
only as passing pains, and kept on with his work.
Another, who had been hunted off to the woods, was
found there frozen to death, in the attitude of prayer.
A missionary on the upper Ottawa was roasted over
a slow fire, hot axes were placed about his neck and
head, and in mockery he was baptized with boiling
water. Yet to his last breath he implored divine
protection for his tormentors. After the capture
of Fort Ignace, on Lake Simcoe, the missionaries
Lalemant and De Brébeuf were cruelly used.
The former was covered with bark, roasted, and
partly eaten before his voice ceased in prayer. His
companion enraged the savages by his indifference,
for he seemed careless of suffering, though they
kept him alive for three hours to endure it, and at
the last they ate his heart, in order that his courage
and fortitude might pass into their bodies.

It was such heroism that subdued the savagery
of the red men and turned them into poor, dull,
ambitionless people, to the comfort of the pale-
faces, who are now able to cheat them in trade
without the risk of so much as a prod in the solar
plexus. The contrast between the conduct of the

French explorers and that of the soldiers and dealers
who arrived later is a contrast between religious
France of the seventeenth century and Brumma-
gem of the nineteenth. Even the Hudson Bay
and Northwest companies have not escaped cen-
sure, for it has been alleged that when a gun paid
for as many beaver-skins as would reach to the
muzzle of it, the skins packed flat and the gun
held upright, the barrel of the weapon grew and
grew with each successive year until the Indian,
after he had bought it with the peltry, had to bor-
row a file and cut off a foot of useless metal. And
it is a fact that when certain red men received pay
in five-dollar bills they readily exchanged one of
those pieces of paper for two silver dollars, for
they could not read the number on the bill.

Missionaries encouraged the building of shrines
and churches, and people who had visions or
heard voices were invited to commemorate the circumstance. Our Lady of the Snows, for instance,
appeared to a Breton cavalier who had lost his way
while hunting on Trois Rivières, and lighted him
to a forge, where he found shelter. In return for
this mercy he was induced by the priests to rear
a shrine to her at Ville Marie, "the city of the
mount," and so it came about that the Church of
Our Lady of the Snows was erected on "the
priests' farm" in Montreal.

There is a faint and melancholy fear that the
missionaries did a little cheating, from purely re-

ligious motives. It has been set forth that the giant devil who infested Les Islets Machins, in the St. Lawrence, was not an entirely disingenuous creation. The Jesuits are charged with telling the Indians that he used a pine-tree as a club, that he sprang upon people who were fishing in his neighborhood or innocently paddling up and down the river, and, discovering by an instinct that never erred, which of them had not been baptized, he brained them forthwith, sparing only the Christians. This tale led to so many conversions that the giant fled in disgust, for lack of occupation. So, too, the report that Cap de la Madelaine, on the St. Lawrence, was haunted by a Magdalen who cried all night for Christian burial, may have had its deterrent effect on the thoughtless or immoral among the women of the settlements. The *braillard de la Madelaine* has been otherwise ascribed to the soul of a murderous wrecker, to a priest who allowed a babe to die without baptism, and to a little boy that alone survived a wreck, though only for a few hours.

Was Christianity taught before the time of the Jesuits ? Did the Norsemen teach it ? When Cartier landed at Gaspé Basin on the St. Lawrence, and planted a cross on shore with great solemnity, he saw with surprise that the natives made obeisance to this object, as one with which they were familiar, although this was in 1536, and Cartier was supposed to be the first white man in that region. The narrative of the Indians was to the effect that long before, when they had been troubled by a pestilence, their old men had a medicine dream, in which there appeared before them "a man exceedingly beautiful, with a cross in his hand, who bade them return home, make crosses like his, and present them to the heads of families, assuring them that they would find therein a remedy for all their ills." This was done; it worked a cure, and the cross became a talisman from that time forth. Was the "beautiful man" a remembered description of Christ, or was it one of the "white men clothed in wool," of northern tradition, who were undoubtedly Norse explorers? Respecting these latter, the Milicites, or Meliseets, tell of a visit of tall, pale strangers who drove away the red men, built houses of stone, swigged mighty draughts from horns, shouting as they drank, and were overwhelmed by an earthquake that changed the course of the St. John River. The Micmacs—by some alleged to be the lost Beothuks of Newfoundland—tell of a woman's dream, long before Cartier's landing, in which she saw an island floating toward the land with trees upon it, and creatures dressed in skins. Next day the island appeared in fact, but it was a ship; the trees were masts, and the creatures were men who spoke in a strange tongue, making signs of friendship. One man, dressed in white, lived among them for a time, and tried to teach a new religion, but, although he found some listeners, the wise men refused to heed him, because the dream had been granted to a woman and not to a medicine-man.

Unqualified praise can be given to the missionaries of all sects and of no sect that have sought for the elevation of the red man, but they have sometimes discovered that he was less of a savage than he looked. The conduct of Chief Joseph, of the Nez Percés, in the war so cruelly and unjustly waged against him, was admirable in its forbearance. Instances of generosity and self-sacrifice are many. A Canadian clergyman, relating to a company of Blackfeet the measures common in civilized states for the care of orphaned children, explained that if his own children were left fatherless his property would be sold, or managed by an executor for their benefit, so that they might continue to secure board, clothing, and education. The Indians were both amused and astonished. "The white people are savages," said one. "When any people die in our camps and leave little children, we take them into our lodges. The best piece of buffalo meat we give to them. We clothe and train them. They are our bone and flesh. They have no father or mother, so we are all fathers and mothers. White people do not love their children. They have to be paid for loving orphans." The respect in which the aborigines hold their ancestors, at least when the latter are dead, is in contrast with the lack of honor that the dead sometimes have from the civilized. There is a cave at Mistassini that the Indians never approach closely, lest they should seem to spy on the ghosts of their fathers, who were buried there in other ages, and who still sit there, holding councils.

And seldom do the Indians hear from the missionaries an eloquence equal to their own. Listen to this prayer of a Piegan to a mountain manitou: " Hear, now, you Chief Mountain, you who stand foremost; listen, I say, to the mourning of the people. Now the days are truly become evil, and are not as they used to be in ancient times. But you know: you have seen the days. Under your fallen garments the years lie buried. Then the days were full of joy. The buffalo covered the prairie, and the people were glad. Then they had warm dwellings, soft robes for covering, and the feasting was without end. Hear, now, you Mountain Chief. Listen, I say, to the mourning of the people. Their lodges and their clothing now are made of strange, thin stuff, and the long days come and go without the feast, for our buffalo are gone. The drum now is useless, for who would sing and dance while hunger gnawed him? Hear, now, you who stand among the clouds. Pity, I say, your starving people. Give us back those happy days. Once more cover the prairie with real food, so that your children may live again. Hear, I say, the prayer of your unhappy people. Bring back those ancient days. Then will our prayers again be strong. You will be happy, and the aged will die content."

A FEW MONSTERS

IN common with other parts of the continent, and the seas that wash their coasts, the Dominion and its waters have been peopled with strange creatures, some of them the more terrible because they evade sight, touch, definition, and bullets. Now and again the sea-serpent rears his head, snorting, from the brine, and puts for shore at a pace that shames our torpedo-boats, and elderly maidens at the watering-places convincingly resign themselves to hysterics. He—perhaps there is also a she, though it does not seem possible— usually proves to be a porpoise, a sunfish, a white whale, or an octopus ; still, " you can't generally 'most always tell, sometimes," and one of the times might have been when he was not a porpoise, but the sea-serpent. The largest devil-fish known, taken on the Newfoundland coast, had a reach of forty feet, and there is no doubt about him, for he was pickled and carried to the States. Either of his arms would have made a more than respectable snake. But all hope has not been abandoned of catching the veritable sea-serpent—the one with eyes like saucepans, with a grinning mouth set with stone-drill teeth, with a weedy mane, with stripes and spots more vivid than a mid-century fashion-plate, and with a braying voice like that of a mule or an agitator. Now and then he leaves his habitat and wallows overland to fresh water. He was seen, for instance, in Skiff Lake, New Brunswick, where he succeeded in stretching himself to a length of only thirty feet.

Rattlesnake Islands, in Lake Erie, indicate by their name what desirable places they must have been to live away from, but the snakes that remain, if, indeed, there are any, are as nothing to what they were when the early explorers visited the group, carrying their imaginations with them; for, said they, the islands bristled with a kind of snake that " blew from its mouth with great force a subtile wind," which whoso breathed must die.

There were some rare birds in this country, too, beside the Indian thunder-birds that flashed terrible glances out of their eyes and made the heaven resound when they shook their iron wings. There was an eagle of portentous size that preyed on human beings when it lacked fawns and bear-cubs. They will show you, beside the deepest reach of the Ottawa, a cliff falling for hundreds of feet into the river, with no beach at its foot. It is Oiseau Rock, and to its top this eagle flew with a pappoose, the frantic mother climbing after it and bringing the child away in safety. This, by the bye, is a legend that is common the world over.

It is a different sort of bird of which the Thlinkeets, of British Columbia, tell in their creation myth. This bird, Chethl, the Great Crow, is almost a deity. With his wings he beat back the rising waters. Then, when his uncle tried to kill him, he called on the floods and deluged the earth, flying up to heaven afterward, where he stuck his bill into a cloud and hung there till the water had gone down. At a later time he got hold of the three boxes in which were kept the sun, moon, and stars, wrenched the lids off, and let the contents shine into the frightened eyes of men.

In all Canada you shall not find a creature so fearful as the giant Gougou, who lived on the St. Lawrence, at Miscou. A ship's mast in our day would barely have reached to his waist, and, saving that he had two eyes, he was a very Polyphemus. He would wade into the river when men were rowing or sailing past, pick them up by thumb and finger, put them into his sack, go ashore, and draw them out to eat at his leisure. The shrill whistling that he made sometimes put the canoe-men on their guard, and they would hurry in at some wooded cove until he had fed or gone to sleep before they dared to resume their journey.

The devil, from whose machinations men will ever pray to be delivered, is master of a hundred subtleties, and changes his form to cheat men's senses. We meet him in "Faust" as the black dog; in "The Monk" as the terrific form with baleful eyes, bat's wings, and an air of malignant triumph; we find him tempting some men and bullying others; now he is the fiend, and anon the gentleman. But where else than in Canada will you find him working for the Church? St. Augustin, in the province of Quebec, is the one place on earth that he has favored in this fashion, and we are still in the dark as to why he did it. He took on the shape of a monster black horse, with the strength of ten usual horses in his thews, and hauled all the heavy stone for the foundations of the church that was built in that village in 1690. Was he looking for a chance to kick the priest? Did he expect that a mason or two would mount his back, that he might rush into the St. Lawrence with them? Did he intend to damage the foundations after he had helped to lay them, that the sacred edifice might tumble about the ears of his enemies? Anyhow, he did the work, and did it well, and that is not the first time that his designs against mankind have failed.

Belle Isle and Quirpon, in the icy strait between Newfoundland and Labrador, were peopled by so many devils that the French sailors would not go ashore unless they had crucifixes in their hands. There was a peculiar species of griffin, also, that was destructive, and that doubters of a later age assert to have been wolves, for as late as 1873 these animals were troublesome along the coasts of the strait, and several persons were killed by them.

Possibly some of the sprites on Prince Edward's Island have four feet, because the mice are troublesome there. There was a plague of these little animals in the seventeenth century, and one in Pictou in 1815. They ate everything, stripping the fields bare; then, for lack of other provision, they starved by thousands.

Richmond Gulf, on the eastern side of Hudson Bay, was the abode of water spirits or some manner of evil creatures who vexed the waves so that they boiled and tumbled without a wind, and it was a sad thing for people in light canoes to get across those waters. At certain stages of the tide a great whirlpool was seen, and the creatures sat on the bottom, among the grinding stones, under the roaring vortex, waiting with upreached hands for the hapless canoeman who should be sucked below the sea, that they might feed on him. Before rowing through the narrow entrance the natives performed ceremonies to appease these evil ones, after which they dropped tobacco into the water, believing that the monsters would smoke it and be calmed and grateful long enough to enable the boatmen to reach shore in safety.

In some quarters the *ignes fatui*, or will-o'-the-wisps, are lanterns carried in the hands of spirits or demons. At Grand Falls, New Brunswick, where it is claimed that these lights have actually been seen, the Indians declare them to be the uneasy souls of dead folks who are hunting for their bodies, which they desire to occupy once more. If you would be without fear of the goblin of the Jack-o'-lantern, in French Canada, you must stop squarely in his path and ask him, "On what day of the month falls Christmas?"

The imp answers, in the Yankee fashion, by asking, "Well, what day is it?"

And if the traveller gives the date, the imp will fly before him, but if he does not remember, it were better that he had held his peace, for he will presently be torn in pieces.

SOME NAMES

IN the names of places we often find as great a puzzle as in the names of people, yet if we could go to the bottom of the mystery we might discover an incident or a faith of some account; in fact, much history has been written in names, while a public temper or humor is often disclosed in the same way. In eastern Canada all the saints in the calendar, and some who do not belong there, have fastened their names to the French villages, recording the occupancy and rule of the land by a religious folk. If we go west and find places called Hell Roaring Creek, Last Chance, Hardscrabble, Silver King, Whoop-Up, and that sort of thing, it indicates a people whose motives are less religious than material, and who succeed in getting fun out of difficulties. The devil has fared in the West as well as the saints in the East, in which more peaceful district others have had in a few cases to take the brunt of his unpopularity, for Devil's Head, New Brunswick, was named for a settler named Duval. Hard luck for Duval! Old France and

Myths and Legends

Old England have often been drawn upon, while the strong, quaint, often musical speech of the aborigines is perpetuated in too few lakes and rivers. Anglicism of names sometimes results oddly, as in the conversion of Chapeau Dieu to Shapody Mountain, and of Portage du Rat to Rat Portage. Though the two latter are the same, yet locally the French rat stands for muskrat, and the same word in English does not. Montreal is the Royal Mountain; Smoky Cape, or Cap Enfumé, is so called because of the mists that toss about it; Quebec is " Quel bec !" (" What a cape !") that being the exclamation of its discoverers (unless it is true that there is an Indian word, Quebego, meaning narrow river), while at Ha-ha Bay the Frenchmen laughed with joy at sight of the green expanse after their voyage up the Saguenay. We have forgotten what haunted Bleak House, where the commandant of Quebec once lived, but we know that Sault de Matelot, in the same city, is so called because a sailor, who had been relieving at a tavern " the enforced horrors of a long sobriety," leaped off to escape a troop of yellow giraffes and pink monkeys with horses' tails.

Lachine, or La Chine, means China, because the St. Lawrence was first thought to be a northwest passage to that land. This is the old name, but in other cases such changes have been made by later comers that it is hard to recognize the originals. The Portuguese Baya Fondo is not so different from

the Bay of Fundy, the Shubenacadie, haunted by
ghosts of fishermen caught in its tides, is heard
under the common "Shippenackety," we guess that
Blow-me-down is Blomidon, but who would suppose that Acadie was the Micmac word Quoddy?
In fact, some believe that the name was borrowed
from the other side of the sea, to denote the discovery of a New-World Arcadia.

The turbulent Newfoundlanders, who, being
mostly Celtic, are thorns in the sides of the Canadian and English governments, have not recorded
in their names the fires, the riots, the shootings,
the lurings to wreck, the extermination of the Boe-
thuks, or other incidents that have made the history
of their island exciting, and the traveller wonders
what may have been the original meanings of Exploits, Topsail, Killigrew's, Joe Batt's Arm, Seldom-
come-by, Little-seldom-come-by, Fogo, Brigus,
Hell Hill, Quiddy Viddy, Bally Haly, Maggoty
Cove, Heart's Content, Bay of Despair, Dead
Islands, and Rose Blanche.

Because Cartier happened to reach it in a time
of sultry weather, we have the Baie des Chaleurs.
There is little doubt that Stanstead, province of
Quebec, is named after one of the three Stansteads
in England, yet it is alleged that the surveyors who
laid off the township were a drunken lot, and were
often heard calling to their chainmen, and even to
their theodolites, to "stan' stead'" (stand steady),
when it was their own legs that were out of plumb.

And, apropos of thirst, More-Rum Brook, in Yarmouth County, Nova Scotia, has been a name of dread to prohibitionists, and is likely to be changed to Smith's " Crick" as soon as they can acquire sufficient influence, as in its present form it is wicked. Sundry years ago, when a surveyor was going over this region, his chain-bearers and others constantly clamored for strong waters, finally refusing to budge until they had some grog. The surveyor had sent to a distance for the rum, and told his reprehensible associates to drink from the brook until they got it. That is how it came to be More-Rum Brook.

In upper Lake Huron lies the chain of Manitoulins, large islands now occupied by graziers and farmers, but formerly a favorite visiting-place of the Indians. They never abode there long, for they looked on the islands as dwelling-places of the spirits of the earth, water, and air, spirits that required reverence and propitiation, and they dared not attempt familiarity. Manitoulin means spiritland, or land of the gods. Manitoba, likewise, preserves the name of the Manitou, or Great Spirit. That name applied originally to Lake Manitoba, whose waters the Indians believed to be stirred by the spirit.

Moose Jaw is only a contraction of " Place-where-the-white-man-mended-his-cart-wheel-with-the-jawbone-of-a-moose," which was thought to be too numerous a name for busy people. Calling River commemorates an echo, and Pipestone River

refers to the material from which the red men make
their ceremonial pipes. Pie Island and the Sleeping Giant, known to voyagers on Lake Superior,
have reference only to the outlines of those heights,
but the Petits Ecrits was so called because of the
picture-writings found on the face of the rock,
representing men, animals, and canoes cut in the
lichen. West of the Wild-Cat Hills Ghost River
flows past the column-like mountain of Devil's
Head. Old maps call the river Dead Man's Creek.
The Assiniboins are responsible for both names,
since they declare it to be haunted by the ghost of
an old chief who rides up and down its banks on a
horse. Devil's Lake, near Banff, was a resort of
malignant spirits, and Cascade River, its outlet,
was the scene of a murder in which the victim's
head was struck from his shoulders. A cave on
the Bow near Canmore is haunted by a spirit, and
is held in much regard by the natives. Near Banff
is Stony Squaw Mountain, thus called from the
tradition that when an old man of the Stony tribe
lay ill and helpless in his lodge at the foot of this
height, his old wife took his weapons and did a
man's work as hunter, killing enough big-horns to
feed them both until he recovered. Dr. James
Hector, exploring the Canadian Rockies in 1857,
was kicked by his horse in the shadow of Mount
Stephen. Hence we have Kicking Horse Pass.
The name Wapta, applied to the stream that flows
through it, means only river. Wait-a-Bit Creek

was so called by the first explorers, who were constantly fetched up with a short turn by a brier that grows thickly along its shores. When caught by the thorns, the victims called to their companions to " Wait a bit." The Arctic-looking Hermit Mountain on the north side of Rogers' Pass takes its name from a shape of stone far up under the sky. It looks like a cowled hermit talking to a dog. Close by is Cheops, recalling the Egyptian pyramid by its form as well as its name. Mount Grizzly explains itself, and Asulkan means wild goat.

Sibilants multiply as we near the Pacific, for the Siwash—probably a corruption of Sauvage—intersperse many *s*'s in their weak, choking, clicking language, as we find in Spuzzum, Spatsum, Scuzzy, Snohomish, Squallyamish, Shuswap, Sicamous, Spallumsheen, Sumas, Skagit, Similkameen, Osyoos, Spokane, Semiamoo, Swinonish, Stillaguamish, Nooksak, and Snoqualmie. These uncouth names often have agreeable meanings, however. Lee's Post, on Pincher Creek, suffered so from the cold that its name came to be Freeze-Out. Slide-Out, on Belly River, was convenient to hiding-places to which traders in unlawful whiskey " slid out" when the mounted police approached, and at Stand-Off the traders kept a band of marauding Indians at bay. Polly Cow's Island, in Katchewanook Lake, is named for an Indian girl who is buried there. Handsome Jack, an Otonabee River Indian, had courted her, but, believing that she was not strong enough to do his housework, he married a more buxom damsel, and Polly pined into her grave.

Juan de Fuca, the old Greek pilot, found the strait that bears his name in 1592, but for a century or more thereafter this region was half mythical. Bacon thought it a safe place for his Atlantis, and Swift for his land of giants, Brobdingnag. The old Indian, Spanish, and Russian names were complacently wiped off from the map by Mr. Vancouver, who fixed his own name on a great island, while Puget Sound and Mount Baker celebrate a couple of his shipmates. Mount Tacoma was called Mount Rainier to flatter an Englishman who never saw it. Captain Gray, of Boston, was leaving Puget Sound as Vancouver entered it in the Discovery, but any names that the Americans appended to the islands, capes, and mountains were not allowed to stay.

TROUBLES ON THE ST. LAWRENCE

THE St. Lawrence is a river of many mysteries and troubles. Blood has often mingled with its waters, the blood of French and English, Christian and savage, soldier and martyr. From the lakes to the gulf its surface has been vexed by the keels of fighting fleets, and its shores have echoed to the roar of cannon. So late as 1838 it was a scene of hostilities, for in that year the British ship Sir Robert Peel was burned among the

Thousand Islands by a harum-scarum band of men who wanted to establish a republic in Canada. "Bill" Johnson, leader of this company, kept out of sight for some time after, his daughter Kate rowing him from one island to another, and keeping him in food during the search that the Canadians made for him. Part of the time he was at the Devil's Oven. It is told of Johnson that he was trapped on Wells Island by Captain Boyd, of the English army. "I'm fairly caught," he confessed, "and you've had a long row after me, so you must be thirsty. Take a drink and rest yourself." The officer dropped upon a bench and took a good tug at the outlaw's flask, while Johnson lighted his pipe and, holding the coal in a tongs over a barrel, remarked, in a matter-of-fact way, "Shall I go with you, or will you stay and go to hell with me? This barrel is full of powder." The captain excused himself, and scrambled for his boats along with his men, for Johnson had put the coal on the barrel-head, and it was eating into the wood. In a minute there was a big explosion, and a great smoke rolled from the cave-mouth. Captain Boyd hoped that it meant the last of Johnson; but that reprobate was out of sight in a new hiding-place before the oars of the red-coats were fairly in the water.

These islands have been famed in Cooper's "Pathfinder" and in the verse of Thomas Moore, who also celebrates the village of Sainte Anne in his "Boat Song." Near Prescott is the windmill, now a light-house, where a company of "patriots," under lead of a Polish exile, held out against Canada for several days, in the belief that the province needed to be "liberated" from something or somebody, while many Americans sat watching on their own side of the river, occasionally saying "Hooray!" There are tales of perilous descents by fugitives and Indians of the rapids that tourists view languidly from steamer-decks. Even now the habitant on its banks shudders when an owl cries, for he remembers the stories told by his grandmother, in the firelight, of *feux follets* and *loups garous*, which are demons that watch for the souls of the unrepentant and the unbaptized. On the pass of the Long Sault, on the river's left bank, occurred one of the stoutest fights in history. Learning that a large war-party of Iroquois had set off to destroy the infant colonies of Montreal and Quebec, the Sieur des Ormaux, better known by his baptismal name of Dollard, hurried away to stop the advance, and at least gain time for preparation. He had only sixteen white men and two faithful Hurons, and his shelter was of the hastiest and slightest; yet for three days of hunger, thirst, and sleeplessness this Spartan band withstood the assault of at least five hundred savages, greedy for their blood, and, although every man in the defences died, the Indians were so convinced of the futility of war against so brave a people that they went back to their homes. In the stillness of the night is it the rumor of the rapids, making the Long Sault, that is heard, or is it the sound of battle that nature would forget but cannot while evil spirits dwell on earth?

Nor have all the wicked spirits run away from the travellers with red guide-books, nor hidden among the trees when they saw the train or steamer coming, nor covered their ears or glared in envy when they heard some frenzied stranger making remarks into a dilatory telephone. Old residents near the Cape of Crows will tell you that the blackbirds that flap and squall among the mists are devils and bring bad luck to sailors, while there are bigger devils in the clouds that swirl around the cape, and devils in the earth likewise, for this region is occasionally shaken by earthquake. In 1663 an earthquake along the north shore was attributed by the Indians near Montreal to the return of the spirits of their ancestors from the happy hunting-grounds. The poor souls wanted a change of diet. As there was not game enough for both the living and the dead, the Indians fired their muskets to scare their parents back again. And, sure enough, the dead and good Indians ceased from troubling after a few months, and went back to the Sand Hills. That was a year of great distress to the people along the river. Every time the earth shook some of them remembered that they had not said their prayers, and others hurried to confess that they had sold fire-water to the Indians. The frightened

Beyond Our Borders

ones were either driven to drink or turned from all but enough of it. There were many land-slides, and the river ran white as far as Tadousac. "Meteors, fiery-winged serpents, and ghastly spectres were seen in the air; roarings and mysterious voices sounded on every side." The Pointe aux Trembles and Les Eboulements preserve in their names the record of these quakes, while, for strange reasons, the Isle of Orleans has been full of goblins ever since.

The Montagnais tell of a giant, Outikon, who, being evil, fled before the cross of the missionaries from Les Islets Machins, where another cannibal monster succeeded him, and found a home at Lake Mistassini, where the Nashkapiouts live, who never pray and never wash; and to show his rage at Christians he stamps his feet every now and again, shaking the hills to their foundations. It used to be said that there was a volcano on the Height of Land, south of Hudson Bay, and that the earthquakes followed its eruption.

The various saints who are invoked on such occasions do not keep the imps from congregating about the Pointe de Tous les Diables in its glooms and storms. Behind this cape is Cartier's land of gold and rubies, peopled by white men clothed in wool. (Legendary vikings?) Farther north is a race that frightened back the first explorers, a people who had only one leg apiece and not a stomach among them all. They lived on scenery. Better

59

such than some of the more usual red men of a later date. There were the Hurons and Senecas, for example, who, after living in peace together at Hochelaga for years, suddenly fell to cutting one another's weasands and barbering one another's hair. This was a little before Champlain's arrival, and the traditionary reason for it is that a Seneca chief had refused to allow his son to marry a Huron girl. In high wrath at this slight, the young woman promised herself to any one who should kill the old man, and on these terms she was won by a young brave of her own tribe; but in the war that followed the Hurons were nearly exterminated.

And what shadowy craft beat about the turbulent river, with its sea width of mouth, in night and storm, or flit among the fantastic pictures of the mirage! There is the Flying Dutchman, who has been known to put in among the bays in the access of a fearful thirst, and sail away again, gnashing his stomach with his fists and talking improper language. And there is Roberval, who ascended the Saguenay and never came down in the flesh. He, too, skims over the river, against the wind, and with no wind. And Henry Hudson, abandoned by mutineers, with his son and six faithful sailors, in his open boat, amid the icy waters that bear his name in mocking compensation for his suffering,—does he not work his way up the St. Lawrence when, on every twentieth year, he sets off to hold revel in his beloved Catskills? In autumn the giant rock of Percé, through whose now fallen arches sloops used to sail, looks down on a phantom ship that has been cruising up and down the bay since 1711. It is one of the ships of Admiral Hovenden Walker that was hurled in a gale against Cap d'Espoir,— ignorantly yet fitly Englished into Cape Despair. Walker had captured an old sea-dog, one Jean Paradis, and had ordered him to guide his ships to Quebec, that he might surprise the French in that stronghold. Paradis stoutly refused, and in the attempt to ascend the river not only the phantom bark but eight transports were smashed on the Isle of Eggs, and a thousand red-coats slept on the bottom that night. This ghostly ship had the captain's wife on board, and as it strikes the rock an officer and a woman in white are seen at the bow, clasped in each other's arms, while the air is filled with wailing as the form of the vessel cracks and fills. The rock itself, three hundred and fifty feet high, has its own " haunt,"—a water wraith who climbs to the top and cries among the flocks of seabirds.

Something is remembered of old Gamache, the wrecker, who has not troubled mariners much, it is true, since they found him dead in his cabin on the Isle of Wrecks, but who had been seen entertaining the devil off Anticosti, and who when chased by government cutters appeared to envelop his boat and himself in blue flame and dance off across the river, regardless of call or shot.

Myths and Legends

More dreaded than these spirits is the woman of the o'er-kind eyes. She, too, affects the region of the Percé Rock, and appears in the twilight putting off from shore in a light boat, rowed with a singularly noiseless stroke by a man whose face is never clearly seen. She asks a passing captain to give her fare as far as Quebec, and, as these rivermen are seldom so pressed that they cannot slack up for a passenger, the skipper backs his mainsail and takes the woman aboard, while the ferryman who has brought her rows away into the mist. She is queerly dressed, and wears a blood-red scarf,—one that is yet no redder than her lips. And immediately the woman begins to make eyes at the captain. Her interest seldom fails of a return, for a tenderness toward the sex is a fatal weakness in sailors, and soon the two are deep in talk in the shadow of the sail. Whether it is that the captain does not see the green light in her eyes, the cat-like gleam that sends a shiver through the crew, or whether the vessel goes wide of her course because all eyes are on the woman, it certainly happens that before eight bells have gone for midnight on passing vessels the ship is pounding to pieces on a reef and with a shrill laugh the woman has disappeared.

Beyond Our Borders

AMERICAN ELEPHANTS

THIRTY years ago buffalo fed up and down our plains for thousands of miles, the herds sometimes a league across and seven in length. Now these great animals are practically extinct,—slaughtered for the amusement of "sporting" men, who left them to rot on the earth and the Indians to hunger for lack of buffalo meat. Not in like way, nor from mere love of blood, yet even more completely have our elephants been killed. Elephants? Ay, truly. Some of the largest, strongest, most savage of the tribe had their home in this Western world during the age of men. Their skeletons have been found in our marshes, and the separate teeth and bones were a cause of dispute and wonderment among the wise men of recent centuries. Cotton Mather, discoverer of mares'-nests and witches, mentions a thigh-bone seventeen feet long! and Governor Dudley told him that it pertained to a giant "for whom the flood only could prepare a funeral; and without doubt he waded as long as he could keep his head above the clouds, but must at length be confounded, with all other creatures." Afterward it was decided that the bones must have belonged to a colossal lion that ate two or three horses at a meal and roared so when he was hungry that the earth shook. Not until Cuvier's time was it agreed that the monster was a species of elephant, that it was extinct, and that it would have eaten neither man nor horses when alive. Old beliefs die hard, all the same, and it is hardly more than fifty years since a Southern " scientist" fixed up the bones of a mastodon in the likeness of a human being, raised it on its hind legs, covered its head with raw hide, and proclaimed it a giant. Another mastodon was grotesquely put together and advertised as the Biblical leviathan, which was supposed to anchor itself to trees by its curved tusks and sleep on the face of the waters. On the Pacific slope the bones of mastodons are found in the gravels, mingled with human bones and stone arrow-heads, showing that men and mastodons lived together, for the elephantine species survived here later than in Europe. In Mexico not only are the bones found, but there are sculptures in which the elephant is represented, and our own Indians portray it in the forms of pipes and in drawings scratched on stone. In Louisiana the red men said that crows had gone to feed on the flesh of an immense animal that had died near the stream they called, because of this incident, Carrion Crow Creek. A mastodon's thigh was exhibited to Cortes as that of a giant, one of a race of evil men whom the Aztecs had succeeded in destroying, after long years of war. In South America similar traditions existed. On the Paraná it was said that the creature burrowed in the bluffs, but in the pampas of the Argentine states it was a Titan again, and " Field of Giants" and " Hill of the Giants" are names that occur there.

Beyond Our Borders

The Delawares had a legend of a wholesale destruction of bear, deer, elk, buffalo, and other animals by the mastodons, which they called "big buffalo;" but before the mischief had gone far the Great Spirit grasped his lightning, stepped out of heaven, the prints of his feet being left on a rock at Big Bone Lick, and killed the monsters right and left. One old bull was tougher than the lightning. As the bolts fell on his forehead he shook them off, and for some time he stood, daring the Great Spirit. At length a stroke fell on his side, and smarting and trumpeting he galloped off toward the northwest, clearing all the rivers and the great lakes in powerful leaps, and there in Alberta, or British Columbia, he still lives, with a few subdued associates. Beside these creatures, the natives say, all other animals are as insects; their skin is proof against arrows, and they have "an arm" that they use as we do ours,— of course, a trunk. Still farther north, in the region of the great, lonely lakes, we hear that the fathers of the Indian tribes had to build their houses on piles in the water, like the ancient dwellings of the Swiss, in order to escape assault from the elephants, who ravaged the whole country.

Myths and Legends

HIDDEN GOLD

Was ever a place or a time where and when the people did not believe in hidden wealth? There is a peculiar charm in the rare, the hinted, and the unseen that leads some classes to conceal even their wisdom, while others reveal it only to the initiated. In common with the United States, the British provinces were hiding-places for the gold of pirates, of misers, of adventurers, and of fugitives, and ever and anon it enters some head, that might be better occupied, to search for this treasure. Money is spent in the seeking, but little is taken in return. Hard-minded men say the reason is that there is none to be taken. Certain who are more open to conviction declare the reason to be a pernicious activity of ghosts and goblins in guarding the hoard, for it was a practice with pirates to kill one of their comrades and bury him atop of the chest or keg of doubloons, that his spirit might haunt the spot and scare away intruders. Any self-respecting pirate of this nineteenth century would be so disgusted by this treachery of his shipmates that when he came up out of the sand and found himself dead he would bid all his comrades go hang—as they would be sure to do anyway—and would trudge away to a warmer clime and more congenial occupations. Captain Kidd, who really did bury one box of valuables on Gardiner's Island, New York, where it was found, was consequently suspected of having salted the whole Atlantic coast with crowns and cob dollars, but if so he died keeping his secret. A rumor that a part of this wealth was deposited on the shore near Halifax has created some anxious guesses as to where.

Probably the most touching spectacle of confidence exhibited to the gaze of nations was that offered by the people who dug over Oak Island, near Chester, Nova Scotia, in search of this treasure of Kidd's, for they went down into the earth a hundred feet. As if busy pirates had time to dig graves of half that depth for their earnings! But they found masonry and timber, and do not guess their meaning.

A few miles away, near the Dutch town of Lunenburg, are the Ovens,—sea-worn caves in a cliff of gold-bearing rock,—that were much likelier hiding-places for treasure, because a great fear of the Ovens has existed since the time when an Indian, being swept into the biggest of them, was carried to the interior of the earth and presently cast up among the Tuskets, with his geography mixed and his shins bruised. Dark Cove and Money Cove, on Grand Manan, are reputed burial-places for a part of the Kidd gains.

Dead Man's Cove, sometime known as such to the people about Grand Pré, was one of Kidd's banks, and in after-years an effort was made to resurrect the treasure, a fortune-teller having given minute directions where to find it. It was a calm, clear night of moonshine when the seekers, after long work, struck their spades against a crock, and, opening the lid, felt their hearts dance within them, for it was full to the brim with Spanish dollars. As they plunged deeper to free the pot from the close-packed clay, one of them found that the iron had pierced a skull,—the skull of the murdered watcher. Almost on the instant there fell a bolt of lightning, accompanied by an appalling roar of. thunder. A blast of wind blew out the lanterns and tipped one man over, so that work ceased then and there. It is said that if one of the seekers is killed on the spot the spell will be lifted. Some gold is alleged to have been taken from a farm on Campobello by adventurers who promised to share it with the owner of the property if they found it. Perhaps they didn't find it. Anyway, they never happened around to share it.

Then there was the Frenchman Clairieux, who buried several boxes of money on Grand Island, in Niagara River, where a handful of ancient pieces was found two centuries later, and Fontenoy, another Frenchman, who buried his money—he had made it by cheating the Indians—in a brass kettle at Presque Isle, near Detroit. At the ancient forges on the St. Maurice River—which are the oldest smelters of iron in America, unless that distinction can be proved for the smelter at Principio, Maryland—the French authority was represented by a governor who lived in a stately château near by. When the English took Canada they heard rumors of the manufacture of shot and cannon in these forges, and forthwith a detachment of red-coats appeared before the place, demanding the surrender of everything and everybody. The governor was absent at the time, but Demoiselle Poulin, a young relative, who spoke for him, threw the keys into the river rather than give them up. The English then entered the château and the forge by force; but it is said that the delay caused by Demoiselle Poulin's obduracy was long enough to enable the servants and workmen to bury many of the valuables about the premises. So, when dim lights and shadowy shapes are seen about the ruins, the traveller knows that the old governor and his domestics are trying to discover where they hid their gold.

It is sad that the great block of lapis lazuli should have disappeared, for it was "worth ten crowns an ounce." It lay two or three miles off the island of Grand Manan, and was a guide to mariners aiming to enter St. John River. An officer, who broke off the piece that was valued as above, and the veracious Charlevoix, are authority for this rock. It is worth dredging to the surface, maybe.

And as Mount Washington had its carbuncle that lighted the clouds with a ruddy glow at night, so the great cliff of six hundred feet that guards the entrance to the Basin of Minas has its enormous

Diamond of Blomidon. It is seen flashing from afar, but every attempt of seekers to wrest the gem from the mocking spirits of the crag has been a failure. Copper you find there, and agate, amethysts, garnets, and beautiful zeolites, but the diamond dims as you approach it, and close at hand fades utterly from view.

Wreck, more often than Piracy, threw wealth on the shores of Sable Island, "land of sand and ruin and gold," "the charnel-house of North America." Gales uncover the skeletons of castaways, but the winds and waves have buried only the more deeply the crocks of doubloons and pieces of eight that perhaps the high-seas-men did not put here. Sarcastic, indeed, is the name of "French Gardens," as applied to this spot of blight, where the forty convicts sent as slaves to the new colony were set ashore by De la Roche, to await a call that never came, except from death. Only a dozen escaped this call, and five years later they were taken off, a shaggy lot, half turned to beasts in appearance, if not in nature. It is guessed that the only available riches of the island are in its berries and wild pigs.

On Fisguard Street, Victoria, British Columbia, stands a dilapidated house of two stories and a ghost story. Who or what the ghost is the people are forgetting; but they recall the Australian who bought it twenty-five years ago when he arrived from the gold-fields of the antipodes, and it is alleged that some of them prowl about the yard when the weather keeps the police in-doors; for, in spite of its ghost, its spiders, and its rats, the place has a rare interest for them. There is Australian gold in the yard,—a pot of it. The Australian had an ignorant horror of banks, bonds, stock, mortgages, and the usual interest-paying investments, so he committed his wealth to the earth, taking it up and increasing it from time to time. When he died he enjoined his wife never to reveal its hiding-place. She refused to sell or lease the property. Hence the visits of folks with shovels and divining-rods.

When gold-hunters went to the rich fields of the Klondike they heard reports from the Indians of a "Too-Much-Gold Creek," whose sands were yellower than those of Pactolus; but the natives themselves had forgotten, and the others, though they moved the name to another stream, never found just where the water flowed. It has taken its place on the maps of other days,—the maps on which one finds the islands most affected by mermaids and the seas vexed by serpents and krakens.

HOW ONE BEAR LOST HIS LIFE

IN the folk-lore of certain tribes Brother Bear is a gentle and sagacious creature, who frequents the settlements with the same freedom as if he were a dog. He slides on the ice with the children, carries them on his back, and is glad of scraps after dinner, though he prefers fruit, vegetables, and honey to meat, when he can get these dainties. The Indians encouraged his friendship because he kept their camp free from refuse, and also drove off the wolves that so greatly vexed the maritime provinces. Indeed, there is a claim that bears have never been killed for food in the East, even when food of all kinds was made scarce by raiding armies of French and English. This may have been true among the Passamaquoddies, whose totem was the bear, and who refuse to sit at a table where bear's meat is served, although even they may be egged on to self-defence, as Nick Lewi was when he was overhauled by a bear who had stepped into four separate wild-cat traps and had one on each paw, which enabled him to box tremendously, and who succumbed only after repeated stabbings.

It does not often happen to a hunter to get off so easily in an encounter with a wild animal as a Melicite Indian did in the New Brunswick woods when he met a bear. He was a calm person, as one must be who lives by the hunt, and these Indians

have a splendid nerve. The white man thinks he
does pretty well when he brings down his prey at
a hundred yards, and he wants a magazine rifle and
dynamite bullets at that. Until recently the savage
did his killing at such short range, with knives and
spears and arrows, that if he missed his aim he
might die for it. But this adventure occurred in
later times, and is best told in the Indian's own
words: "One time I go huntum moose. Night
come dark, rain and snow come fast. No axe for
makum wigwam. Gun wet, no getum fire. Me
very tired. Me crawl into large hollow tree. Find
plenty room. Almost begin sleep. Bimeby me
feelum hot wind blow on my face. Me know hot
bear's breath. He crawl into log, too. I takum
gun. She no go. I think me all same gone,—all
eat up. Then me thinkum my old snuff-box. I
take some snuff and throwum in bear's face and he
run out. Not very much likeum, I guess. Me lay
still all night. He no come again. Every leetle
while, every time, bear he go ' o-o-O-ME !' sneezum
over and over, great many times. Morning come,
me fixum gun and shootum, dead. He no more
sneezum, no more this time."

THE ISLE OF DEMONS

STRENGTH and courage were often exhibited by the women who were among the early immigrants to this country,—delicate creatures reared at the court of France, some of them, and knowing little but luxury and ease until they came to these shores. A typical " new woman" of that kind was Marguerite de Roberval, niece of the harsh old Sieur de Roberval, " the little king of Vimeu," who came here to possess the land and flog the natives of it into the religion of love and charity. The girl had plighted her troth to a young cavalier who had enlisted among the adventurers on this expedition. It was of course impossible that their love-making should escape notice, and old Roberval was so incensed about it that when his ship arrived at the Isle of Demons (Quirpon, near Newfoundland) he set Marguerite ashore there with her nurse, and only four guns with their ammunition to support life, while he held on his way; but the lover sprang from the deck with gun in hand and armor on his back and swam to shore, where the three exiles ruefully or vengefully watched the departing ship. By their united efforts a hut was built, and here a babe was born to Marguerite. For a little time their state was not so ill. Then came the cold, the game grew scarce, privation and anxiety told upon them. The cavalier was first to go; next the infant; lastly, the nurse. Marguerite buried them.

74

Beyond Our Borders

She was alone. Some women would have resigned
themselves to despair, and truly this woman had little
to live for. Not only was she without human company, but imps and spirits walked over the island,
peered out of the mist, whispered in the night,
called and whistled in the gale. These evil ones
had horned heads and wings and "howled like a
crowd in the market-place." At last a sail appeared.
She heaped her little fire with brush and made a
smoke, which struck terror to the crew, for this
was the Isle of Demons, and the smoke was of the
eternal burning. And so they sailed away. Hoping,
despite her grief and misery, Marguerite fished
and hunted, skinning the animals that she shot, for
clothes, and keeping her hut stanch against the
gales, praying when the fiends shook the door and
muttered strange words at the window. In the
third winter another sail appeared, and again she
heaped up brush and sent a column of smoke aloft.
This time the crew were scared, especially when
they saw the woman's figure gesticulating franti-
cally on a rock, but the officers forced them to
anchor and make a landing. They were honest
fishermen, and never imagined at the first that this
brown and lonely creature had been an ornament
of the gayest society in Europe, but they took her
back to France with them, strong, sedate, resource-
ful now, and she regained her kin. If she felt
any bitterness toward her uncle she was able to
take a satisfaction in hearing shortly of his failure,

He went swelling to the New World as "Lord of Norembega, Viceroy and Lieutenant-General in Canada, Hochelaga, Saguenay, Newfoundland, Belle Isle, Carpunt, Labrador, the Great Bay, and Baccalaos," with five shiploads of convicts in his train, this precious company having been assembled to develop the country and convert the red men. Roberval was a hard master; perhaps he needed to be, and he so ill-treated his rag-tag following, giving them scanty food and plenty of hard work at forts, mills, and shops, shooting, hanging, and beating women as well as men for the least offences, that they mutinied, and his life often hung in the balance. Presently the food gave out, and the proud Sieur was fain to eat fish and roots boiled in oil,—he who had dined with kings. Scurvy set in, and the wretches died pitifully, yet unpitied. Roberval was recalled, and according to one report he was struck down at night by an unknown hand before the Church of the Innocents, in Paris; but others believe that he re-covered and made a second venture for wealth and power, his cruel, haughty spirit again defeating its own aim, so that he died, leaving none to mourn him. As he went to his death among the black and lonely reaches of the Saguenay, did he shrink aghast at the memory of his misdeeds? Mingled with the sounds of wreck and storm that faded on his ear, did he hear the moans and calls of the strange creatures on the Isle of Demons to whose keeping he had com-mitted the girl he should have loved and sheltered?

THE FIGURE IN SMOKY HUT

SABLE ISLAND, haunt of convicts, pirates, and such wild creatures, who were landed there centuries ago, is a mere bank in the solitary northern seas that froth against it, tearing and rebuilding its shore, and in high tide threatening to engulf it. There are now no inhabitants except the light-keepers, for so many crimes were committed there in the old days, especially by wreckers, that permanent settlement was prohibited. It is still a graveyard of ships, over one hundred and fifty having met their end there, but castaways run no risk of murder. Strange tales are told there of a heroic friar, of one of the fugitive judges who condemned Charles I. to his death, of men left alone to perish who became like wolves, and if a sailor had to choose a spot to be wrecked upon, this key of sand is one of the last to which he would consent.   .

In the eighteenth century the British transport ship Amelia, with treasure and a guard, went to pieces on the sands of this dread spot, and few survived the disaster. Those who did succeed in getting to the mainland told of villains who had shown false beacons and robbed and killed the crew, and their strange tale was promptly investigated by government. Captain Torrens, of the navy, was despatched to the scene of the wreck to gain all possible knowledge of it, and, if might be, to apprehend all who were engaged in the crime. He found the island without trouble. The trouble began as soon as he had found it, for his ship ran her nose into it, and bade fair to stay, although she was eventually freed from the sand and kept off at anchor. No inhabitants were found, except wild hogs, which the sailors were glad to shoot for food. Going over this almost desert in search of relics that might furnish some clue to the outlaws, Captain Torrens arrived at the squalid shelter known, probably because of its ineffective ventilation, as the "smoky hut," and pushed open the door. To his astonishment, the place was occupied. In the dim light he saw a woman, young, fair, with pain and sadness in her face. She seemed to have but just been rescued from the sea, for her long hair and her simple white dress clung to her figure, and were as if dripping with moisture.

"Beg pardon, madame," said the captain, peering under his· hand to see into the dark, for the sun had set in a threatening sky, "but are there any others here?"

The woman remained motionless, with eyes fixed on his own, and said no word.

"Is it possible that a ship has come ashore and I did not see it? Pray, how long have you been here? Can I do anything for you?"

The woman raised her hand. The first finger was gone, and its stump was mashed and bloody.

"Ah, you have been hurt. Wait till I bring

my surgeon." And he turned to go back to his ship. Hardly had he taken five paces before the woman had slipped out at the door—a thistle-down floating in the air could not have been lighter—and ran away. Happening to look back at the moment, the captain saw her. "Now I understand," he said to himself. "The poor creature has been crazed by her suffering and by her life alone in this place," and calling after, he begged her to stop. She did not slack her pace, which was marvellously swift and easy, and, fearing that she might do some violence to herself, he gave chase, telling her that she had no reason for alarm, and asking her to accept the shelter of his cabin. The woman ran until she reached a pond in the centre of the island, where she seemed to dive, for, although he searched carefully through the reeds and long grass, Captain Torrens discovered no trace of her, not even a bent blade to show that she had passed. Going back in perplexity, he was the more bewildered on seeing at the door of the "smoky hut" the same woman that had disappeared at the edge of the pond. There was something uncanny in it. He began to wish that he were not alone. Yet he strode resolutely to the shanty. A wan gleam of twilight rested on the still face of the woman, who looked fixedly upon him. He staggered back and became almost as pale as she. "Lady Copeland! It is you!" he exclaimed, in a strained whisper.

The woman nodded.

" I thought you were dead."

Again the woman nodded.

" You were killed here—by the wreckers ?" he gasped.

She nodded again.

" I understand. They threw your body into the pond? Horrible! And your finger? Yes, yes. I see. They cut it off to get your rings. Rest assured I will do all I can for your repose. Shall I search for your body and take it to England? No? Then my chaplain shall read the service at the pond. And I will hunt down the villain who robbed you, and send your jewels to your family."

Again the figure nodded, and the captain could see that a peaceful smile had come upon the face. The wind drove up a little cloud of sand. He closed his eyes for an instant to shield them, and when he opened them he was alone. Hastening back on shipboard, he fetched out the chaplain, had prayers said, weighed anchor, and, acting on such clues as he had gathered, he set sail for Halifax, where he recovered from a money-lender the gems that had been stolen from Lady Copeland, despatched them to her family, then proceeding along the Labrador coast he caught the wrecker who had slain her and hanged him at the yard-arm.

THE SHADOW OF HOLLAND COVE

IN 1764 came the first white settler to Holland Cove, Prince Edward Island,—a surveyor, one Captain Holland, who gave his name to the place where he had set up his habitation. With him presently appeared a woman, of Micmac origin on her mother's side, but her father was a French count, belike, for she was tall, distinguished, and in mind and bearing unlike the majority of half-breeds. Racine was the name whereby she was best known. Of her history the captain's associates knew nothing, or wisely professed to know nothing. During the winter after his arrival the captain was frequently absent on hunting and surveying trips, and on one of these excursions he was gone so long beyond the appointed time that Racine undertook to cross the cove on the ice, to see if she might not find some token of him or meet him the sooner. Such, at least, was the supposition. It was an unwise venture, for the ice was infirm, and, falling between two floes, she disappeared. Holland mourned her loss on his return, and attempts were made to find her body, but without avail.

On a still night in the following summer the coxswain of the captain's party was wakened by a sound of low voices in the sitting-room, and, knowing that all hands had turned in, his curiosity was roused. Lighting a tallow dip, he peered into the room, and to his surprise saw Racine. Her position made it seem as if she were seated on the knees of a figure in the captain's easy-chair. The voices were subdued until they were almost whispers, so that the steady drip of water from the woman's clothing could be heard distinctly. At the approach of the coxswain Racine arose and fled past him into the garden, going as silently as possible, yet leaving an odor of sea-damp and a trail of moisture along the floor. There was quite a pool of brine before the chair. To the spectator's surprise, the chair was empty. Had it been vacated while his eyes were on the retreating woman? He stood puzzled, uncertain, and seemed to hear the words, " Why doesn't he come? I must meet him," receding from the open door. Then he heard a splash at the shore. This roused him, and he called up the house, Captain Holland arising with the others. In ten words he told what he had seen, and all hurried to the water, but again nothing was seen or heard. There were the puddled wet, the track of a soaked dress, the open door. Who had been there? With whom met? Still, they think nowadays it was a ghost, and that all who see it will die of drowning. If you disbelieve in spirits and have a faith that you will die in your bed, you may care to watch at Holland Cove on the night of the 14th of July, at the hour when the tide is high.

THE FRIAR OF CAMPOBELLO

CAMPOBELLO ISLAND sounds well, but is prettily absurd, and the change from the original and distinctive title of the Passamaquoddies, which was Ebawhoot, is pleasant only to people who like weak names. It has more history than an island measuring only three miles by eight can usually boast, for many are the tales of pirates, of wrecks and wreckers, of haunters and of war; as in 1866 the romantic region was menaced by all the terrors of bombardment. A band of Fenians assembled at Eastport in that year, determined to take the island away from Canada, crush its population of eighteen or twenty, and annex it to Ireland; but they got into a discussion and finally didn't. Here Admiral Owen, proprietor of the island, used to pace up and down in his gold lace and buttons on a quarter-deck that he built over the ledges. Here is the rock of the Friar, scarred by the shot of British war-ships at practice; for sea-captains were not brought up on Indian legends. This friar was never a monk. He is a petrified lover. Foolishly he fell victim to the charms of a squaw, and when the husband of his copper-colored enchantress discovered the fact he drove him into outer darkness. So stony was his despair that it completely changed him, and there he is at this day: skedapsispenabsku, the stone manikin.

Another accounting for the figure is this. A young Indian of courage, and his wife of grace and beauty, lived on the cape above the Friar, and would have lived happily had it not been for the parents of his wife, who not only insisted on living with her and being cared for, but on commanding her as if she were still unmarried. A trip to St. John River having been proposed by the parents, the young man refused to go with them or to allow his wife to go. She was divided between two duties, as she fancied, and was in much grief. Neither her father nor her husband would concede any point, and the time set for the journey was near. Now, the young man had medicine power, and he did what he could to increase it, until, feeling that he could work his will, he asked his wife to walk with him to the shore. While she sat there he threw his command upon her, and she sank to sleep; then she grew rigid, death-like, and soon she was stone. "I told you I would never part from my wife," he said to his father-in-law. "Come with me and see how I keep my word. There is your daughter. She will never move or speak again. I look on her and bid you fare-well." And, putting all his magic power into the effort, he began to lose his human outline, to harden and turn gray. And in a few minutes he, too, was stone.

This myth of conversion is wide-spread, and on the other side of the continent we find an opposite

phase of it. The Chinooks point to Mount Ikanam as the body of Ikanam, creator of the universe,
self-petrified; while on the Yukon, above Klato-
klin, or Johnny's village, are two mighty rocks
heaved sheer for hundreds of feet above the water.
These are husband and wife. Being incompatible
in temper, the man kicked the woman into the
plain and drew the river out of its old bed to run
between them.

With that infernal spirit of destruction that dif-
ferentiates men from other animals, a crowd of
fishermen succeeded in tumbling the Campobello
husband into the bay, while the British captains
pounded off the head of the wife with cannon.
Along come other destroyers who tear up the old
names and old traditions, set up Jonesvilles and
Jimsonhursts, and hold five o'clock teas amid the
ruins of Indian romance.

TWO MELICITE VICTORIES

SUNDRY miles of the country watered by the
St. John—the river of that name in New
Brunswick, for it is applied to other waters; indeed, there are not saints enough to go around—are
and long have been the haunts of the Melicites, and
although they now wear trousers, read the papers,
and make a dollar or so a day as canoemen, they
boast of many achievements in war. Especially
venomous were the Mohawks, and two of their

victories against those people were unusual. Near
Muniac a peninsula juts into the St. John. It is a
long way around, and a short cut is offered across
the isthmus. The Melicites knew this and the
Mohawks did not, and through the device known
to theatrical managers who give a "cheap numer-
osity to a stage army," the invaders were turned
back and no lives were lost. Finding their enemy
encamped in force on the shore opposite this point,
evidently intending an attack on some villages below that were peopled only by women, children,
and old men, the braves being absent on a search
for deer and Mohawks, a little company of six
Melicites proceeded to multiply itself. The men
had three canoes, and in them they paddled down-
stream as fast as possible and as far as possible
from the hostile camp. But they did not go home.
They turned around the point, out of sight behind
the trees, then scrambled across the isthmus, embarked, and came down once more, the boats being
well strung out. As boat after boat went by for
half a day, the Mohawks, who had had no idea that
there were so many hundred Melicites, became
thoughtful, then sad. They felt that they had been
lured away on a dangerous errand, and, so deciding,
they packed up their belongings and returned to
their own habitations.

The victory at the Grand Falls of the St. John
was won by equally clever strategy, but it had its
tragedy. Indeed, there have been many tragedies

in this gloomy chasm, with its seventy-foot plunge of waters, from the times when the Melicites used to fling their prisoners over Squaw Rock into a black depth two hundred feet below, to these later days when lumbermen have been drawn into the torrent and their bodies never given back to the sight of men. Two or three centuries ago, at least, the Mohawks descended the river to do injury to the people who dwelt beside it. At the mouth of the Madawaska they paused for a few minutes to wipe a village out of existence. A few of the people escaped, but all on whom hands could be laid were killed, excepting only a squaw. Her life was spared on condition that she would act as their pilot down the stream, for they knew that there were dangers to navigation between them and the populous Melicite town of Aukpak. The woman gained their confidence by leading them safely over some rapids, and, as the current was strong and they were constitutionally opposed to work, they roped their canoes together and allowed the river to carry them. Their guide occupied a place in the first boat, and was warned that she would die if she misled them. Suddenly the shores came together in a savage gap, and the current grew more swift. The squaw looked straight ahead with impassive face. And now a deep roar was heard. She told them it was a stream falling into the St. John. Then, as the fleet swung about a point, the misty gulf disclosed itself, while a thunder of water stunned them. They realized their danger, and rowed with frenzy for the shore. But it was of no use. They were in the river's grasp. The squaw gave a loud cry of triumph, there was a faint crash of splintering canoes on the tooth of rock below, then victory and silence.

THE FLAME SLOOP OF CARAQUETTE

"HEAVEN save us all and shield us from harm," is the prayer of the people who live along the Bay of Chaleurs, and especially of those Brunswickers who fish upon it, when they hear that the flame sloop is on her cruise again. Never is that apparition reported but some dweller on the bay gives up his life within a week. The sloop is seldom seen except by sailors and fishermen, but the gleam of it penetrates far through even stormy air, falling over the landscape in a pale, phosphorescent glow, as if the northern lights were out, and fading while one looks about him to see where it comes from. Those who see it fairly and live to tell about it say it is a sloop-rigged craft, all made of fire,—a vision out of hot hell on the cold waters of the Laurentian gulf. Its sails are sheets of flame, its shrouds are like lightning, its hull, mast, and spars glow like brands. On the deck are the crew, charred corpses, stiffly walking the red planks, hauling at the blazing halliards, and climbing the white-hot shrouds. Various are the explanations of this phenomenon. Henry Hudson perished lonesomely in the vast bay that keeps his name, the victim of a mutiny, and this may be a vision of the fate that befell his crew in working southward, even though the ship itself reached England. Roberval ascended the Saguenay, and in one version of his history he never came down. Is this a revelation of what ensued among his discontented men? According to one dim rumor, Verrazzano, the Florentine discoverer, was killed by Indians near Louisburg, Cape Breton, and his crew, attempting an escape, may have drifted down the coast to meet this strange destruction. The omnipresent Kidd has infested this bay at times.

But a tale has gone the rounds of the Chaleurs villages, that shortly after the nineteenth century was born a small vessel went ashore on the south side of the bay, near Caraquette, New Brunswick. It was believed that crew and freight went to the bottom with her, until certain articles known to have been on board were found to be in the hands of a few fellows ashore, who were looked upon askance by their neighbors as men who smuggled, diced, drank too much, had even sailed in a pirate ship and set false beacons inland to lure well-freighted barks ashore. So it was whispered about that these fellows had more knowledge of the sloop's wreck than they were willing to impart. There was no direct evidence, but the circumstantial proof offered by their mysteriously earned property was sound enough to take a warrant on. Some leaky-mouthed villager told them that the officers were coming, and, hurriedly gathering their effects into a small vessel of their own, they stood away to sea. Had they intended any usual business they would have waited until a stout nor'wester had blown itself out, but their lives were in hazard, and their first hope was to get out of the Bay of Chaleurs. On the very next morning parts of their vessel began to come ashore in the breakers, and before the sun was down the body of every one of those guilty men had been flung upon the rocks. This the people believed to be a certain indication of their crime. What brought them to their end? Some act of carelessness? The upsetting of a stove or lamp? Or was it a stroke of lightning? Whatever it was, it worked an act of vengeance, and the souls of the wretched creatures are doomed to haunt the scene of their offence, swathed in such flames as the good priests say must be their everlasting portion.

Beyond Our Borders

THE ACADIANS AND EVANGELINE

WE shall never be quite at the truth about the Acadians, the French settlers in Nova Scotia, for the reports of the differences between them and the English are colored by race and religious prejudice. Certain it is, however, that on taking possession of the country the British regarded these farmers with suspicion, and that they burned their homes and drove them into exile with such haste that many families were separated, never again to be united. The French set forth that this was the act of a tyrannical governor and an imbruted soldiery. The English allege that the Acadians could not be trusted; that under guise of neutrality they were plotting against their conquerors and watching for an occasion to restore French rule in the Dominion. At the dawn of the twentieth century the breach, though narrowed, is still unhealed. Among the charges brought against the Acadians is that of angering the savages against their new rulers by telling them that the English were the men who had crucified Christ. Although the farmers along Minas Basin persisted that they had no part in the war which culminated in the fall of Louisburg under the guns of British regulars and Yankee militia, they were ordered, under penalties, to aid the winning party. One British officer told them that unless they furnished wood for his camp he would tear down their houses for fuel. Another said, "If you don't take the oath of fidelity I will batter your villages with my cannon." Cornwallis, on the other hand, assured them that if only they would be peaceable and loyal they might retain their religion and be "the happiest people in the world."

Several acts of these French settlers were not those of a peace-loving or a neutral people. They made trouble at Chebucto; they incited the Indians to the raid on Dartmouth, in which many of the villagers were killed, hurt, and kidnapped, their homes looted, and a third of the settlement laid in ashes. At the end of the war the Acadians who had escaped arrest refused to take the oath of allegiance and claimed the right to be let alone. Vicar-General La Loutre, their clerical leader, so hated the Protestants that, like the Russians retreating before Napoleon in a later time, he burned one of his towns—Beaubassin, a place of a thousand souls —that the English might not take it. It was a wretched season, and were it not for certain picturesque incidents attending the deportation and dispersion of the Acadians, of whom several spent the rest of their lives vainly seeking their families, and of whom "three ship-loads were sent to Philadelphia," one could wish that its record might be lost.

Best known of these episodes is that of Evangeline, the heroine of Longfellow's poem. She, at least, was an innocent sufferer in the clash between the races, and it is her story that, more than any other factor, has caused the action of the English to be condemned with expressions of horror. Evangeline Bellefontaine and her betrothed, Gabriel Lajeunesse, were of Grand Pré, whose few ruins on the south shore of Minas are a common show for tourists. When the British seized their village and burned their homes they expected to be sent away together, but in the haste and confusion they were separated, and, without the slightest clue to the whereabouts of her lover, Evangeline set off on a search for him. She sought from Maine to Louisiana, daring roughness, illness, and fatigue, and at last reached a home on the Teche on the very day that Gabriel had left it to prosecute his equally vain search for her. After other years of wandering, broken in spirit, hopeless, yet willing to live for the good she might do, Evangeline became a nun, and was assigned to a Philadelphia hospital. A pestilence was raging. People were dying by hundreds. On a Sunday morning she found in the hospital a new victim. It was Gabriel. A cry, a kiss: he was gone. Yet life was less bitter to her from that moment.

Myths and Legends

THE TOLLING OFF GASPÉ

WHEN it was learned that the English were coming, the good folk of Grand Pré hid many of their simple treasures, for to their minds, inflamed against the invaders, to be an Englishman was to be little else than a robber. Strange sights had been seen in the air, strange sounds had been heard in the twilight, and the people feared. Knowing that the English were heretics, their first care was to save the church properties, the communion-cups and host of silver, the embroidered vestments of the priest, the sweet-toned bell that called them to matins, mass, and vespers and rang the restful Angelus across their well-tilled fields. These objects were placed in a vault, and, according to one version of the tale, were stolen on the very next night by the crew of a strange vessel that landed here. A gale sped the departing craft, and as she lifted across the waves the boom of the bell came back across the seething water. Accursed in this theft, the vessel got no farther than Blomidon. At the foot of that great crag she was shivered into pieces, and there among the sands the treasure is.

But the oftener told story of the bell is that it was put aboard a rescue-ship, the Tourmente, that it might be carried with the other church belongings to a chapel near Gaspé. The sight of the rich silver, the gemmed stole, the candlesticks, incense-burner, and altar ornaments, that might easily be

converted into money, roused the cupidity of the
captain and his lawless crew : so, instead of deliv-
ering the treasure at Gaspé, they set the priest
ashore and sailed away. Standing on the beach,
the good father pronounced a curse on ship and
crew, and hardly had he turned away ere the sky
darkened, a wind came up that increased to a hurricane before the canvas could be taken in, and
presently the vessel was hurled against a rock and
was broken in two. Not a soul survived ; not even
the girl passenger who was on her way to join her
lover. And now the tolling bell of a spectre ship
is sometimes heard by the people of Gaspé. It is
a vessel squat and square, sailed by a skeleton crew
in pigtails and petticoat breeches, and the boom
of the stolen bell, that hangs high on her foremast,
is so dire in meaning that passing sailors tremble.
The form in white that wrings its hands on the
deck is that of the girl who was to meet her lover
only in death, for his shadow, too, is seen on a
cliff, feeding a phosphor beacon-fire, and as the ship
careens below he leaps to her rescue and disappears
beneath the waves with her in his arms. To see
this ship as it cruises up and down the gulf, especially when it flies by in dead calm or against the
wind, her binnacle burning blue, her funereal bell
tolling, is to meet a storm within an hour. If you
follow that lamp and bell through the deepening
murk, hoping to gain safe harbor, you will be hurled
on the same reef on which the Tourmente perished.

THE RIDE TO DEATH

A MONG the Indian gardens of fable was the lake country of the Blue Mountains, in Nova Scotia. A certain reverence for the spirits of its woods and waters made the Micmacs who dwelt there jealous of the advancing white men, yet they had received so many benefits at the hands of the French people that they could not refuse help to the latter in their extremity. For Annapolis Royal had been thrown into panic on the news that the English had burned Grand Pré, seized its farms and live stock, and sent all its people captive to other lands. Already the English officers had disarmed the Acadians, so that they could not even shoot ducks for food, yet with deportation to follow capture the Annapolitans determined to risk the harshness of the wilds rather than the cruelty of their fellow-men. Collecting what they might of their goods and stock, they set off for the Blue Mountains. Sometimes they suffered a lack of food, several babes died of hunger and exposure and were buried beside the trail, cattle fell by the way, and the nights were filled with dread when the growling and squalling of beasts came from the bush. Having no guns, they were without defence, except that of clubs and stones, but they reached the Micmac settlements just as a troop of English arrived within striking distance. The Indians beat back the pursuers and cared for the

Acadians until they could help themselves, sharing fish and game, and building huts to shelter them. And friendship was strengthened between the red men and the white.

Among the French was a girl named Rachel, whose lover, Joseph, had disappeared on the day of the flight. Whether he had fled with another party or been deported to the southern colonies none could tell, but there was a fear that he had resisted the English and had been killed. A young Micmac sued for Rachel's hand, thinking that her heart was free, but she would not listen to him. Long he paid his court, but with no effect until the young man's father took on a tone half threatening. He reminded her how the French had been befriended by the Micmacs in this flight, and what ingratitude she would show if she behaved with coldness toward his son. Her own people also pleaded with her. Their lives depended on the friendship of these Indians; it was certain that she never again would hear of her white lover; in this marriage she would be gaining favors for all her people; beside, the hunter was a well-appearing lad, who had been Christianized, and might be won to the ways of the Acadians, as well as to their faith. Worn with these persecutions, indifferent in her sorrow, feeling that she had no friend, Rachel consented, and a day was fixed for the wedding.

The log chapel was decorated with flowers, all

the people, both pale and dark, gathered to feast and dance, the priest awaited the couple at the altar, when a commotion arose without, for a young Acadian was come, eagerly calling for Rachel. It was Joseph. He had been carried with other ex-iles to Philadelphia, had but just succeeded in finding this remote colony of his people, and was filled with disgust and rage at discovering the apparent faithlessness of his *fiancée*. In a few words the girl explained that the marriage was not of her seeking, and begged him to take her away. The Indian, who had been haughtily regarding his rival, bade him begone, for he would not suffer the disgrace of giving up his wife to any man. The older heads were shaken sadly, because matters had now gone too far to be undone. The wedding must take place. The girl must dress quickly and follow her dusky groom to church. In a few minutes five little girls, wreathed in flowers, went to her door, whence she was to walk to her bridal. The Indian became impatient. He knocked; he called. There was no answer. He flung open the door; the place was empty. Instantly the village was in an uproar, the Indians clamoring for pursuit and revenge, the Acadians declaring their innocence, the old priest urging peace. A few bent grass-blades and broken twigs showed that the flight of the lovers had been toward the outlet of the lakes, and when the Indians reached the water Joseph and Rachel were seen in a canoe paddling down the river with all haste. The pursuers quickly embarked and gave chase. Believing that capture was certain, Joseph picked up his gun and was about to shoot his Micmac rival, but Rachel begged him not to fire, for the Indians might revenge the act upon the innocent. He dropped the gun and resumed his paddle. Presently they noticed that the Indians had fallen back, and their hearts bounded with a new hope, for liberty now seemed secure; but in another moment they knew the reason for this abandonment: the roar of a waterfall was heard, and their canoe was whirling toward the brink with growing speed. The paddles were useless. The lovers' lips met in a kiss; then, clasped in each other's arms, their voices joined in prayer, they rode into the abyss, to death.

In another version a happier ending is reached: the runaways leave their canoe at the head of the rapid and hide among the trees. The birch is found empty and crushed among the rocks below. Thus prosperously starting a belief in their death, they travel safely afoot to Halifax, where they beg the captain of a British ship to give them passage to the southern colonies, and in the warm, fertile lands of a more peaceful country they live happily for long years.

THE GENERAL WITH AN EAR

STUDENTS in the university at Fredericton, New Brunswick, are in no wise different from the pupils of other schools, although it is not recorded of them that they ever put a cow into the chapel belfry or enlivened a lecture on geology with cannon crackers. But they did break the law with a gun on several occasions. This gun belongs to the university, and has had a way of going off on unexpected nights, causing the alarm of housewives in the town and the utterance of distressing remarks by usually moral householders. The students had organized a glee-club, which for its own safety's sake did most of its singing in vacant farms and grave-yards, even defying the ghosts in silks and peri-wigs that vex the hermitage, and one night it shifted the scene to a place in the woods, having noticed certain threatening exhibitions on the part of citizens near the places of its other rehearsals. As it happened, they had posted themselves beside the grave of a certain French general, and they had not been at work more than ten minutes before this officer scrambled out of the earth with hair on end, tears in his eyes, and distraction in his aspect. He adjured them by all they held sacred—if people who made such noises could hold even the ten com-mandments sacred—to go and sing to the others. If only they would let him alone he would tell them where a cannon had been hidden with which they could create a less terrible noise, though a louder one, than they were engaged in making. They accepted the bribe, imperilled their lives and those of other people by practising elsewhere, and found the gun, so that Fredericton had, for a time, two kinds of disturbances instead of one.

THE DEFENCE OF ST. JOHN

ALTHOUGH it has always been a mission of womankind to astonish and perplex dull men,—that is, all men,—one cannot read the history of the maritime provinces without a fresh experience of wonder and admiration, with occasional moments of doubt, it is true, at the exploits of the sweethearts and wives of immigrants and habitants. And beauty is added to their courage by the modesty of it all, for not one of them clamors for her rights, or summons a band of shrieking sisters to suppress the tyrant, man ; though, goodness knows, the tyrant often needed suppressing the worst way. And it was France—religious, conventional France —that gave these daughters to the New World; France, that held the sex in social abeyance and reared its girls to dance and sing and work embroidery, and charm, and pray in convents, but not to fight. We had, withal, a dozen Jeannes d'Arc in this country in the old days who would have done as much for their people as the original Maid of Orleans did for hers had they enjoyed an opportunity.

Such was Madeleine, daughter of Lieutenant Verchères, who at the age of fourteen withstood a siege, by Iroquois, of "Castle Dangerous," on the Richelieu. With only three despairing men and two little boys to aid her, she held off the savages for a week, until help arrived from Quebec.

Such was Demoiselle Poulin, who refused to surrender the forges on the St. Maurice at the bidding of the English.

Such, in quieter, more womanly ways, were Hélène de Champlain, Marguerite de Roberval, and Evangeline Bellefontaine.

Such was Madame Drucour, wife of the governor, who served the guns at Louisburg, firing three shots at the English every day, to inspirit the jaded soldiers to fresh resistance in the siege; and her bravery won favors for her countrymen from the enemy after the surrender.

But the most conspicuous act of courage was the defence of the fort at the mouth of the river St. John, New Brunswick, against the brutal, mean-spirited Charnisay. In 1643 Charles La Tour was a prosperous trader who had set up his station at this point, and his neighbor, D'Aulnay Charnisay, had a post across the bay at Port Royal. The two ruled Acadia jointly, though each had his half, so that there was no excuse for friction; but La Tour's material success aroused the jealousy of the other, and he worked for his removal. As a result of his reports, the king was persuaded to lend himself

to the schemes of the mischief-maker, and author-
ized him to arrest La Tour for treason. Conscious
of his right, La Tour declined to be arrested; on
the contrary, he strengthened his walls and secured
enforcements from the Protestant town of Rochelle.
Charnisay persuaded the king to crush the rebel,
and when the royal troops arrived he blockaded
the port against his brother governor. In a fog
La Tour and his wife escaped to Boston, whence
he came back with five ships filled with sympathetic
fighters, and soundly thrashed Charnisay, but carelessly omitted to hang him.

Smarting under his reverse, the beaten man
waited until a partial peace had been arranged and
La Tour had withdrawn on a hunting and trading
trip, before investing the fort, with an idea of
starving it into surrender. Two monks, gaining
entrance to the place, were unmasked by Madame
La Tour and shown to be spies; but to express her
contempt she put them out as if they were not
worthy of punishment. They returned and announced the absence of La Tour to their chief,
who, fancying that he had merely to fight with a
woman, made a general assault, only to be beaten
off. For three days he boldly sent his followers
to be shot by the woman and her little garrison;
then, finding that he was not a match for her, he
corrupted one of her sentries with money, and so
bought his way into the fort he could not capture.
She met him so sturdily after he had entered that

he offered honorable terms of capitulation, and she accepted them in order to save her little band; yet no sooner had the papers been signed and the defenders laid down their arms than this incredible creature fell upon them, had them bound, and, singling out one of their number to act as executioner, hanged them, every one, save him who made the noose. He would have hanged the woman, too, but that he feared the rebuke of his king. As it was, he put a halter on the neck of Madame La Tour, and compelled her to see this slaughter of her servants and soldiers. Her husband impoverished, calumniated, and driven into exile, her friends and money gone, her mind filled with the memory of this outrage, the woman lived but three weeks after the capture, and Fort La Tour, with fifty thousand dollars' worth of plunder, passed into the hands of Charnisay. Strange, indeed, was the sequel to this siege. Charnisay, in more or less disrepute,—rather more than otherwise,—did not live long to gloat over his mean victory. He was found strangely dead in a shallow river near Port Royal. And, would one believe it ? the successful suitor for his widow's hand was La Tour. " Your husband and my wife disagreed," said he, " but that time is gone. Let us live in peace."

BROTHER AND SISTER IN BATTLE

BRAVE as the French were, and skilled in war, they forgot much in this country, and in various decisive conflicts with the English were overmastered in strategy and strength, if not in courage. It may be that the imagined remoteness of the military works on our frontiers, no matter of whose holding, lulled their garrisons into a false sense of security, for it is sure that in our day such an assault as that of Ethan Allen on Ticonderoga or that of Wolfe on Quebec would be out of the question. And it was the lack of a guard that led to the capture of St. John by the English. The attack was made early in the morning, while most of the French behind the walls were sound asleep. Alarmed by shouts and firing, the soldiers tumbled out of their bunks, grasped their sabres and matchlocks, and had made a sortie before they realized that they were undressed, or knew how large a force they were to meet. The neglect to post guards enough was a fatal one, and no heroism could redeem it.

Among those who served at the guns of the fort with furious energy was a woman, and an Englishwoman at that. Two years before she had wedded a French officer while on a visit to relatives in Paris, and when he was ordered to Acadia she elected to follow and share in the hardships of a soldier's life in a new land. The rebukes of her relatives, the appeals of friends not to side against her own country in the impending war, even the warnings of her husband that her step involved difficulty, if not danger, were of no weight with her. Personal love outweighed all else.

One of the first to fall in the attack on St. John was the young French officer, her husband. She grieved only for a moment. Rage succeeded regret. She went from one man to another, shrieking encouragement and orders, sighting and firing the cannon whenever a rift in the sulphur clouds showed the red flag of England or the scarlet coats of its defenders, and crying for revenge,—a spirit of war incarnate. Loud cries, increased firing, and a hurry of men told her that the besiegers had forced an entrance. The fight was to be hand to hand. Wrenching a sabre from the grasp of a fallen officer, she pushed her way into the front of the band, and, as the storming party appeared, carved and slashed lustily. In the smoke and din and pressure the invaders hardly knew or heeded that she was a woman until one of their lieutenants ran forward and grasped the arm of a stalwart trooper who was about to lunge at her with his bayonet. "Stop, for God's sake, man! Spare my sister!" commanded the officer. At these words the woman's arm fell, her sword clanged to the pavement, and her face turned white. "Brother!" she murmured, and sank, half fainting, into his arms, while the red-coats, with a yell of triumph, passed through

the gate and over the walls. Down came the lilies
of France, and up went the cross of St. George.
The day was won, and the defender of St. John
was a woman once more. Neither she nor her
brother had known that the other was in the battle. Her appeals in behalf of her husband's soldiers were heeded, and when the soreness in her
heart had healed she was married again, to an English officer, and became the revered great-grand-
mother of several Blue-Nose families.

THE GOLDEN DOG

UNLESS it may be the citadel, nothing is better
known in Quebec than the Golden Dog. It
is a gilded relief representing a dog, of doubtful
pedigree, lying on the ground and gnawing a bone.
An accompaniment of text informs us, on the animal's behalf,—

> Je suis un chien qui ronge l'os,
> En le rongeant je prends mon repos.
> Un tems viendra qui n'est pas venu
> Que je mordray qui m'aura mordu.

Which has been fairly done into English in this
manner:

> I am a dog that gnaws his bone.
> I crouch and gnaw it all alone.
> The time will come, which is not yet,
> When I'll bite him by whom I'm bit.

Myths and Legends

The purport of which in our time would be
that the dog is "layin' low," like Br'er Rabbit,
and watching his chance. This panel, let into the
front of the post-office, pertained to the house that
formerly occupied its site, the house of the Chien
d'Or, built in 1735. It passed through many fortunes, for it was at times residence, church, shop,
post-office, Masonic hall, and coffee-house, and here
Horatio Nelson met the girl he would have married,
—landlord Prentice's daughter,—swearing that if
he couldn't have her he would leave the service;
but he couldn't, and didn't, and it may be that he
fought all the harder for his disappointment. Here,
too, one Badeau, a merchant, was found hanging to
a nail, dead. Who put him there, and why, will
never be known.

The builder of the place was Nicholas Philibert, a Bordeaux man, who was seeking his fortune
here as a trader. He was a decent sort of fellow,
but, like every one else who had money or the hope
of it, he was wronged and swindled by Bigot, the
Royal Intendant, the thirteenth and last who held
that office. This Bigot was a curious mixture of
craft and tyranny, greed and recklessness. His
principal aim in life was to get money, but he gave
a good many hours a day to spending it. The
splendor of the entertainments in his palace, with
its four hundred and eighty feet of front, and his
generosity to his favorites, were in strange contrast
to the stony indifference he showed to suffering

among his soldiers and the poor. So constant were his drafts on the royal treasury that the Queen of France innocently asked if the walls of Quebec were made of gold. Although another man was the ostensible manager of it, Bigot was the owner of the great shop and warehouse where food and furs were bought low and sold at extortionate prices, and which, bearing its ill reputation as widely as the town itself was known, was called "The Cheat." In times of famine he fattened in proportion as the country starved.

The owner of the Chien d'Or was outspoken in his condemnation of the governor, and he refused to help him in any schemes of plunder. Bigot resorted to sly and small punishments. Whatever the injury he did to Philibert, the victim feared him too much to retaliate at once, yet the threat implied in his golden dog was more courageous than direct assault, because it published his enmity and invited repression. He gnawed but a dry bone of revenge to the last, and never had a chance to fix his teeth in the throat of his tormentor, for one of Bigot's officers, who had been quartered upon Philibert as an annoyance, picked a quarrel on a trifle, and spitted him with a rapier on his own door-step. One version of the tale has it that Philibert's widow placed the golden dog above her door as a threat and an advertisement of the wrong she had suffered. Be that as it may, Philibert's brother—some say his son—came from Bordeaux

to visit his wrath on the assassin. The murderer
had fled, but, getting upon his trail, he followed
him up and down the earth, spending months in
the quest, until he had run him to his hiding-place
in Pondicherry, in the East Indies. There he
challenged the slayer, and, falling upon him with a
fury that was the wilder for its long repression, he
cut his heart in two. Nor had things gone well
with Bigot, for the reports of his misdoings were
not long in reaching King Louis, who had him
sent home in arrest, clapped him into the Bastille,
and appropriated the wealth for which Bigot had
sinned so industriously. The governor had among
his considerable harem a certain Madame P., whose
husband had been sent abroad to discover riches,
and after his release from the Bastille this woman
allowed to the fallen magnate a small pension, which
sufficed to keep body and soul together. So the
once powerful and greedy and splendid representa-
tive of France came to his end meanly, with time
and reason for repentance.

THE GRAVE IN THE CELLAR

THE Intendant Bigot built a spacious château
for himself about five miles from Quebec,
at the foot of Charlesbourg Mountain. The ruin
of the Château Bigot, or Beaumanoir, lasting to our
time, has borne an evil reputation for spooks, and
is one of many places thought to contain hidden

treasure. In the cellar is a grave surmounted by a stone marked only with a letter C. This initial is understood to stand for Caroline.

In the eagerness of the chase Bigot was separated from his companions one evening, and plunged into a part of the wilderness he had never before explored. His quarry having escaped him, he came to a sudden sense that he was lost; that he had taken no account of bearings; that he knew not which way was north, south, east, or west, or whether Quebec lay before or behind him. He sank on a fallen log to wait until the rising of the moon should give some clue to his whereabouts, when his ears caught a soft but steady footfall. He held his musket ready, for he thought of bears, and, seeing a shape approaching, was about to fire. The figure advanced into a little twilit opening, and, lo! it was a graceful and handsome girl, dressed in the garb of an Indian. He accosted her in his best manner, and prayed her that if she knew any trail out of the wood she would lead him back to his château. This she could, and did, readily enough, and, finding the young woman to be even more attractive in the light than in the shadow, the Intendant persuaded her to enter his home and rest. Whether force, fraud, or affection kept her there is not known, but she never left the château. Caroline, for that was her name, was a half-breed, the daughter of a French officer and an Indian mother. She quickly won a place in what passed

for the affections of Bigot that had never been
gained by his other favorites, and in the comfort
and seclusion of her richly furnished apartments on
an upper floor she found certain amends for the
gross and common life of an Indian village.

She had been installed as mistress here for some
time, and had grown accustomed to her place.
Those about her seemingly held her in esteem.
On a night when there had been no roistering and
no festivity, when the brook sang its song sleep-
ily and the moon poured its white light through
the Gothic windows, the quiet of the house was
broken by a shriek of agony coming from Caroline's chamber. Bigot, being first to reach it, received into his arms the drooping form of the girl,
who made an attempt to speak, but, failing, pointed
to the dagger that had been plunged into her breast,
then breathed her last. A servant reported the
brief vision of a shadow on a private stair leading
to the room. No clue was ever gained to the
criminal or the cause of the crime. One surmise
is that it was the father of the girl, who hated
Bigot. Again, it was fancied that it might be her
mother, maddened by her shame. It might have
been some foe of the Intendant, striking him in
what he believed to be a vulnerable point in his
usually hard heart. It may have been Bigot. The
general belief is that the assassin was Angélique
des Moloises, an adventuress of Quebec, who had
decided to marry Bigot herself, not that she loved

him, but she wanted to rule New France. She was jealous of the sweet-natured Caroline, and may have had reason for bitterness toward the Intendant. An old version of the story makes her responsible for the murder, but has it brought about through a gift of flowers to the half-breed girl, the bouquet having been poisoned by the Canadian Borgia, the notorious La Corriveau, with something resembling the *acqua tofana* of Italy.

THE MOUNTAIN AND THE SEE

IT'S of no use to try, you can't get away from it in Quebec,—that old yarn about George III. and Dr. Mountain. Every guide-book tells it, every guide repeats it, and every visitor is supposed to laugh the first eight or ten times he hears it. Some people pretend that they can whistle it. So you may as well know the worst and have it over at once. The episcopal see of Quebec was a fat benefice, and many prelates were willing to sacrifice toast and tea and other domestic luxuries that they might assume the charge of it, for a vacancy had occurred, and several eyes looked longingly, with anxious side glances toward the king. Among the willing ones was the Reverend Dr. Mountain, of London, who, having the king's ear one day, when George had been greatly comforted by port and flattery, made this remark: "Your majesty can fill the see of Quebec by faith."

"How, by faith?" inquired the head of the Church.

"You can say, 'Be this Mountain removed into that see,' and it shall be so."

George III. meditated for some minutes, and was finally about to take his afternoon nap, when suddenly he turned, broke into a roar of laughter, merrily punched the clergyman in the back, and shouted, "I see it! I see it! Sea: see. Ha, ha, ha! Well, the Mountain shall be removed to that see." And it was.

The moral of which appears to be to make yourself explicit when you converse with royalty, and to request favors only after it has had its dinner.

THE SIN OF FATHER ST. BERNARD

IN his native France Father St. Bernard was merely important enough to be suspected of lacking sympathy for the Revolution, without having either the wealth or the title to justify such an enmity; for he was a second son, and it was his elder brother who would fall heir to the honors and riches of the family. Being a ready and eloquent speaker, and not by instinct a fighter, he had accepted the usual alternative for the army, and entered the Church. At the breaking out of the war against aristocracy and religion in his native land, his friends prevailed on him to seek the peaceful shores of the New World, and, provided with letters to eminent prelates in Quebec, he set sail for that city, where he was presently installed as chaplain in the convent of the Ursulines.

The nuns became very prompt in their devotions when the handsome, dark-eyed, rich-voiced young priest entered on his duties, and one of the first offices that fell to him was that of accepting as a member of the order a young woman of rare beauty who, in a season of melancholy following her orphanage, had resolved to take the veil. Her relatives had tried to dissuade her from this step, the mother superior and the priest had cautioned her against a haste that she might repent; but she was firm in the decision to which she had held through her novitiate, and as Sister Louisa she was installed as a member of the holy community. His duties often obliged Father St. Bernard to hold interviews with this nun. Her modesty, gentleness, and innocence commended her to his manhood, as her cultivated mind had appealed to his intellect and her piety to his priestly function. At first unconscious of the reason, he sought more frequent occasions for meeting her than the others, and when at last it dawned upon him that he loved this girl the time had passed for cure. Often while he ministered at the altar his eye roved to the figure he had learned to distinguish among all others of the host, and he lurked in the shadow of columns, prayerfully, greedily watching her as she passed to her devotions or knelt to the Virgin in appeal for strength.

For in her heart the same battle was being fought that raged in his. She had read love in his eyes and answered it. Nature, that knows no creeds, no law, no prohibition, had put her command on both, and it overbore their promises to heaven. When, with hesitation and shame, he declared himself to her, she left her hand in his and only turned away her head. Could it be, he asked, that she could forgive him, that she could condone, that she could love? She sank against his breast. In a delirium of joy he clasped her in his arms, kissing her again and again, until the ringing of the Angelus brought them to themselves with a shock. It was the last service they attended together in the convent, for they fled that night, were married, and found an asylum in the United States.

Seven years passed,—years of sometime happiness, dimmed with regrets and fears. In their most blissful hours they were tortured by the recollection of an unkept trust and broken vows. Spectres of dishonor walked with them in their garden, and dreams of punishment haunted their sleep. The time came when the hours of repentance outnumbered those of gladness, and their talk fell often on the days in Quebec when they were innocent and served God with clean hearts. "Oh," cried St. Bernard, at last, "is it impossible to conjoin the religious life and human love? Must our passions always be our masters? Hapless partner of my sin, I pray that you may never feel this wretched state as I do. God must despise me, for I despise myself."

The violence of this renunciation—for so she construed it—astonished and alarmed the wife, who, with a sobbing cry, fainted on his shoulder. She awoke in a delirium, and several days passed before her reason returned to her. Lying on her pillows, pale and thin, she lifted her sad eyes to him, as he bent anxiously above her, and said, faintly, " We have erred in loving, but reparation is in our power. We must part. Do not weep. Be strong. Be true to your oath."

It was decided to return. He prostrated himself before the bishop, asking if heaven still held mercy for such as he, and the good old man received him into the Church again, as a shepherd would receive a strayed sheep into the fold. He resumed his robes, and was assigned to missionary duty on the frontier among the Indians, who learned to trust him, and even held him in affection before his days of usefulness were ended. His wife, taking again the name of Sister Louisa, re-entered the convent as a penitent with a truer knowledge of the world than when she had taken the veil, and a softer feeling for transgressors. She became the most sad, most silent, most pious of the sisters, and when she died they buried her, at her own request, in the corner of the convent garden where Father St. Bernard had first clasped her in his arms.

LAROUCHE HAD HIS WISH

ON tithing day Davy Larouche, of St. Roch,
—a fat, merry fellow, with whom the
world always went well,—is up betimes, sprucing
himself at the glass. "Aha! you are going to
see the girls again?" cries his wife,—"you, who
were that foolish and bashful that I had to do half
the courting."

"Get along with you," chuckles Davy. "Don't
you know this is the day to take tithes to the curé?
You wouldn't have me meet his reverence in a
blouse. If the weather had been a little better
there would have been more for him, and that
means more for us. We can stand it, but some of
the neighbors feel the pinch a little."

Larouche ate his breakfast, loaded his sacks into
his sleigh, lit his pipe, and in a contented spirit
drove off toward the village, singing. The Canadian habitant is among the few left on earth who
sing without being paid to. In passing through a
wood his jocund voice seems to have attracted the
attention of a man whom Davy had never seen
before, a stranger to the country, for he was not
dressed for rough life or cool weather. He was
a fair-complexioned man, of thirty years, maybe,
with long locks falling over his shoulders and the
most beautiful, searching blue eyes ever seen. He
wore a flowing blue robe, belted at the waist.
Without knowing why he did so, Davy stopped

short in the road, and stared with consuming curiosity, not unmixed with awe.

"Peace be with you," said the stranger, in grave,
sweet tones.

"The same to you," stammered Davy.

"Where do you go?"

"To the priest, with my tithe."

"You had a good harvest, if this load represents
one bushel in every twenty-six."

"Pretty good; but if I could have made the
weather—ah! then we should have seen a harvest!"

"Be it so. Hereafter you shall have such
weather as you wish."

The man in the robe stepped aside to make way
for Davy's sleigh, and the farmer, as he passed,
turned to look at him once more, but nothing could
he see of him. He allowed the fat old horse to
take his own snail pace, he had fallen into such a
state of wonder upon this promise, and a questioning if the stranger were an angel or a lunatic.

Next year at tithing-time Davy harnessed no
horse, but took his offering in a handkerchief. He
was neither plump nor merry, and he did not sing.
Midway in the wood he gave a nervous start, for
the stranger had again stepped from among the
trees and raised his hand, as in blessing. "Peace
be with you," said he.

"Thank you," answered Davy, scratching his
head and putting his bundle behind him. "I need

it. I'm at odds with all the neighbors, and what to do I don't know. They will have it I'm a sorcerer, because every time I've happened to wish for a certain kind of weather we've had it. The sun has been hot at the wrong time, and the rain has been cold at the wrong time. We've had drouths and freshets, and the seed has been washed out of the earth, and crops have dried and withered and rotted and been torn with wind, and I don't know what all. The stock hasn't fed as it should, and even my family's gone against me."

The one in the blue robe smiled. "You are convinced, then," said he, "that God knows better than his children what is for their good? Your wishing power is gone, and next year your tithes will fill your sleigh again."

And Davy Larouche trudged on, wondering.

THE HEART OF FRONTENAC

IN the court of the Fourteenth Louis there was but one man who could rival him in grace or looks, at least in the opinion that was whispered behind the palace doors. That was Louis de Buade, Count of Frontenac. Louis placidly regarded himself as the handsomest man in France, and he had a woman-like hatred of a rival. In fact, he was so secure in this pleasant self-estimation that it never occurred to him to look for a rival until he chanced on one of his favorites, Madame de Montespan, in something too earnest converse with this Frontenac. In that moment his vanity received a serious blow. He kept his eye on these two people, and put his spies upon them, gaining an increased assurance that it would be for the peace of Paris if the impudent fellow could busy himself with affairs at some distance from the city. Le Grand Monarque was not usually suspicious, and the Montespan had wonderful control over him, but this time he was decided, and Frontenac was sent to Canada. Three women viewed this exile with varying emotions. The queen had hoped that Frontenac would succeed with the Montespan woman, that she might claim a little of the king's attention herself. The Countess Frontenac had hardened her heart against her husband when she realized that in marriages of state love has no place, and that even if she were disposed to respect her lord, he cared nothing for her. She refused to go with him to Canada, and remained at home. As for the Montespan, nobody knows whether she was glad or sorry, but, whichever it was, she applied herself to ruling the king with increased severity, and had Louis been a more sensitive man he would probably have made a declaration of independence and abandoned her more promptly for Madame de Maintenon than he did.

Frontenac was made governor of Canada, the king not caring to proclaim his motive baldly, and, while he maintained in Quebec a state worthy of his position, his dignities were solitary. He was urbane toward his associates and toward those who called to see him about matters of state, but he never broke his silence respecting affairs in France. Louis lived to an aggravating age, his stormy career of war and his wasting ambitions seeming but to toughen him, and Frontenac, hopeless of a return, though he was allowed to make one brief visit to his native land, died in 1698, a lonely old grandee. They buried him in the Recollet church, near the Place d'Armes. A surgeon removed the heart of Frontenac, enclosed it in a metal box, and sent it home to his widow. She coldly refused to receive it, for in life it had never been hers. The next ship took this handful of unfortunate dust back to Quebec, where it was placed in the coffin, and for a century remained undisturbed. When the Recollet church was burned the box containing the heart was among the few things that escaped destruction.

THE DEVIL DANCE ON ORLEANS

WHEN Marie Josèphe Corriveau, of Quebec, was condemned to death in 1763, by one of General Murray's courts-martial, everybody said that she deserved it. She had killed her first husband by pouring melted lead into his ear. Number two she choked with a noose, which he succeeded in casting off, and after he had forgiven her for this discourtesy she beat his brains out. To other people it was rumored that she had given subtile poisons. Her guiltless old father tried to save her by alleging her crime upon himself; but the only result of his plea was to get himself hanged without saving her. The execution occurred on the Heights of Abraham, but the body of La Corriveau was encased in an iron cage and swung from a gibbet near the site of the temperance monument at Point Lévis. Some say that she was never hanged, but was shut in this cage to perish of cold, hunger, thirst, and madness, and that her groans and cries lasted for several days, growing weaker and weaker, until at last only the creak of the chains was heard. This creaking was said to be the call of the body for interment, and it excited such terror that the young men of the district cut it down and buried it at night in a spot where, eighty-seven years later, it was discovered by the parish grave-digger —and sold to Barnum. The cage on being opened was found to contain only a thigh-bone.

But burial did not silence the creature. She somehow got out of her cage and her grave and walked after people who were late on the road,— blue, brown, withered, with tangled locks, an altogether fearful object. Among these late goers was citizen Dubé, a truthful man, never timid in the daytime, nor at night either, if he could get rum enough. It was his fate to be abroad in the small hours on the south shore of the river. He had prayed for the peace of the Corriveau in passing, and, seeing a bluish light over on the island of Orleans, concluded that something was astir there : so, tethering his horse on a good patch of grass, he huddled in his cabriolet and watched the light for very comfort. Not but that he knew of the *ignes fatui*, the fool fires or will-o'-the-wisps, that were carried by the devils over on Orleans to lure people into swamps and fly off with their souls as they were drowning, but this light was brighter than the will-o'-the-wisps. And now he could see figures moving. Their aspect did not quiet him. They were of uncommon height and size, were bony, hare-lipped, and pig-snouted, had tusks, and flourished long tails. Had not the night been uncommonly clear and he uncommonly sharp-sighted, he could not have seen these handsome fellows at that distance, nor could he have heard their remarks about him unless his ears had been wide open,— proof enough, as he afterward submitted, that he was not drunk. The demons, for such they doubtless were, began to dance and sing. Their voices brayed and growled and cackled, and they sang a fool song to the effect that they would soon have Dubé for supper. Their master, a huge creature in a cap with a spruce-tree on it by way of feather, pounded a mighty pot with the clapper of an unblessed bell, holding the vessel up toward the goggling farmer, to show in what they intended to boil him ; but, though he was disturbed, Dubé did not lose his self-possession. " You rascals," he bawled,

" you'll get none of the pork that lards my ribs for your supper."

They answered only with gibbering laughter and capered the higher. Then two fleshless hands caught him by the shoulders. It was La Corriveau out of her cage. His hair crawled over his scalp like worms, and he sweat ice-water. " My dear François," squealed the hag, " do me the favor to dance with my friends."

" You limb of the Old One, is this what I get for praying for the quiet of your soul ?"

She laughed—the sound was like a wind playing over empty bottles—and butted him with her unfleshed head. " Take me over to the island, there's a dear. I must meet them, and only a Christian can ferry me, for the river is blessed." Here she tickled the unhappy man under the chin with her claw-like fingers. Dubé pulled away from her. " Get over as best you may, old gallows-bird," he cried.

" Dog of a Christian, bring her here, or it will be the worse for you," clamored the imps.

" Yes, my dear; obey the gentlemen," croaked the bare-bones.

" But how in the dev—how, in the name of the good Sainte Anne" (here a shuddering silence fell), " am I to get over ? I have no boat."

" Then I'll strangle you, and fly across on your departing soul."

Dubé saw the blue light flame up, saw the company leap in a more frantic dance than before, and heard the screech of the vampire as she sprang at his throat. He gurgled a prayer and tumbled in a heap in his cabriolet. When his senses returned to him he sneezed himself into a sitting posture. He was alone, and it was a chilly morning. Dawn was flushing the east. He reached for his bottle, for he sorely needed spirituous comfort, but the Corriveau had emptied it. Nor did he fill it when he got to town. He was a light drinker after that adventure, and died in an odor of sanctity which, his neighbors held, was better than that of alcohol.

THE DEFIANCE AT ELORA

ELORA, with its cascades, its ravines, and its overhanging cliff,—one of the many Lovers' Leaps, where an Indian girl stepped into eternity to end a hopeless love,—and its buried horde of purple wampum, giving rise to tales of hidden treasure, is destined to be widely known for its romantic and beautiful setting. Of especial interest is the " Broken Fall," with a beetling pulpit of rock standing against the rush of waters at its base, for to this pertains a myth of daring equal to that of Ajax. In common with most other Indians, and with the Greeks, the Ojibways believed in guardian deities of mountains, forests, rivers, lakes, seas, and clouds. Nations and people invest their gods with their own qualities, so that a military nation will pray to a fighting god, a money-loving race will have messages from their god to get land and gold, the god of some tribes is a fiend, the God of Calvin was a tyrant, and the God of our own time is a God of love and mercy. The Indian appreciated the world's beauty and lived close to nature, yet in loveliness and brightness he saw as little that is gentle, that spoke of justice, order, law, and love, as if he had been civilized. He lived by shedding the blood of animals, and it was an easy passage from that to shedding the blood of men. Hence he believed in gods that loved destruction, and sacrifices were sweet to them.

Considering these facts, the courage shown by the Ojibway chief who lived in a cave here at Elora was wonderful, yet because of it he triumphed. The manitou of the river, like the spirit of Niagara, was angered by the settlement of people on its banks, and his voice in the fall roared incessant protest. Now and again, after rain or snow melting, he hurled such volumes of water over the cliff that wigwams on the shore were destroyed, canoes were swept away, and the Indians were restrained from hunting and fishing until the flood subsided. To keep this genius of the stream from too serious mischief, sacrifices were made to him, the usual victim being an Ojibway girl. Keechimatik, who ruled here in 1750, was struck by the modesty and beauty of one such girl who had been brought to his cave, bound, that she might be devoted to the manitou. The people were deaf to the appeal of her old mother that she be allowed to take her daughter's place, for her life was nearly over, whereas the girl had all to live for and might become the founder of a noble family. Already the river god had seen his intended victim, and was howling and hissing his demand that she be thrown to his embrace. The elders of the tribe advanced to seize her, when the chief sprang forward and with raised arm bade them desist. "This maid shall not be given to the god," he cried. "I claim her for myself."

Turning to the fall, the chief resumed, "Too many of our people, O manitou, have we given to your keeping. I see you rising in the spray, I feel your cold breath on my face; you have called the thunder birds out of the south to strike at us, and their black wings are spreading across the heaven. I hear your voice in rage, and our medicine-men who know its speech tell us that you demand this woman for your prey. It shall not be, for she is my wife." Cutting the cords that bound her, the chief raised her to her feet; she fell on his breast in gratitude, and the people hurried away from the coming storm, fearing an instant punishment for this act. The tempest passed, and none was harmed.

What the god could not enforce he could gain by fraud. He visited the wife in dreams, charging her to slay Keechimatik, because he was faithless to her. The husband had gone to the pool to fish.

Little did he reck of the woman's changed heart, for she, under spell of these visions, had concealed herself behind the islet in the fall. A twang, a whir, and an arrow transfixes the heart of the chief. He crawls to his cave to die, while she, attempting to regain the shore, is caught in the mad current, and the manitou receives her at last with a howl of triumph.

THE MIRACLES OF SAINTE ANNE

BOATMEN sing prayers and praises to the good Sainte Anne; the habitants kneel at wayside shrines to her; they build chapels to her memory; they make pilgrimages to her finger in Baie St. Paul; and well may they do these things, for she has been their friend in a thousand perils. True, the French have a mediæval honesty of faith, and they pray to many other saints beside, nay, are on intimate terms with them. It is recorded by the proud old family of Lévis, after which they have named Point Lévis (not Levi), opposite Quebec, that when a chevalier of that house was about to salute a statue of the Virgin, he heard a sweet voice from heaven saying, "Cousin, keep on your hat." All through old Canada you find churches where sacred relics—bits of bone or withered toes and fingers—work wonders of healing among the afflicted, and a well-known type of the votive church is that of Bonsecours, in Montreal, where stands an image of the Virgin that has for years exercised a miraculous power of saving sailors in storms and besetments, and they have made many offerings in return.

Yet, of all churches in the colony, that of Ste. Anne de Beaupré (St. Anne of the Bowsprit) is most noted. The name is derived from this circumstance. Two fishermen were caught in a storm on the St. Lawrence, and one was swept overboard and drowned. The other, clinging to the bowsprit, swore that if Sainte Anne would help him to reach the shore he would build a shrine to her. The boat bumped into the land at the site of the chapel, whose erection he undertook forthwith. This first chapel was finished in 1660; the new one, raised by the Pope to a shrine of the first order, in 1876. The healing spring was a separate discovery. It was while working here to lay the foundations for a house that a habitant, Louis Guimont, who had been racked with rheumatism, suddenly found relief. Scoffers said that he had sweat the disease out by hard work, but Guimont scoffed at them in turn, for had not Sainte Anne blessed the spring beside the way and whispered words of promise to him? The fame of the spot went through the country. Increasing thousands go to it on crutches or on litters, and leave them there, together with spectacles, bandages, splints, pill-boxes, cigars, liquor,—an astonishing array of proofs of release from illness and bad habits through saintly intercession. Water from the spring that bubbles forth beside the church is carried away in bottles by the multitude, and is used in the curing of all diseases.

Our saint was the mother of the Virgin Mary, and, under authority of the Pope, in 1876 became patroness of Canada. On her death, in Jerusalem, she was placed in the family vault, whence, in Marcus Aurelius's day, her coffin was torn by the infidels, who were trying to efface all sacred relics and monuments from the Holy Land. One coffin, which they pitched upon the sands, they could neither burn nor break open. It was that of Sainte Anne. Enraged at the futility of their assaults, they dragged it to the Mediterranean and threw it into the water. It refused to sink, and swam to the town of Apt, in Provence, where it lay buried in the sand until a huge fish uncovered it, in the sight of a party of fishermen. They took it up, and discovered it to be the coffin of Sainte Anne, though they could not open it, and their bishop walled it up in a crypt, where it stayed for seven hundred years, with a lamp burning before it. Next the Emperor Charlemagne opened the crypt, in obedience to a vision granted to a deaf and dumb boy, and removed the coffin. After some other centuries the bones were sent to Canada, and they are now exhibited at the shrine of Beaupré.

It was Sainte Anne who saved the wife of Cadieux, or Cayeux, though some believe that it could have been only the Virgin herself. Cadieux was a French immigrant of education, a soldier and adventurer, who had either a disappointing love-affair or had fallen out of favor at court. He had a native thrift, withal, wrote pleasant verse and music, was popular with all sorts in the New World, and traded with the Indians, to his own advantage, when he went to live beside Calumet Falls, near the present village of Bryson. The Ottawas thought so much of him that they gave him one of their girls to wife. While these two were packing furs into their canoe for a semi-annual shipment to Montreal, rumors came to them of an approach of the hostile Iroquois, in war-paint. Hastily finishing the loading of the boat, Cadieux committed it, with his wife and two others, to the torrent. The oarsmen were skilled, but in the rapid and dangerous stream their address would have gone for naught had not the wife prayed to Sainte Anne for guidance. Instantly a figure, shining, silvery, misty, appeared before the prow, as if it were shaped from the spray, and, closely following, as it led this way and that, past shoals and rocks and eddies, the rowers brought the canoe to quiet water. Nor did the saint desert them then, but shone before them all the way to Montreal, where they went thankfully ashore, sold their furs at a good figure, and did not forget the Church when they received their money.

But how fared it with Cadieux all this time?

Heavily. Fearful lest the canoe should be seen and fired on, he and an Indian friend remained to drive back the invading Iroquois. He likewise should have invoked a saint, but he was too busy and eager to remember his duty, so his patron was forgotten. When the marauders appeared, the two fighters dodged from tree to tree, shooting from different points and giving to the enemy an impression that a considerable force was standing against them. Every shot brought down a man; but Cadieux's Indian friend was slain and his wigwam was burned before the band retreated. Knowing that it was likely to return, the white man fled into the forest, and died there of hunger, exhaustion, and " the madness of the woods." His last energies were given to writing " The Lament of Cadieux" on a large sheet of birch bark that was clasped to his breast when the rescue-party found him. It is a sad song that is often heard on the river, where it is sung by the " shanty-men." His memorial cross has been cut away by lumbermen for sacred relics, but the spoilers have tried to make good the loss by carving votive crosses on the neighboring trees. Cadieux's " Lament" is a poem of some length, beginning in this fashion:

> Petit rocher de la haute montagne,
> Je viens finir ici cette campagne.
> Ah! doux échos, entendez mes soupirs;
> En languissant, je vais bientôt mourir.

TADOUSAC BELL AT MIDNIGHT

TADOUSAC, which stands where the black Saguenay rolls from its lonely cañon into the sea-like breadth of the St. Lawrence, was one of the early trading and missionary stations of the French, for this bleak region was rumored to be rich in mineral treasure. Cartier landed here in 1535, and told this thumper after reaching home : " In ascending the Saguenay you reach a country where there are men dressed like us, who live in cities, and have much gold, rubies, and copper." He wanted to be governor, you see. The first stone building in America was put up here, and immediate measures were taken to get the gold and rubies away from the Indians. Poor creatures! They had no use for gold so long as they could have iron, and as to a ruby, they never saw one. They did not even have bones to gnaw sometimes, for as you pass along the Saguenay they show the Descente des Femmes, down which the squaws came one winter and made their way over the ice to a friendly set-tlement, where they got food and carried it to the bucks who were starving at home because they were too dignified to work. These Indians were early reformed, and they loved their helpers and teachers, and so long as the body of Father La Brosse lay in the little church at Tadousac the faithful red men, the Montagnais, who had so often listened to his preaching, never passed up or down

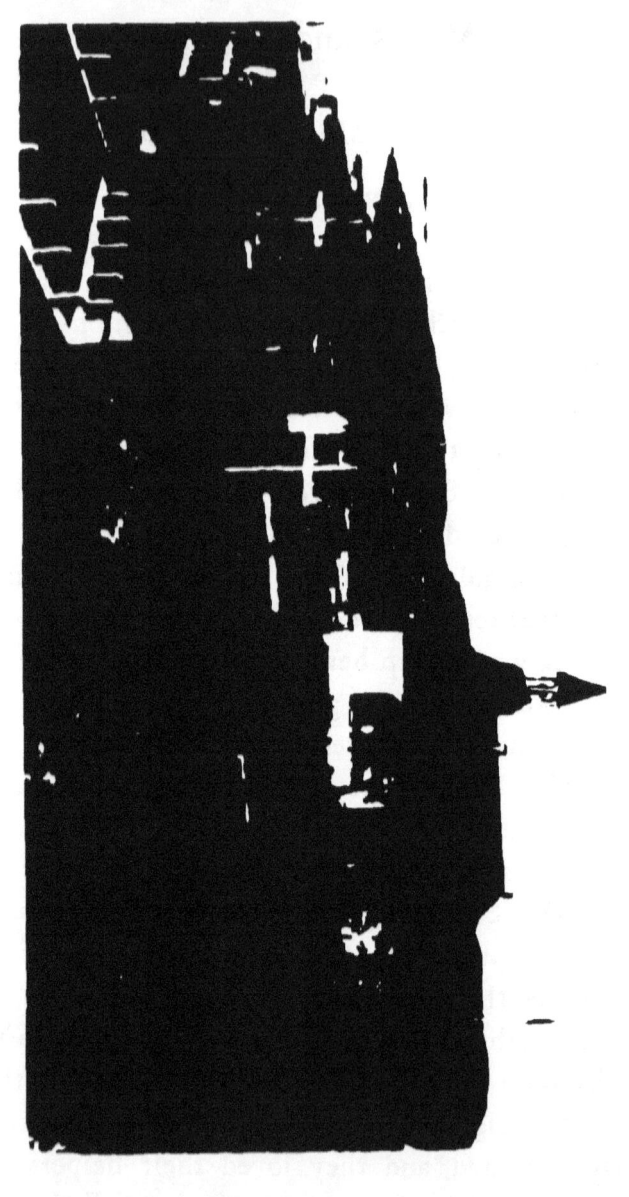

the Saguenay without stopping here to pray. They would fall to the floor and talk to the dead man through a little hole in his tomb, and they fancied whispered answers of advice or comfort. This custom ceased with the removal of the remains to Chicoutimi.

Père La Brosse, last of the Jesuits at this settlement, was taller than common, strong in spite of his seventy years, and, with his white hair falling over his shoulders, was a man of distinguished aspect. The tale of his death is still told among his people, though it occurred more than a century ago. He had been busy among his converts all day, and as night fell he went to the trading-post and passed some hours in pleasant talk with its officers. As he arose to leave he looked with a sad smile over the little company, and said, "Good-by—forever. This is the last of the world for me. At midnight I shall be no more. The bell on the church will tell you so. Come to me, if you will, but please not to touch my body. I desire Messire Compain to bury me. You will find him waiting at the Isle aux Coudres. It will storm, but do not fear. When you go for him your boat shall be unharmed. Farewell, and benedicite."

He was gone. The men stared at one another in amazement. Some laughed nervously and said that the priest was joking. One of them drew out his watch and looked. The time wore on. Their talk flagged, a silence fell, and every face grew anxious. The watch marked twelve. Boom! boom! went the bell—slowly,—rung by no human hand, —tolling for a passing soul. All started violently, and every face was white. Then, in a kind of panic, they hurried to the church. Father La Brosse lay before the altar, his hands clasped in prayer, yet held before his face, as if he had been dazzled by a great light. He was dead. They watched in the gloomy place until dawn, when four hardy men offered to fetch Compain. A storm had sprung up, the ice was crashing and piling, and it was an ugly sea they had to face, but a lane of smooth water opened along its frothing surface and they reached the Isle aux Coudres, sixty miles away, in safety, marvelling. Messire Compain was awaiting them on the rocks, breviary in hand. He knew, he said, why they had come, for the bell of his church, also, had struck at the death hour, and a whisper in the air had told him what had befallen. So he went with them to Tadousac and did his office. And they learned afterward that the bell of every mission where Père La Brosse had served during his busy life had tolled, untouched, that night.

Beyond Our Borders

THE BELL OF CAUGHNAWAGA

STUDENTS of our history are familiar with the incidents of the raid on Deerfield, Massachusetts, on a winter night in 1704, wherein forty-seven of the Puritans were killed, very few got away, and one hundred and twelve were captured, to be transported to Canada. Only one house escaped burning and pillage, and that was defended by seven Englishmen, whose wives cast bullets while the men picked off the French and Indians through the windows and loop-holes. In the march to Canada several of the captives, who showed signs of illness and weakness, were promptly slaughtered. For the brutality exhibited in this "war" the French leader, Major de Rouville, has been greatly blamed, but it is likely that he was unable to control his savage allies after they had tasted blood. Rev. John Williams, pastor of the Puritan flock, lost his wife and two of his children by murder on the long walk, yet when his freedom, his children, and a pension were offered to him if he would join the Roman Church, he refused. All the captives were obliged to attend mass, however, and twenty-eight of the Puritans chose conversion in preference to continued suffering, and, as the chronicler quaintly puts it, this "kindred blood now rattles bad French in Canada, or sputters Indian in the North and Northwest." The French treated their prisoners with kindness, allowing sixty of them to return on payment of ransom. The little daughter of Mr. Williams was kept by the Indians and adopted into their tribe. When de Rouville returned, five years later, to repeat the raid on Deerfield, he was soundly beaten.

But this old story is only preface to another, less well known. Father Nicholas, of Caughnawaga, had secured from his barbarian congregation enough skins of beaver, foxes, otters, and the like to send to France and with them buy a bell for his church. The ship that brought it was captured by the English in 1703, and the bell, after being landed in Salem, was sent to Deerfield meeting-house, where it solemnly tolled to sermons and to prayers, gave note of death, and sounded alarms when fire broke out or hostiles threatened. The "popish" legend on its side was chopped and filed away. To have their bell thus fall into the hands of enemies of their Church was more than the Indians could endure, and it was the thought of this sacrilege rather than race hatred which lent fury to the arms that wielded the knife and axe. Father Nicholas accompanied the raiders and secured his treasure after Deerfield had been laid in ashes. It was carried as far as Lake Champlain and buried. Then, when spring had released the land, a company of young communicants dug it up and carried it to its destination, the Saut St. Louis Church of Caughnawaga, opposite Montreal. As they emerged from the wood bearing this burden on a pole, its clapper pounding joyously, the people in the village, who had never heard such a sound before, sprang up, crossed themselves, and cried, in solemn exultation, "It is the bell!" They went forth in glad procession, wreathed it in flowers, and took it to the church, where for long years it called the faithful Indians to mass and vespers.

THE MASSACRE AT BIC

FEW parts of the inhabited north country have escaped blood-baptism. Causes that in our day would lead to nothing more than a rival political convention, or a few editorial shrieks, or the consumption of Bowery fire-water and some resulting black eyes, were in the old days reasons for murder. No man knew when he was safe, and usually he wasn't. If a brave from South Molunkus looked cross-eyed at the warrior from Memphremagog when he met him in the woods, the insult or the menace was to be atoned for only by the consumption of South Molunkus by fire, the scalping of all adults found there, and the kidnapping of the children. The Iroquois going down the St. Lawrence on one of these errands of objection to the Souriquois saw ahead of them on one of the islands of Bic, opposite the debouch of the Saguenay, a number of canoes and moving figures. Recognizing the people as their enemies, they plied their paddles with energy, to fall upon them before they could escape. It was a hard fate for the Souriquois, for they were mostly women and babes, incapable of defence, and they had not canoes enough for even an attempt at flight : so they huddled into a cave and prepared to slay the first who should enter. The Iroquois landed, traced the Souriquois to the cavern, were greeted with stones and clubs, and, unable to guess how many might be concealed there, they prudently resolved to take no chances. Gathering drift-wood, they piled it before the cave, built a fire, and heaped on grass, weeds, and leaves that made a dense smoke, which blew into the cave and suffocated all within. But this mean victory was dearly won, for, on sighting the war-party up the river, five Souriquois had gone to their villages on the St. John for help, and, defying tire, thirst, and hunger, a large band of men hurried back with them to the St. Lawrence. It was too late, of course, to rescue their sisters, daughters, and children at Bic, but with an Indian all times are ripe for revenge. The murderers, having started on the return march with a false belief in security, relaxed their guard, and during an absence on the hunt the canoes they had hidden among the bushes on shore were seized, together with their load of provision. Thus set afoot, hundreds of miles from their homes, they were at the mercy of their pursuers. The Souriquois hung on their march, and ere many days had harried them all to death. Human bones have been found on the Islet au Massacre, in the Bic group.

Beyond Our Borders

THE DOOM OF MAMELONS

ALONG the lower Saguenay are strange, bare, rounded rocks, the ruined foundations of old mountains long since shaken down by earthquake and ploughed away by glaciers, and heaps of sand, the erosion of other hills. It is from their name that the whole district is known as Mamelons, meaning the place of great mounds. For a century and more it had been prophesied among the Leni Lenape that if any princess of their tribe should wed a white man war and defeat would follow, and the tribe would reach its end at Mamelons. They had come to believe that where the European landed the red race would look its last on the sun. For a thousand years war was waged across these wastes between the Montagnais, or Mountaineers, and the Eskimos of the frozen northland. The Montagnais were helped by the Nasquapees, a small, fine-featured people, keen of sight and smell, disbelievers in the powers of medicine-men, yet a folk who called up the dead, for they were mediums and translated the messages of spirits. They claimed to have come long before out of the East,—Basques, or Iberians. In the last great fight between the red and the yellow men at Mamelons there had been omens: a raven had been on the moon (an eclipse), and the sun had risen red. Scorching heat lay on the sand, so that in the battle many tried to cool themselves by drawing the dead upon them, for the sake of their shadows. Knowing it was to be the last of many great battles, the dead hurried to the help of their friends, and for hours cries and tramplings sounded, and strange buffetings were felt from viewless hands. Hundreds of feet below, the Saguenay foamed red, and still the heat increased and the copper sun shone fainter. In the height of battle the earth began to rock, ashes sifted out of the sky, or, gathering moisture from the sultry air, came down as mud. Darkness fell ; then, with a hollow roar and crash, a long-pent volcano in the north burst into eruption, and every man who had stood on the heaving earth was flung down into his own or his enemy's blood. In the dawn it was seen that only two on the battle-field were alive, and they the chiefs of either party. Sadly they made the sign of peace, and the Eskimo set his face northward, nor did he and his tribesmen ever return to vex the Laurentian people.

The Leni Lenape chief had a daughter who at a later time gave herself to a white lover at the old chief's home near Cape Eternity. When they left it to go down the Saguenay they were nearly caught in the fire that raged from Lake St. John to Chicoutimi and that spread over one hundred and fifty miles of forest in seven hours, but they plunged into the dark flood, gained their boat, and so in time reached the French priest at Mamelons, the place of doom. The wedding was to be at once.

They approached the altar gravely, he strong, confident, she pale and oppressed. When she should have spoken the words that would bind her to the husband, as he pressed the ring on her finger, the girl looked strangely into the east. Her pallor intensified. She had forgotten where she stood. For she saw the millions of the old Iberian race marching through time, carrying their kings and queens enthroned and lifting up their gods. And of all the hosts she was the sole survivor in this western world. The land henceforth belonged to the white people. The chapel bell tolled. It tolled the passing of a soul. It told the passing of a race.

THE REVENGE OF HUDSON

AFTER the mutiny that resulted in the departure of the Discoverie from Hudson Bay, leaving her commander, Henry Hudson, his son of the same name, and two or three followers afloat on its lonely waters, it was supposed that all the occupants of the frail and unprovisioned boat perished during the winter,—drowned, perhaps; crushed in the ice; starved; killed by wolves, bears, or savages. Tradition, however, records the finding of a white-faced lad with yellow hair on the great bay's eastern beach. Whether he had been wrecked there or had wandered from some shelter, seeking food, the Indians who found him lying on the pebbles could not tell. On his breast were tattooed the letters "H. H." in red ink. The men presently took him to their lodge and revived him, for the boy was exhausted and had been poorly fed, not ill, and it was not long before he became as one among the tribe,—nay, one above the tribe, for among the beliefs of the people was that of a white Messiah with yellow hair who should come to them in a strange boat and aid them in their arts and lead them in their battles. And they soon came to know him as "the white god," for he was wise in council, just and demanding justice, prudent, and his teaching and example made them happier and better. He grew to a great size, was quick in the hunt, invincible in fight, and he married the daughter of a chief. He differed from the Mistassini, among whom he thus became a leader, in that he was not brutal or revengeful. After a battle, so that the cause had been won, he ministered to the enemy, and sent them to their homes with food, to be his friends.

In one of the hunts that took the men to the far shores of Ungava Bay, for seal, the people reached the water on a day of storm. Great was the wonder at the spectacle of a ship with broken rudder and torn sails that was driving toward the land. A monster wave lifted her and flung her with a crash on the beach. As the wave receded a figure scrambled along the bowsprit, leaped waist-deep into the frothing sea, and half swam, half waded, to dry ground. He was the sole survivor. A giant he was in size, and he bore a battle-axe. As he saw the red hunters gathering curiously about him he frowned and raised the weapon, but with accord they dropped the points of their seal-spears, to show that he was in no danger from them. For even among enemies, the man who is saved by an act of Providence must be spared, lest by persisting in his harm the anger of the Great Spirit be aroused. To this sacredness of miraculous escape were due the safety of Washington at Braddock's defeat, and that of Major Rogers after his apparent leap down Rogers's Slide. The "white god" advanced with a smile and open hand to meet the shipwrecked one, but as he came before him he stopped and searched his face, his own countenance turning hard and gray and his eyes kindling fiercely as he looked. Then he tore aside his fur jacket and showed the letters "H. H." burning on his breast. The stranger started back in fear, his legs shook under him, his axe hung in a nerveless hand. Then he fell on his knees and begged for mercy in a tongue that the Indians did not comprehend. The "white god" spoke never a word, but he seized his own hatchet from his belt, and with all his great might he struck the stranger on the head, cleaving him to the chin. Then, turning to his people, he said, "He was my father's murderer. Fling his body into the sea, and may he find hell there."

KENEN'S SACRIFICE

BOIS BLANC, on the Canadian side of Detroit
River, was so named for the white wood
that grew there, and that was stripped away under
a supposed military exigency in 1837. This was
the place in which Tecumseh waited till he had
learned the issue of the battle on Lake Erie, and
when General Proctor would neither stay to defend
himself against the Americans nor allow the braver
Tecumseh to occupy the fortifications in his stead,
he scornfully charged upon his red-coat ally that he
was "a fat dog sneaking off with his tail between
his legs, after making a show of courage." The
military importance of the river was recognized
early, and for a long time it was doubtful if the
garrison at Fort Pontchartrain would be kept at the
present site of Detroit or moved across to new
works at Bois Blanc. Had this removal occurred,
Detroit might at this day have been a village and
Bois Blanc a city. A French mission for the
Hurons was established here, but after the English
had resolved to take the land their agents turned
these Indians against their teachers, and nearly pre-
cipitated a massacre of the French troops.

White Deer was the daughter of one of these
Hurons who had died on a mission of policy to
Montreal, while her mother, a white woman, had
been buried not long before. Fathered and moth-
ered by the whole village, the girl grew up in the

affection of all. She had the beauty that is often the gift of half-breeds, and many of the young braves, and some of the old ones, looked on her with longing. After their fashion they threw little sticks in her path when they saw her coming, for when a maid was not averse to the attentions of a gallant she would pick up the stick he had thrown. White Deer stooped to none of them, although she lingered near those of Kenen, a tall, strong warrior, young and handsome, and he was thereon mightily encouraged, so that he followed the girl about and gathered berries for her, and in other ways showed that he would like to wed her and have her wait on him. The gossips had it all fixed, even to the day of the wedding, when Kenen came into camp one morning with a white man on his back. He had accidentally wounded the stranger while hunting, and was in anxiety lest he should die, and the French at the fort, when they heard of the shooting, avenge it on the innocent.

White Deer took her turn at nursing the injured one to health, and, as he was a man of well-stored mind and soft manner, the white blood in her veins declared itself, and she looked into his eyes as she had never looked into Kenen's, and saw her happiness there. More than suspicious of loss in her affections, the Indian dogged them sullenly from place to place, and at last came upon the young man kneeling at her feet and kissing her hands.

Their troth was plighted. Kenen launched on the man a scathing rebuke for his ingratitude, and ordered him to seek his own people at once; then he turned on the girl and poised his knife at her breast. She looked up at him. "No, no," he cried, and flung the blade into the river. "Kenen is like the tempest in his strength, but the lightning of his anger cannot strike the White Deer."

Not long after this a war broke out between the Iroquois and the French, and among the captives taken by the Indians was the white man whom Kenen had shot and the girl had saved. He was condemned to the death by fire, and had been tied to the stake, when a tall man dashed through the shrubbery and stood beside the captive.

"Hold!" he cried. "You have heard of Kenen, the Huron, for he has the scalp-locks of your people at his belt. Many an Iroquois has felt the bite of his axe upon his head. Kenen could take the life of more than one of you even now, and he will do so unless you heed his words, for he comes before you as a willing prisoner to take the place of this captive. Let him go to his people. Kenen is a prize more worthy of you. Go, white man, comfort the White Deer, who waits and weeps for you." And, slashing the cords at his feet and wrists, he set the captive free. "Go, while your path is clear. My canoe is there." With vague words of thanks the rescued one staggered away. Some would have followed, but Kenen stood against them like an oak, and to have chased the pale-face would have cost at least one life, so they waited. When the plash of the white man's paddle sounded up from the river, Kenen flung down his axe, walked to the stake, and folded his arms. And as the white man sped away toward his bride a great pain filled his heart, for he saw the blaze of fagots among the trees and saw the forms of dancing devils circling the fire.

THE CALLING OF ZOÉ DE MERSAC

A SPECTRAL hunt, like the wild chase in the Black Forest by Wotan and Frau Holle, startles the people on the Canadian shore of the Detroit. At certain intervals a dog trots northward over the water, a black dog with drooping ears. Again, it is a phantom boat, rowed by twelve fierce and silent men, also going north. Once in seven years a gaunt horseman rides north, followed by dogs, along the western sky, at sunset, and the people shudder, for they know that among those who see the spectre one must be in his grave within a month. So at least it proved when Sebastian Lacelle hunted near his home at Askin Pointe. He was a sportsman by instinct, "born with a gun in his hand," they said, and on one of his forays he had wounded a deer and followed it through the wood at top speed, to get another and a final shot. Soon he came to a clearing, and there was his deer, trembling and looking around at him with innocent, frightened eyes. He had slaughtered hundreds of animals for sport. He had bent their heads upon their shoulders and cut their throats while they looked into his face, inquiring, beseeching, astonished. He had pounced on them in their death-throes and clubbed and stabbed them. Why did he not do so now? Because a pretty girl knelt before the door of a cabin, and the deer—it was her pet—lay on the ground, bleeding, panting. She was lamenting and caressing the pretty creature, while she tenderly dressed the injury. Lacelle felt a strange tug and softening at his heart. He doffed his hat and offered some clumsy explanation with a hope that, as he had supposed the animal a wild one, he might be forgiven. As she lived in a time when a request for mercy for an animal would have been received with jeers and laughter, it was natural that Zoé de Mersac should grant the pardon with at least a pretended willingness, and, as both had lived a half-wild life, they soon found plenty of matter for easy talk. The hunter went to the woods again next day, and yet again. Their talks were longer and their voices lower at each such meeting. Yes, they loved and were happy.

On the day before the wedding, when the people were discussing at their doors the way the *chasse galerie* had swept by on the night before, the girl was seized with trembling, and her heart shook. She told her fears to her lover. Surely, something was impending. His gun was flung on his shoulder. He laughed at her. To-morrow all would be well. He was off for one more hunt, to celebrate his last day as a bachelor. Yes, he would be careful. He was always careful. See, the ducks were plenty on the river. Wouldn't a nice plump one look well at the wedding dinner? She besought him with tears to stay. He kissed her, and laughed again, "Dead or alive, I'll be back in the morning."

At daybreak Zoé went to the shore, unable to rest, yet cheered by the dewy freshness of the landscape, the softness of the sunshine, the chorus of birds, and, sitting on a boulder,—one of those great rocks that Hiawatha had hurled at his father in the long fight,—she waited long; but Sebastian did not come. Once, indeed, it seemed as if she heard a sigh, and a cold touch fell upon her bosom, so that a chill went through her, and she fled, frightened, to the house. All day long she waited in her bridal dress, despairing, her anxious parents and puzzled guests about her; but he did not come. At the fall of the dark she went out to the shore again, alone. It had grown windy and threatening. Ah, God! how the spectre hunt went by that night, with cries and howls and whistling! The north must have been crowded with spirits. A boat-like cloud whirled past. As it went into the north she saw the leap and quiver of the aurora borealis,—the flames that pour from the end of the earth, for there the old world-fire has never been put out. And again the wind shaped itself into words, like his voice: "I will come for you in a year and a day." She went back to her home. No tears were in her eyes. The cold spot on her bosom would not be warm. Even her heart seemed colder.

In a year and a day the dawn broke fresh, and Zoé asked to be dressed and taken to the river in a chair,—it was so long since she had been out in the sunlight. Painfully, carefully they clothed her wasted form. Her face was white, save for one red spot on the cheek, but she smiled as they lifted her across the threshold, and she looked toward the cloudless sky in rapture. For some time she sat there with her parents, bright and happy, as it seemed. Vapors began to gather and drift up the river toward the north. She eyed them with a curious expectancy. Somewhere was heard the hollow baying of a hunting hound. A cloud shaped like a boat drove past on the breeze. Zoé looked up with a joy in her face that was wonderful to see. "Sebastian!" she cried, and stretched forth her arms. The others looked into the air, wondering. When they turned to her again they wondered no less at the great calm that had come to her,—a calm never more to be broken by the storms or accidents of this world.

THE HEADLESS DESERTERS

TWO soldiers of the British garrison on Drummond Island, of the Manitoulin group, were homesick. They had been stationed at this lonesome post for several years, after the war of 1812 was over, and, having neither the excitements of battle, the pleasures of frontier life, nor the comforts of home, they chafed at their restraints and their remoteness from such of their kind as they most valued. They resolved to desert. Lake Huron, between the island and the shores of Georgian Bay, was frozen. They would cross to the mainland, follow a trail to Toronto, gain United States territory, and take ship for England. On the first clear night after coming to this decision they escaped. The commander of the post was a martinet whose severity was in large measure responsible for the discontent among his men, and he determined to use sharp remedies to prevent this homesickness from becoming contagious. Notice was posted at the barracks that twenty dollars apiece would be paid for the return of each runaway, dead or alive. Some black looks were bent on the commander, and some mutinous talk was heard in barracks, but what of that? Soldiers were cheap, and of little more account than cattle, in his opinion.

A camp of Indians neighbored the military settlement, and the savages often visited the garrison to sell game or pick up scraps of bread. It was not long before they knew of the reward, and two stalwart hunters fitted on their snow-shoes and hurried off on the trail, while it was still to be descried, though dimly, along the wind-swept ice floor. With blood they could buy that more precious liquor, rum. The tracks showed more clearly on Great Manitoulin Island, where the red pursuers shortly found them. They skulked along the shore while the short day lasted, making better time in the bright midwinter moonlight. Presently they slackened their eager pace and went forward with fresh caution, for they saw, just around a wooded point, a glow in the air. The half-perished fugitives had set fire to some drift-wood and were seated on a log facing the flames. So attent and unsuspecting were the soldiers, and so loud was the crackle of the burning wood, that the approach of the murderers was unheard. The Indians were at their backs, their tomahawks in hand. In another moment the heads of the deserters had been smitten from their shoulders. With these ghastly relics tied at their belts the Indians regained the barracks, delivered the proofs of their industry, and received their forty dollars,—a sum sufficient for a long and lurid debauch. So suddenly did the axe-blows fall that the bodies of the soldiers were not jarred from their seats, and did not topple, but remained with hands extended to the blaze. And there they sit on winter nights. Their fire burns blue now instead of red, and shines on uniforms that are mildewed and faded. When the fisherman or hunter puts in at this point, hoping for shelter, he gives one glance at the headless soldiers; then, as fast as his legs will carry him or his arms can pull at the oars, he leaves the gruesome spot. When he passes by daylight no figures are there,—nothing but charred branches.

THE DEVIL'S HEAD

ON a bluff overhanging an inlet of the Lake of the Woods, near Rat Portage, Ontario, is a curiously marked and weathered mass of granite, the ledge resembling a broad, distorted face with staring eyes and savagely grinning mouth. Some larkish persons have used paint to increase the human suggestion of the thing, and persons of weak nerves suddenly coming upon it for the first time have been rudely startled and have been compelled to ask for flasks. Skull Rock and Devil's Head they call it, the names being used indifferently. It is twenty feet high, and of about the same width. The mouth, strangely, is a cave, which may be entered for ten feet and leads to a deep throat in the stone behind. Nearly every miner who enters this region to prospect for metal visits this freak and touches his palm to its forehead for luck; for the first gold-bearing rock discovered by white men in this region was found in the mouth of this great mask. It was said that Indians put it there ; but, while the mound-builders knew the value of copper, and worked it skilfully at the Lake Superior mines before the era of Columbus, there is nothing to prove that they valued gold until the frauds and ferocity of Europeans showed them how much other men could prize it. One miner travelled fifteen hundred miles to touch this face before he began a search for gold in quite another part of the country. The Indians are indifferent to this phase of the matter. They see in the glaring monster the head of a giant who came out of the Northwest to protect them against the whites, and they feel a reverence for it which they used to prove by burying their bravest men in its shadow. Consequently, it is not to them the head of a devil, but of a hero. There are many traditions of warriors who were to help them repel the hated French and English, and until a recent date they read comfort in heavenly signs, and looked hopefully to every strong man of their own race, down to Sitting Bull, to free the land. The comet of 1811 they said was the avenging arm of Tecumseh. The expected Messiah, in whose honor the exciting ghost-dances have been held from time to time, is by some affirmed to be Manibozho. It was not Manibozho who left his skull here in the wilderness, grinning at the faithful, for he was a man of peace and wise counsel. It was possibly a visitant from the happy hunting-grounds. Look west from Calgary to the tumbled Gothic peaks of the Rockies, and you see the Indian's "bridge of the world" leading to heaven. It was from those happy hunting-grounds that the giant rescuer returned to fight once more, but vainly, for his people.

FATHER JACQUES'S VENGEANCE

IN one of the forays of red men, so horribly frequent in the old days, a family of French people on an island on the Otonabee, near Ludgate's Hill, was exterminated, all save a little girl of two years, whom the Indians, in adopting, named Sajo. The Ojibway raiders were perhaps the more cruel in this act because they, too, had suffered from an incursion of their foes about that time, and among the captives who had been led away from their camp by the Hurons was the chief's son, Long Snake. Years passed after these acts of evil, and wounds had time to heal. If the old chief, Swan, sometimes mourned his son, the charm of his white captive, who had become to him as a daughter, softened his grief, and so in time he came to think of Long Snake as dead. A gentler spirit moved the Ojibways, for the "black-coats" had come among them, teaching peace. Father Jacques especially had their love and confidence, for he treated them as men, not as brutes or children, and proved what right-living people the whites could be. Thus, on the day when Father Jacques rowed to the island of Otonabee, where the massacre had taken place, but where the tribe now had a village, the people promised to give a respectful hearing to his appeal, though they had heard it was not to be to their liking. He had come to plead for Sajo's liberty, for she had been seen by a young white settler who loved her and was prepared to offer a ransom in money, goods, or service. No, they did not wish her to leave them. She was their daughter, their sister, and when she married it should be as the chief directed, to one of their own people.

The priest made his appeal to chief Swan: "You, brother, have known the sorrow that comes of severance from those you love. Long Snake was stolen from your home in his childhood. How if I were to tell you that he lives? Should not Sajo then go free? How if I were to bring him back to you? How if at this moment he hears my voice, is awaiting in that thicket and will do my bidding? Long Snake, come forth. Behold your son, O Swan, and you, lad, see your father." The chief gazed long at the young man, grown so tall and strong, and, slowly approaching him, dropped his hands on his shoulders. "It is he," faltered the old man; then, in a gush of that feeling that inheres in every race, savage or civilized, he caught the boy in his embrace. The company remained silent during this scene. At last an elderly hunter said, "He is worthy to be Sajo's husband." The suggestion was caught up in a general acclaim. It was a turn in affairs that the priest had not expected.

"Stop!" he cried. "I have done good to you and have never asked for reward, but I must do so now. I am akin to Sajo, and I demand her as her guardian. She is loved by a pale-faced brave, who will give you many guns and blankets when you let her go. Let her be brought here."

The girl was summoned from a wigwam at the edge of the settlement, for women seldom had a voice in the councils of the tribe, and she made obeisance before the black-robed minister.

"She is worthy to be my son's wife," exclaimed the chief, struck anew by her beauty and grace. "Look, my son, this girl is yours. You, Sajo, shall be still more my daughter than before; you shall wed my son."

"Chief Swan! Chief Swan!" cried the priest, "I beg, I command you not to press this child of the white people into a marriage without love. She is my relative."

"How can the black-coat make his words good?"

"Listen to my confession. I thought, when I was in France, to have been a soldier rather than a priest, and had I so decided I might have come among you not as a teacher but as a destroyer. I loved my cousin, Josephine Disette, and she loved me until she met one Picot, a merchant, my better in wealth. Meeting the two walking arm in arm one evening, I was so struck by her perfidy that I clutched a chain which I had given to her and brutally tore it from her neck. An ivory carving that hung from it remained in my hand. Picot aimed at me with his cane and broke the ornament, a smaller piece falling to the ground. I would have answered the blow but for the appeal in the woman's eye, that brought me to my senses, and I hurried away in rage and shame. I went to Paris and entered the priesthood, coming to Quebec soon after. There I but recently learned that Picot and his wife—my cousin—had lost their money and had come to this land, too. They settled here. The ruin of their home is yonder. They were killed by you, for in those days your eyes were darkened. Now for my proof. On Sajo's breast hangs an image of the Good Son of the Great Spirit. Is it not so?"

"No. There is an ornament, but it has been broken."

Father Jacques placed his hand on the girl's head. "Benedicite, daughter," said he,—"daughter in the church, but cousin in kin. In my youth I vowed a vengeance on your father and mother for a fancied wrong. I redeem you to the world again for your sake, and for the sake of a good man's love. That shall be my revenge. See, my people." Drawing from his breast a little bag, he took out of it a broken ornament of ivory, and placing it against the fragment worn by Sajo it was seen to be complete. It showed the crucifixion with the name in gold, "Josephine." "In the name of the Good Son, whose likeness is there, I claim my kinswoman." And with no word of protest, though with sad eyes, the Ojibways saw the departure of their daughter.

THE BONNECHÈRE AFFAIR

THE Blackfeet had camped on the upper Ottawa, near one of the Hudson Bay Company posts, in the first half of the present century, and among them was Big Moose, famed for his size and power. As he had looked love on Little Fawn, and she had declared her willingness to be his wife, it is surprising that her parents did not give the girl to somebody else. Some time before the marriage occurred, Big Moose entered the camp bearing in his arms a fair-haired stranger, a Scotchman in the employ of the Hudson Bay Company, who had fallen while traversing the wood and wrenched his ankle. As the fort was some miles distant, no attempt was made for several days to move the injured man, and much of the care of him fell to Little Fawn. He was a handsome, heartless fellow, who struck up a desperate flirtation with his nurse, after the manner of his kind, while Big Moose vainly played his bone pipe in the twilight before her lodge. The Indian was not sorry when the stranger was able to

go back to his own people, carrying with him—
though Big Moose did not know it—the heart and
honor of the girl who was shortly to be his wife.
The wedding was celebrated with the usual re-
joicings, and, in spite of White Fawn's thought-
fulness and silence, the couple were apparently
happy.

The supply of food grew short that winter, and
the more stalwart of the tribe had to bestir themselves to get meat, Big Moose being happy in the
assurance that when he returned from the long
hunt a child would greet him. True enough, the
child was there, but it did not greet him, for it was
dead—dead on its mother's breast, and she, too,
was dead. The babe had yellow hair. The Indian
swore an oath against the white betrayer.

Five years passed. John Rigby had become a
prosperous smith in the village that had grown up
about the second shoot of the Bonnechère, a few
miles above its meeting with the Ottawa. His
daughter Jessie was his idol, and he had taken a
pride and pleasure in ministering to her tastes,
sending as far as to Boston for the books she wished
to read. Her favorite place of study was an island
in the stream, near the fall. It was summer, and
she sat there poring on a favorite volume, obliv-
ious to all about her. The path to this island was
across the dry bed of the stream, for the water
had been dammed above, in order to shoot down
the logs that made the chief industry of the place

and region. So absorbed was she in her book that she did not see the slow rise nor hear the lapping of the water as it overflowed its channel near the left bank and began to fill the dry space which she had crossed an hour before. She was roused by a crash. Her escape was cut off. Down came the logs, and with them the "river drivers," a swearing, quarrelling lot, coarsely dressed, smelling of liquor, with Dan McDonald in the lead, a fair, fearless fellow, a bold fighter, a bit of a thief, and a mystery, for it was thought he had once been a gentleman. A mass of timber came against the upper end of the islet with a shock, and the girl shrank with a scream. Dan saw her. Jumping, swimming, scrambling, he gained the patch of ground, caught her as a swirl of water swept her from her feet, and, bidding her rest her hands on his shoulders and trust in him, he swam down the stream to safety. He took her home, then, and returned to work. A trifle like a ducking did not worry him.

Yet his life changed from that day, for in that brief service he had met her look of appeal and gratitude, and he loved her. No more gaming, drinking, ruffling, and late hours. He confessed the sins and follies of his past life and asked her help to keep him a better man. He must soon leave the village to raft the lumber down to Bytown, the Ottawa of a later time, and could not see her for some weeks. Would she say good-by to him? Certainly, and would wish him a safe and pros-

perous journey. Would she—could she—care a
little bit that he was going away? Yes, she had
enjoyed his calls, and would be glad to see him
again. Then—could she love him? Whatever
her answer was, it is certain that within an hour
they went out for a walk in the moonlight, and in-
stinctively turned toward the cascade where they
could see the island on which they had met; certain, too, that they stood there for a long time,
with clasped hands. As they looked into the
water, a drunken Indian lurched by and growled a
curse. It was Big Moose. A vague fear came
upon them both.

The next night Dan is on board the raft, drifting down the dark river,—drifting toward a darker
river than he sees. He is watching the stars in
the water and dreaming of happy days to come.
A dark form steals from behind the little cabin of
the raft, and in a minute Dan is roused from his
meditations by a clutch of hands at his throat. He
succeeds in turning, and strikes wildly at Big Moose,
whose glaring eyes he can distinguish in the starlight, as well as the glint of a knife that the Indian
is holding in his teeth, awaiting the chance to stab.
In their struggle both fall into the water. Some
days go by before Jessie hears that two bodies have
been found on the Ottawa, a white man's with fair
hair, and that of an Indian who bit upon a knife
and clutched the other's throat.

HE WENT BACK FOR HIS GUN

GITCHE GAUZANI lived on the north shore of Lake Superior, not far from the place where great Manabozho rests. Before he had become an old man he died of an illness, and they prepared to bury him, like the others who had gone, with his head to the west, since it is in that direction that they journey toward the land of the sleeping sun and the happy hunting-grounds. The usual bows, arrows, blankets, dishes, knives, spoon, pipe, meats, fruits, and ornaments were brought to put into the grave with him, for these things are needed, they believe, in the long march to shadow-land. Gitche Gauzani looked so life-like that his family refused to allow him to be buried, and it was just as well they did so, for in four days his soul returned to his body, and he awoke. He had come back for his gun. He had a fine one, and he wished it to be buried with him, but his relatives had taken a liking to it, and had insisted that a bow and arrows were good enough for a dead man. So he had set off along the broad road of the dead. Ah, yes, it was beautiful, but he had no gun. There were fields of richest vegetation, many groves, birds without number filled the air with song; he reached the misty valley— misty because the river of women's tears ran through—that spread around the shining, tranquil city of the departed, and there were buffalo, moose, deer, antelope, and other game that walked beside him, fearless, for he had no gun. Recalling his dying request to his friends, he started home to get it, and then he met the endless procession of pale, tired people travelling toward the city of the dead. They were complaining bitterly because they had been overloaded with presents that they could not use. One burdened man offered a gun to him, but the ghost of Gitche Gauzani wanted its own, and it struggled on to the place where it had been liberated from the flesh, in time to stop the burial. Great fires seemed to rise around his body to keep him back, but he made a desperate leap through them, and awoke. He was not entirely glad to be on the old earth again, but he improved his chance to advise his people. He insisted that in future they must give to the dead such things as they had been attached to, and not trouble them with miscellaneous luggage of which the survivors were anxious to be rid.

KWASIND, THE STRONG

ON the shores near the Sault Sainte Marie lived Kwasind, the Strong. His parents often blamed him because he did so little to help them and engaged so seldom in the sports and work of his people. They said he was dull, selfish, and did not respect his elders; but the reason for his reluctance was that he spoiled everything he touched, he was so muscular. Once when e had been ordered to take in his father's fish-net and dry it, he wrung it out, and in doing that he broke it into pieces. Then it was seen that he was too strong to work, and they let him alone. He amused himself, nevertheless, with other kinds of labor than that of the camp. He threw fallen trees out of the trails and clearings as lightly as if they had been weeds. He would pick up rocks that Manabozho had thrown at his unrespected parent and "shy" them into the river as boys cast pebbles. He would dive and stay under water for an hour, fighting the beaver and helping Manabozho to clear the streams, so that they would not overflow in snow-melting time. He did so many things of this kind, and bragged so much about them, that the fairies, the pukwujinee, feared him and resolved to have his life. "He will do so much for men that nothing will be left for us to do," they said. "He will undermine our power and drive us into the river, where our wicked cousins, the neebanawbaig, will have us."

Now, the strength of Kwasind was in his scalp. Struck there he was helpless; only, the right missile must be used. He could resist stones and arrows, but the soft fall of white pine cones he could not endure. This the fairies learned, and they perched among the trees, dropping pine-seeds as he passed, but missing him, and he, supposing that squirrels were at work, paid no heed. The only way in which it appeared that he might be hurt was in a general attack. So, after storing a quantity of the cones at the point of red rocks, they awaited his coming, for they knew that on warm days it was his custom to float down the river on the current, half asleep. Presently he came gliding by in his canoe, and the cones rained upon him. As he sat up to see what was the meaning of the assault, one of the missiles struck him fairly on the head, and he fell from his boat and sank, never more to rise. Then the fairies laughed and capered and were happy once more. The hunters used to hear them in their dancing, until the white men came and drove away fairies and hunters together.

THE CURSE OF SUCCESS

NOT only did Hiawatha, or Manabozho, affect the shores of Lake Superior, but many spirits of good and evil inhabited the woods, and the Indians point to the birch-trees that have spoken and the rocks on which local gods have sat. A great boulder opposite La Pointe bowed to the young Otamigan who, believing it could have been moved only by his protecting god, never passed without laying on it an offering of tobacco. Here, in Kitchi Gami, the Big Water, swam Great Otter, the first thing to cross the world after this planet was made. At the first step in his journey he reached ice; at the next, swamp; at the third, water; at the fourth, flowers sprang about his feet. But most strong, most dreaded of the lake gods was the evil one, the Matchi Manitou, the great creature who lived at the bottom of the lake, sometimes taking a fish's form, sometimes appearing as a serpent. None but the wicked besought him, for he was full of guile. An instance of his dealing is found in the tale of the Indian who dreamed for eleven successive nights that a voice had commanded him to go to the lake edge, strike the water with a magic stick, and repeat certain words to it. Then he should find power that would enable him to secure health, wealth, and happiness. On the eleventh night he woke his squaw, saying, "Listen! Do you not hear drums clashing on the water?"

She did not hear any other sound than that of the surf lapping on the shingle.

"The drums are there. They call me," he exclaimed, and hurried from the lodge, while she, fearing that his mind was touched, crept after, cautiously, and watched him from the shadow. He bent over the lake and began a weird chant in words she could not understand, keeping time with blows of a medicine-stick upon the waves. At first the water merely splashed, but after a little it began to eddy, circling wider and wider, faster and faster, with deepening roar. Fish, frogs, waterfowl, and lizards were drawn into the whirlpool and were pulled down into its black throat; the rim of the whirl began to ascend the beach ; it lapped about the man's feet and rose to his knees ; the ceaseless rush of the tide made him dizzy, and he could barely hold his footing ; yet still he sang and pounded, and demanded that the king of fish appear. At last the monster was compelled to obey the summons. His huge bulk heaved above the surface, and, fixing his baleful eyes on the man, he cried, " What do you wish with me ?"

" Give me the magic power to be rich and well and happy."

" Happy ! You shall be strong, rich, feared, a great hunter. What more do you need ? You see on my head the charm. Take it. But you shall give me one of your children in exchange. It is agreed ?"

The man reached forth his hand and took from between the creature's horns a red, flower-like object, that crumbled to dust in his grasp. " That," said the Matchi Manitou, " is power. Make twenty little boards, sprinkle the dust on each, give to each the name of a benefit you wish, and I will tell an opposite harm from which you shall be shielded. Whenever you need more power come back and summon me again. So long as we are joined in our work against all other men I shall hear you call and your power shall be renewed. Remember, each time I am called I have one of your children."

The great mass sank heavily in the vortex, and

the lake was still.   Floating off his little boards,
the man wrapped up what powder he had left and
plodded back to his tepee.   His wife was dead,
overcome with horror at what she had seen and
heard.   The curse of success had begun to work.
For an hour the enchanter grieved, but there was
little softness in his nature, and he hurried the
funeral of the woman that he might begin his new
career unchecked.   In a day or two one of his
children was drowned.   The Bad God had taken
his pay.

Though obscure till then, the man took on importance in his tribe.   He increased in size and
strength, and did such killing in war and the hunt
that they made a chief of him.   He read the future
so clearly that he became the leading prophet.
His spoils in war and his levies in peace so grew
that he had to build the largest lodge in the country to hold his furs, his arms, his embroidered
clothing, his wampum, his copper implements and
ornaments, his store of maize, dried fruit, and meat,
his carved pipes and tobacco.   He had more dogs
than any other man.   He took two new wives.
He painted his face and dyed his feathers with
more brilliant colors than his neighbors had ever
seen.   His lodge-covering was gay with pictures.
With each increase in strength he assumed more
command, until at last he became a tyrant, obeyed,
but only through fear, met with dark looks, followed with scowls.   When he was absent people

gathered in knots and whispered. He returned to the lake for new strength and new favors, and one after another his children disappeared. At the last he called to Matchi Manitou in vain, for he could offer no more sacrifice. He began to waste, fever laid hold on him, the wives he had bought as barter fled when they thought it safe to do so, for they had never loved him, his wealth began to melt under pressure of his needs, his proud spirit failed, and the common scorn was no longer whispered. Deserted, feeble, filled with pains, impotently raging at his fate, he resolved on one last appeal. He went to the lake, beat it with his medicine stick, and began his chant. Yes! he was heard! Again the water began to swirl; it rose about him, it swept him from his feet, it whirled him to the vortex, and with one despairing cry he was sucked into the depths.

THE DEATH OF WAHWUN

AS you ascend the river Mawenetechemon, in northern Ontario, you pass the fall "where Big Otter sleeps," the Indian of that name having been buried beside it after he had been swept over the plunge of water. Next you cross the widening called Lake Weendawgoo, where the storm spirit lives; and, lest you rouse his wrath, you must go reverently and in silence. Then you come to one of those forbidding districts peculiar to the northern streams, where bare rocks, sand-hills, drowned trunks, and black ooze almost surround the spread of the dark river. Here is "the place of death." In this lonely spot lived Wahwun, a powwow, or wizard, who for no reason except to wreak his evil nature put spells and troubles on the people of his tribe. He was endured because he was feared, until he caused a mysterious illness to fall upon their chief, when they resolved to suffer no more of his tyrannies and to punish him for those he had inflicted. The avengers chose a windy night, when the sound of their footfalls would be lost in the strife of the elements, and, stealing to his tepee, they rushed in and pinioned him before he could reach his medicine-bag to "spell" them. The medicine-bag was destroyed, and he was tied to a pile of fagots that were set on fire. As the flames crackled around him he scowled and hissed at them, snake-like, and cried, "May the evil spirit curse you! May your hearts faint in battle! May your scalps hang in your enemy's lodge! May the evil wind come out of this marsh and blight your corn and frighten off your game and kill your children!" More he could not say, but with a roar of hate gave up his spirit, which was presently seen as a black cloud hovering over the lake. For years the people suffered under his curse, and even now the place is avoided in the night.

THE DEVIL'S HALF-ACRE

NORTHEAST from the reservation given to Chief Brant for his services to the English troops, and for some time known as Wellington Square, was a clearing of no large area, with a log cabin on it that had been built and occupied by a man and a woman, both of gentle manner, well appearing, and quite alone. Few people ventured into that region eighty years ago, except the trappers, although a trail led near the clearing from the head of Lake Ontario to an inland trading-post. On a June day the woman sat sewing in the door, but every now and then she dropped her work, as if to listen. She was of French type, dark, with a rich, out-door complexion, soft eyes, and a winning smile, for as she looked down the path she did smile, in expectancy. At some distance could be heard the crack of rifles: the Indian hunters were about; but to these sounds she paid no heed. She sang a gay little French song softly to herself and smiled again. Suddenly a crash sounded in the thicket, and a hunted doe fled by like an arrow. At the same moment a loud report came from among the trees. The deer sped on. The woman half arose, toppled, fell forward on the step, and a stain of red trickled away toward the earth. Hurried steps sounded among the shrubbery, following the direction taken by the doe, and the sun moved toward its setting: very slowly it went down that day.

Beyond Our Borders

In the twilight a man's voice called across the field, "Lois!" then, in a higher key, "Lois!" There was no answer. The man advanced eagerly. For an instant he stopped. He had seen the shape on the step, and a shudder went through him. His gun dropped from his hand, his game-bag slipped from his shoulder. With a toss of his head he flung off the spell of a fear that was closing upon him and ran to Lois, so still, so cold, with face down upon her arm as if she had fallen into a tired sleep. "Lois!" he cried, "what is it? You are hurt! Ah, my love, *ma chérie*, open your eyes. See, it is Paul come to you. Will you not speak to me?" He begged, he wept, he embraced her yielding form. At last, a little sigh. With almost a laugh of joy he caught her up, ran into the house with her, and placed her on the bed. He bathed her face, he warmed her with fur wraps, he tried to force hot drink into her mouth, but without avail : a slow, slight breathing was all that betokened life.

Just at dawn she awoke and gazed into his face. He, who had tried to look comfort into the eyes of others in like case, knew the meaning of that gaze, and his head fell forward upon her hand, while he was shaken with sobs. "It is the punishment, Paul," she said. "We have sinned, almost beyond forgiveness,—you against the Church, breaking your priestly vow, I against my husband. Pray— pray for me—and for you——"

And Paul Daudet, runaway priest, prayed as he
had not prayed since he had striven against temp-
tation. As the sun came up he closed the eyes of
Lois and went out. It was a different world from
yesterday's. His Eden was become a hell. A
grave would soon hold all his happiness, but he
would not go away. He, who had deceived the
most trusting, generous patron of his Church, how
could he go back? Unaided he made the coffin
and dug the grave, and at its edge he said the funeral
service. The time was dull and the world was
cold after that, yet he lived on, alone, growing old
fast, so rude, so gruff, that the Indians feared him.
How he subsisted, when, where, and how he died,
none can say, but in time he disappeared, and they
called his little garden " the Devil's half-acre."

MEDICINE HAT

ON the south fork of the Saskatchewan, where
the prairies begin to feel the effect of the
upward pitch of the distant mountains and to rise
into the long slant that we call the plains, stands
the promising town of Medicine Hat. It is a
name with a character of its own, and already the
people who prefer such begin to shudder at the
ondrawing of the vandal who will demand its abo-
lition, and by dint of some service in parliament,
or church, or the local grocery business, will secure
a change in his own behalf. Then the unhappy

place will become a Smithburg, a Jonesville, a Browntown, or some other exasperating inanity, like a hundred thousand other inanities between Hudson Bay and the Gulf of Mexico. Such a change will be all the more a pity, because the present name throws a light on the ways and thoughts of primitive people. Know, then, that medicine means more to an Indian than to us. We think of it as something diabolical that is good for us,—queer anomaly!—but the Indian distinguishes as "good medicine" and "bad medicine" anything that he fancies will change his fortunes for better or worse. Imagine that Lo is hunting antelope and meeting no success. Presently he finds the top of a tomato-can, and shortly after he gets a crack at his game. Can he doubt that the piece of tin gave the luck? Not he. In this he is as reasonable as many of his white brothers. He wears that fragment of tomato-can about his neck with his other jewelry, and it is "good medicine."

Well, several years ago there was a Blackfoot chief who lived here off and on, hunting sometimes and making war on the Crees betweentimes. He had much joy and profit in a head-dress of feathers, that he called his medicine hat, for when he wore it he had good fortune—if he had luck. Ah, 'twas a dark, dark day when he met the Crees near the site of this town. He fell upon them with great industry, smiting, slaying, scalping, fairly beaming with satisfaction; but just as the enemy was in flight a gust of wind whirled out of the west, caught the magic hat, and tossed it into the Saskatchewan. Instant was the effect: the poor chief lost all confidence in himself and his cause, and with victory in his reach he forbore to grasp it, "skedaddling" over the plains in a panic, followed by his tribe. And thus befell the evil that leaves its record in Medicine Hat. Do you, reader, ever wear a medicine hat?

GHOST WOMAN AT THE BLOOD CAMP

CHIEF HEAVY COLLAR, of the Blood tribe, left his camp, on the site of Fort McLeod, with a war-party, to exterminate a few acquaintances in the Cypress Hills, but, finding that his departure had been reported to the enemy, there was nothing for it but to jog home again. On the South Saskatchewan, above Seven Persons Creek, he left his party to kill a buffalo, and while roasting a slice of the meat he thought, "If one of the young men were with me I would send him back to that hill for some hair from the buffalo's head, so I could clean my gun with it." In a minute a shag of this hair blew toward him and fell at his feet. Tramping up the stream to St. Mary's River, he crawled into a bunch of rye grass to sleep. But all night he was conscious of faint, strange noises, and he was troubled. At dawn he found that he was lying beside a skeleton:

a Blackfoot woman had been killed there in the preceding summer. Next day he went as far as Belly River, where at nightfall he made a fire in the shelter of a tree that had come down in a freshet. The skeleton had been following him, for now he saw it, seated astride a branch, whistling and swinging its legs in time to the tune. Four times he prayed the thing to leave him, but it only whistled the more, looking up at the stars in a complacent manner, until anger got the better of fear, when Heavy Collar fired at the skeleton, and it fell backward, screaming, " You have killed me again! Dog! there is no place on earth where you can hide from me." All that night the chief ran from the skeleton, its angry words dying in the distance, then approaching and lending the fresh energy of fright to his jaded frame. At daylight his companions saw from the Belly River buttes the two figures approaching, and, descending to meet their chief, they began to chaff him for bringing back a stranger wife. Yet as they looked about they discovered no woman, and only the footprints of Heavy Collar could be seen along the ground. Then he knew that his senses had not deceived him, and that he was haunted.

On regaining the camp a feast of welcome was set in nearly every lodge, and, leaving his own tent, to eat with a neighbor, Heavy Collar saw a bear walk out of the brush, as if attracted by the odor of food, and he threw a bone at it to drive it away. "You killed me once, and again you are killing me," cried the creature; for it was the ghost woman in that guise. He shouted, "A ghost bear is upon us!" whereon all the people in the camp crowded into his tepee and listened as the ghost tramped about, grumbling, outside. First she turned the wing, or flap, at the top of the lodge, so that the wind would blow the smoke of Heavy Collar's fire back into the tent and strangle the people. They, hearing her threats to kill them, began to pray to her. After a time the chief's mother lighted a pipe and offered it in propitiation, and as the ghost backed away the woman followed, still extending the pipe. Heavy Collar ran out and seized his mother about the waist, but she was drawn on as by an invincible power. Another man caught him, and he in turn was held by another, until the whole village was on the march. Suddenly the pipe fell from the old woman's hands. She was dead. The ghost was satisfied with one life, and melted out of sight, never to be seen again.

THE BLACKFOOT EDEN

NAPI, Old Man, first to be born from nature's creative forces, built the mountains, levelled the prairies, caused trees to grow, made the Teton River, rested on a hill above it, leaving there the outline of his form, then walked northward, building the Sweet Grass Hills with rocks that he carried. Now he covered the earth with grass and fruits, constructed some animals, " little brothers" he called them, and made of clay a woman and her son. In four days this clay was able to walk and speak, and the woman, having seen that the brutes were mortal, asked of her creator if she and her companion would always live. Said Old Man, " I had not thought of that. If this buffalo-chip floats on the river, people will rise again four days after they die. If it sinks, there is an end to them." The dung floated. But the woman was dissatisfied. " Let it be as this stone decides," she said. " If it floats we will live forever." The stone sank, and the son died. So, because of a foolish woman, all must die. But she had other children, very poor, very ignorant, save for what Old Man gave and taught them. They had no weapons until, moved by pity at the sight of several men gored to death by buffalo, Old Man invented the bow and arrow, and taught them to make fire by rubbing sticks, and to make utensils of stone.

At the north end of the Porcupine Mountains he stopped to make another tribe of men, which he did by designing mud images, blowing on them, and commanding them to be people. The animals were following in his track wherever he went, for they understood him, talked with him, and served him willingly, but the new people ate them, and in order still better to appease their hunger he made buffalo enough to occupy the northern plains, for this original Eden was, roughly, the country extending east of the Rocky Mountains for a hundred miles or so, and between the Yellowstone and the North Saskatchewan. Still moving northward, Old Man paused at the meeting of Bow and Elbow Rivers to create another family and teach and provide for it. At Red Deer River he stretched himself on the earth for another sleep, and there you may see the imprint of his form. On waking he moved still farther from the warm lands, where people grow lazy and timid, and climbed to the summit of a tall hill. It was steep, and he amused himself by sliding to the foot, the place being known to this day as Old Man's Sliding Ground. In after-times he set aside this Eden for the Blackfeet, Bloods, Piegans, Gros Ventres, and Sarcees, warning them, when others came, to fight them back. They did so until white men entered the region with friendly protestations, and now the Indians have no land, no game, no place in the world. Had they obeyed Old Man it would have been different. But Old Man has not died, and never will die. He has removed to the mountains in the west, beyond the vexing sight of smelters and locomotives, and when he is sorely wanted by his people he may come back.

THE WICKED WIFE

WHEN Fort Edmonton, on the North Sas-katchewan, was built by the Hudson Bay Company, a number of Snake Indians were found living among the Piegans of the district, and The Egg, one of the Snake squaws, married a white employee of the company. The presence of these Snakes so far from their old home fell about in this way. A Piegan, who was good, brave, and rich in ponies, had but one wife, whom he loved so much that he cared nothing for other women. While picking berries at a distance from their camp they were surprised by a war-party of Snakes, and knowing that he would be killed if captured, while his wife would be spared because of her beauty, he left her—since it was impossible for both to escape—and galloped back to his people. With six of her relatives he undertook her rescue, and followed the warm trail of the marauders for several days. When at last they came to the Mis-souri the man swam across it in the darkness and waited in a hollow to see the women when they should come to draw water. Among the first was his wife. He sprang from his hiding-place, kissed her, and in a hurried whisper said, " Come, swim the river with me. Five of your relatives and your brother wait for us in that wood." She hung back, saying that she wanted to get the pretty things that had been given to her, and to steal a horse ; and on a promise that she would do this, the husband re-crossed the river.

She was a faithless creature. She had already learned to love her captors, and she betrayed the little band of rescuers into their hands. Her husband, who alone was taken alive, the others being scalped, was, at her instigation, tortured by fire and boiling water, and bound to a tree with black-ened face, that he might be given to the Sun. When camp was broken, an old woman who had lingered behind, out of pity for him, cut his bonds, gave him food, and promised that she would mark the trail followed by the wife. Then he went back to the north. Great were the anger and grief when he bore the news of death, defeat, and du-plicity to his people, and quick was their revenge. The trail had been marked so well by twigs that they were soon in sight of the Snake camp, and, stealing into the lodge of the kind old woman, the husband clapped his hand on her mouth, that she might not scream, and kissed her. So soon as she had been quieted, she told him that his wife was not only with the Snakes, but had become chief among them, as she was believed to be " a great medicine." Having bidden the beldam to draw aside her friends and relatives, and charging her to say that she had been told in a dream to do so, the Piegans fell upon the camp with a whoop, and killed nearly all that were in it. The wife was decorated with the scalp of her Snake lover, and made to dance on burning brush until she fell and died. Then the old woman and her friends were summoned from their retreat, and as a reward for what she had done they received half of all the horses and plunder in the village. On the next day the Piegans started back to Canada, and as they had won the hearts of this company of Snake survivors, the latter followed them, married among them, and became as Piegans.

FOURTH OF JULY AT YALE

IN the early days at Yale, on the Fraser, the place was peopled by a rough crowd of six hundred Yankees, who had been drawn into the region by the discovery of gold on American Bar. The "foreigners" in this company were few, and the Americans managed the town affairs in their own way. On the Fourth of July after their arrival they decided to celebrate the independence of the United States. They were on British territory, but what odds ? Nobody was there to object. Oh, but stop ; there was one objector, a cockney, known as "Bloody" Edwards, who freely flung away his h's and did not mix pleasantly with his neighbors. Having imbibed strong waters and fired salutes until their patriotism was at a high pitch, the miners decided to call on Edwards and "initiate" him. That worthy saw the crowd approaching with fife, drum, and colors, and he stood at the door of his shack, waving a small British flag and roaring for Hold Hingland and the queen. The flag was like the proverbial red rag shaken before a bull, except that it was John Bull who was shaking it.

"Naturalize him," cried one.

"Swear him in. Make him take the oath," shouted another.

They proposed the oath of allegiance to the United States. Edwards refused it with profane and contemptuous remarks about the republic, and another "bloody hooray" for the queen.

"Duck him in the Fraser," commanded the Irishman in the party.

"Yes, baptize him as an American citizen."

The Briton remaining obdurate, he was hustled to the river and cast in with a mighty splash. He cheered for England as he arose to the surface and struck out for shore. The crowd laughed, and, considering the incident closed, prepared to return, but the Irishman had a century of inherited hate to satisfy, and, bending over the bank as Edwards had almost touched it, he thrust him back into the cold, muddy water, shrieking, "Drown him, dom him! Drown the son of a gun!"

Emerging a second time from the swift current, the Briton cheered again, but weakly, and swam more slowly. The Irishman again stood ready to force him under water.

"The darned fool don't know enough to give in," commented one of the bystanders.

" It isn't fool ; it's grit," answered another.

" Drown him ! Kill him !" howled the Celt.

A tall Yankee advanced to the bank, thrust his elbow into the Irishman's stomach, with some advice to get away, and, lending his hand to the tired swimmer, pulled him out. Nearly all followed him to the nearest cabin, a little concerned when they saw how weak and chilled he was. After being stripped, rubbed, clothed in dry raiment, and entreated in a friendly manner, a bumper of spiced rum was poured out for him, in which he was at liberty to drink anybody's health. He drank it for his own. The little red flag they induced him to give up, that they might raise it with the stars and stripes. As the flags of the two nations lay spread on the shingle, where they were to be tied together, one of those blasts of wind that so often belch through the cañons caught them, twisted them into one, and sent them high into the air, soaring like an eagle, a spot against the snowfields. Said one old miner, solemnly, " God has joined them two flags together."

And millions say to that, " Amen !"

DEATH OF THE GREAT BEAVER

NORTHEAST of Fort Reliance, at the upper extension of Great Slave Lake, are two mounds known as Beaver's Lodge and Muskrat's Lodge. These, the Indians say, were inhabited by huge animals that have no likeness on earth in our time. The beaver, who was as large as an ox, had done such harm among the villages, with occasional help in mischief from his friend the Rat, that the red people swore to endure it no longer; so, giving over all other business, they set off in a resolve to do him to death. He was hiding in his mound when they came upon him, and they sent a volley of arrows through a rift in the rock that pricked him in a hundred places. This frightened him badly. He went down into the river by a hole in the earth that had an opening under its waters. Crossing without coming to the surface, he took refuge in the home of his old partner the Rat, who, seeing his plight, refused the shelter of his lodge, for he was willing to keep out of conflicts with the destructive creatures that occupied the skin houses on the shore. In wrath at this reception the Beaver pulled his recalcitrant friend into the water and belabored him so soundly that the Indians saw the disturbance and hastily rowed to the scene of it. The Beaver dived under their fleet and reached the lake without drawing breath, but his hunters kept sight of him in the clear water, and as he emerged they filled his hide with darts and spears, and a running attack was kept up all the way through the narrows until he was killed. When the Indians returned, the Aheldezza, which had been a gentle stream, had become a fierce torrent, broken by falls and rapids impossible to ascend except by portages, and they had no sooner reached the Beaver's house than they were swallowed by a whirlpool. This account is thought by one explorer to figure the history of a great natural convulsion, such as the breaking down of the hill dam that formerly kept Great Slave Lake at a level with Lakes Artillery, Aylmer, and Clinton-Golden.

WHY THE MOUNTAINS WERE MADE

WISUKATCAK, in the Cree myths, is a demi-god, like Old Man of the Blackfeet. He lived on the plains with his father and mother, who often quarrelled, and he had a little brother. In one of the domestic wrangles the father went wild with temper and cut off the mother's head. Filled with apprehension rather than with grief, the murderer said to Wisukatcak, "Take your brother with you, and go away as fast as you can. If your mother's head follows you, keep it off, for it will try to harm you. Here is a flint, here a fire steel, and here an awl. If you see the head, throw first the flint, then the steel, then the awl, and repeat this word," And he revealed to him a magic word of great power.

The children trudged away toward the west. Soon they heard a rustling in the sage, and saw their mother's head rolling swiftly over the ground, and as it came near they could hear it calling to her

children. The elder boy repeated the magic word
and threw the flint behind him. "Let a wall of
rock rise up across the earth," he cried. And instantly the earth heaved and vast mountains swelled
from the plain to the sky, with the children on the
western slope. These were the Rocky Mountains.
It was a long time before the head could scale this
range, but it did so at last, and went rolling toward
the sunset as an antelope would gallop. The boys
saw their danger again, and the elder, repeating the
magic word, threw the steel behind him, and commanded, "Let a fire rise up and stretch across the
earth." And with appalling reports the craters of
Shasta, Tacoma, Hood, Baker, and the rest opened
along the coast, and shot their ashes and lava to the
zenith. This checked the progress of the head for
an hour, and it was scorched and blistered, but it kept
on presently, through the showers and streams of
molten rock, so that it was soon at the heels of the
boys again, calling as before. Wisukatcak threw
the awl behind him, repeating the magic word, and
ordered that a hedge of thorns should spring up to
reach across the earth. It did so, and has since
spread, so that we have the cactus with us at this day.
Even this barrier the head broke through, and went
rolling after the children. Arrived now at a large
river, probably the Columbia, they saw a pelican
in the water, and Wisukatcak hailed him, "Grand-
father, take us to the other side, for our mother is
chasing us to kill us." The pelican took them

over. Then came the head, demanding the same service. "I am going after my children," it said. "Carry me over, too, and you shall have me for a wife." The pelican did not exhibit any enthusiasm over this proposition, but after some urging he stooped at the shore and allowed the head to roll upon his shoulders, and, with a caution to it to remain still, he arose, slowly, to a great height. When poised over the middle of the river, where some sharp rocks jutted above the surface, he threw off his burden with a sudden lurch, and the head, falling on the rocks, was smashed into pieces. The brains are the masses of foam that float on the surface of the water in times of freshet.

THE PLACE OF DEAD MEN

ON a small affluent of the upper Assiniboin is a pleasant plain with an unpleasant memory,—the place of the two dead men. Here a quarrel occurred between two brothers that ended in a tragedy, one of them drawing a knife and slaying the other. Fratricide was held in such abhorrence by their tribe that with one accord the spectators fell upon the murderer and killed him, burying him beside his victim. From that time no Indian camped upon the place, for the dead men kept their peppery tempers and would greatly disturb the traveller who stopped near their graves.

The lad John Tanner, who was stolen from his

home on the Kentucky River in the early part of this century and taken to Canada, adopted the Indian mode of life, took an Indian wife, and became a hunter. While camped near this haunted spot he heard its story, and resolved to show a better courage than the braves, by spending a night there. He pushed his canoe to the shore, ate his supper, and rolled himself in his buffalo-skin to sleep; but soon two dead men walked out of the darkness and squatted by his fire. They spoke no word, they did not move; they looked steadily at him out of their round, fishy eyes until he could endure it no longer and sat up; whereupon the watchers vanished. Presently he fell asleep, and the dead ones returned in his dreams, but now they not only stared, they gibed at him and poked him with sticks. He tried to resist, to rise, to cry out, but in vain. One of them told him after a time that he would see a horse fettered at the top of a low hill that stood near, adding, " There, my brother, is a horse which I give you to ride tomorrow. And as you pass here on your way home you can call and leave the horse and spend another night with us."

The day, which had never before seemed so long in coming, broke at last, and the dead ones were seen no more. Tanner arose as soon as it was light enough to go on, drew his canoe among the bushes, in perfect confidence that the promise was to be kept, ascended the little hill, and found the horse, which he mounted and rode to a trading-station not many miles away. But he never could prevail on himself to return to the place of the two dead men, and his people had a worse fear of it than ever.

HOW THE INDIANS BECAME RED

THE Okanagans—who once figured in an unofficial publication as the O'Kanaghans—believe in Skyappe and Chacha, the good and bad spirits who are constantly moving through the air, watching all men, and they also tell of a heroine, one Scomalt, who was great and strong and ruled the island where the first men lived. This was long, long ago, when the sun was so young that it was only as large as a star, and there was very little earth to live on. This island was far in the east, and was settled by white giants. War arose among them, and the noise and slaughter so exasperated Scomalt, their queen, that she drove the rebels to the end of the island, broke it off, and pushed it out to sea. This fragment, with its inhabitants, now too busy worrying to fight, drifted for many days, and was so swept by storm and so lacking in food that one by one the people died, all but a man and his wife, who deserted the derelict, for it was water-logged and sinking, and paddled day and night in their canoe until they came to America,—then an island fringed with rocks,—and landed on what is now the territory of the Okanagans. From them came all the people of the western world. But, alas! they were no longer white. After their days of exposure to the sun they had been burned red from head to foot. Here the descendants of this pair shall dwell until the lakes and ever-flowing rivers deep beneath us shall melt the foundations of the world and it will float away again, that time to ruin.

THE POOL OF DESTRUCTION

SOMEWHERE off the coast, probably off Vancouver, was the Charekwin, a vast whirlpool where meeting ocean currents tossed and circled, and in the centre of the flood the waters were sucked down with hideous roaring and lamentation. Hardly less fearful were the cries of those who were committed to the deep, for the vortex was the mouth of hell, and those who had lived in evil met their end in water burial, so dreaded that the coast Indians would readily die any other death than that by drowning. On the coast of California lived the Hogates, long ago. There were only seven of them, and they dwelt in houses, like white men, for they were strange to the red people, who say that they came from another land in a boat. Large and strong were these immigrants, with fierce appetites, as the kjökken-mödding, or "kitchen-midden," attests, which they left on the height of Point St. George, near Crescent City. There are shells of mussels and bones of elk, seals, and sea-lions by the ton. In killing the ocean creatures they used a harpoon fastened to their boats by a long line, and once, having thrown this weapon into an unusually large sea-lion, the value of their prize decided them to take a risk rather than cut the raw-hide rope, when the monster set off with the speed of a tidal wave toward the northwest. But if they had thought to tire him they were mistaken. Hour after hour they rushed over the sea, beyond sight and comfort of the land, and soon the roaring of Charekwin sounded across the waves. Too terrified to attempt an escape, or knowing the hopelessness of such an attempt, the men awaited their end in silence. Now they could see spirits tossing on the wind that rages above the caldron. Their time on earth was limited to minutes. But the Father of Life had had little reason to reproach them, and he would not abandon them in this extremity. As they reached the in-fall of the waters the rope broke : the sea-lion was drawn under, struggling mightily, but the boat arose softly into the air, circling as it had circled about the mouth of hell, ever rising; and so the seven Hogates reached heaven and became the seven stars,—the Pleiades.

Myths and Legends

YEHL, THE LIGHT-MAKER

A THLINKEET living in sight of the great
Alaskan peaks had for a wife a woman so
bright and fair that he was exceeding jealous,
though it was all so dark on earth that he could
barely see except by fire, or by the beauty of the
woman herself, for the heavenly lights had not been
set, and in the gray the few other beings groped
sadly, trying to find sound earth to live on. This
wife was so faithful that she could not so much as
suppose a cause for jealousy, and she made the
state of her husband worse by beaming pleasantly
on all strangers and holding them in cheerful, innocent talk. He kept a flock of red birds hovering near his lodge, that they might report to him
what she did and said and who conversed with
her; and her willingness to be with others angered
him so that he made a box, at last, and hid her in
it. Because his sister's children had merely looked
at her, while this rage was on him, he had slain
them every one. The bereaved mother walking
on the shore excited the compassion of the fish,
who put their heads out of the water to ask what
ailed her, and the whale, the counsellor of his tribe,
bade her swallow a certain pebble on the beach
and drink some sea-water, for she should then bear
Yehl, a son nobler than those she had lost. She
obeyed, and the prophecy came true. In a place
removed from her wrathful brother she brought up

196

her boy to differ as much from him as he could. He was to do good to men, and to relieve the cold and dark by setting fires in the sky. He grew up resolved in this course, and when he gained his age and strength he went to Baranoff Island, where the wicked man lived, and after biding his time until that ferocious relative was absent, he crept into his lodge, dragged out the box in which the beautiful woman was caged, and was about to open it, when the Thlinkeet returned, and, catching him at his merciful business, rushed at him with spear and club.

Yehl struck up the weapons, and after a struggle escaped, and some time went by ere he came out of his hiding in the shrubbery to attempt again the liberation of the fair victim. Possibly the Thlinkeet believed that his enemy had been mortally hurt in the fight, for he relaxed his guard, and Yehl surprised him in a deep sleep. First he opened the box that held the stars and moon, and they floated lightly up to their places in the sky. Then he opened the box that had been the living tomb of the innocent wife, and with a look of rapture she, too, sped into the skies. Amazement sat on every face, for she was light itself; and now, for the first time, the beauty of the world disclosed itself in her smile. Her husband, waking, saw the empty boxes, the shine in the sky, the triumphant Yehl beside him, and with a roar of anger he rushed away to the mountains. The people, who had been used to groping by the light of comets, were so terrified at the fire of the newly risen sun that they rushed into the sea,—some of them,—and in mercy Yehl changed them into fishes, that they need not drown; others, leaping into the air, out of their wits, he turned to brightly colored birds; while those that ran to hide in the woods became deer. The rest fell prostrate, hailing him as deliverer, light-creator, and while he stayed on earth they worshipped him.

THE SHELTER OF EDGECUMBE

AN Indian and his wife quarrelled, not unusually, and their fights ended in victory for the stronger, namely, the man. In fear of his blows, after one of these misunderstandings, the woman ran like a deer up Mount Edgecumbe, her husband just at her heels all the way to the top; but as they reached that point the spirit of the peak, Ahgishanakon, "the woman who supports the earth," opened the rock and took the woman to her protection. "Back!" she cried to the pursuer. "Back to the woods and howl your anger there! Back and prey on meaner creatures, that are less worthy of your bragging when you beat them. You have aimed blows at the one you were bound to shelter, the mother of your children. She shall be forever in my charge, while you shall slink and prowl about the earth for a few years longer in your real character. Wolf you are by nature. Now be wolf in fact." And the man felt himself shrinking and growing uncertain on his feet. He could no longer steady himself. He dropped forward on his hands. His fingers were growing long, his nails becoming claws, his flesh hidden by hair. He tried to cry his protest and astonishment, but only a long, hoarse bay came from his throat. He was indeed a wolf. Howling fiercely, he fled aways and still he haunts the wood ; yet when he catches any animal he carries it to the mountain-top. The distant rumble of the storm is the woman's voice, talking with the manitou, and the thunder is the growling of the wolf as he gnaws the bones of his prey. The manitou of Edgecumbe, Ahgishanakon, saved herself from the universal deluge by catching at this peak, and standing on it held up and saved the world from drowning, too, while her brother, Chethl, struggled so hard to rise out of the water that wings appeared on his shoulders and he became the osprey.

HOW SELFISHNESS WAS PUNISHED

BEFORE Sitka was dreamed of there lived on its site, one summer, a Thlinkeet, with his wife and mother. It was a time of suffering and hardship, for the fish stayed off the coast, the game had gone far over the mountains, and neither net, trap, nor arrow brought a morsel to the lodge. The Thlinkeet fished and hunted all day to no effect, and he could carry home nothing but an occasional bark pail of berries, roots, or young sprouts, to boil for soup and greens. His mother, who was nearly blind, and could not see to pick the berries, grew daily more haggard and weak, whereas the wife kept fresh and strong. Was it a dream that the younger woman was eating every night, and was cooking fish in the lodge? No, the mother's senses were still sharp. Waking and assuring herself that it was not a dream, she feebly held out her hands, crying for a single morsel.

" Your mind wanders. You were dreaming. There is no food," answered the wife.

" But I can smell it. I see the fire. I hear the crackle of its skin. Ha! Now I hear you eating."

" No, I am only chewing gum from the spruce-trees. It makes one feel less hungry."

" I know you are eating fish. Give me some, I beg."

" Then, since you will intrude yourself, take it." And, picking a tail and head out of the scalding fat, she flung them into the outheld hands and shut the withered fingers over them until the old woman's palms were badly burned.

The starving one sobbed herself to sleep. In the morning she whispered to her son what had happened. He said nothing, greeted his wife as usual, and resolved to watch. On the next night when the time was half-way to morning the young woman crept softly from the lodge, followed by her husband, whom she supposed to be asleep. He saw her cut an alder branch, after making curious gestures before it, take it to the shore, and wave it over the sea, repeating some words whose meaning the listener did not know, but which he immediately committed to memory. In a moment the water rippled with a thousand fins,—a shoal of herring coming up to be caught. The woman stooped and plucked out two or three of the largest, laughing quietly as she gathered them in her dress and tiptoed back to the lodge. Her husband managed to reach it before her, and was lying so still when she entered that she never thought of looking to see if she were watched. A fire was soon snapping; the fish were broiling on the coals and sending forth a maddening odor. The woman ate as much as she pleased, threw the rest into the shrubbery outside, and went to bed content. Our Thlinkeet was lucky on the following afternoon in catching a seal that yielded a particularly heavy fat, with which the wife was so kindly plied at supper that she slept soundly until dawn, her husband taking her place as fish-catcher at midnight, and, by copying her incantation, securing a good batch of herring. When the selfish wife awoke and saw her husband and his mother making an ample breakfast and looking at her significantly, she smiled good-naturedly and made an excuse for quitting the lodge. No sooner had she gained freedom than with all her speed she ran toward the mountains, fearing pursuit and punishment. Yes, her husband was following. She climbed a great boulder that lay in her path, but as she reached the top her dress divided into feathers and she shrank to a twentieth of her size. She cried in astonishment and alarm, but her voice had become a hoot. Her husband gained the rock,—her husband nevermore: her witchcraft had reached its end, and the evil forces she had commanded now commanded her. With a heavy flap of wing she arose before the face of the Thlinkeet and flew off into a wood. She was an owl.

THE GHOST OF SITKA CASTLE

WHEN Alaska was a Russian province its little capital of Sitka had sometimes the aspect of a court. It was a scene of gayeties, war-ships anchored in its harbor, officers, soldiers, and sailors brightened its few streets and its gloomy Baranoff castle with arms and uniforms, and social life gained its final charm when the ladies of the governor's household received the visiting military and naval deputations. In those days Sitka was a miniature St. Petersburg in formalities and hospitalities. The great samovar, made in the brass-foundry of the town, was always bubbling in the castle drawing-room, and tea was served to every guest by a maid in the picturesque costume of the Ukraine. When Alaska passed into the possession of the United States the official mansion was gutted by relic-seeking vandals, who even pounded the hinges from its doors, and it might have been destroyed altogether had not an American signal-officer insisted on setting apart two rooms for his own use. He half regretted his choice of a residence when the time had come either to disprove or to verify certain rumors that had been repeated to him before he entered the place, for on that night he surely heard the rustle of a dress moving down a corridor, and caught the perfume of wild roses. All night long somebody—something—was walking in that corridor,—some one in distress; and, suddenly opening his door, he believed that he saw a woman's figure in a wedding-gown, with phosphorescent gems in her rings, slowly twisting her hands together. Just then the moon flashed from behind a cloud, and no such thing was there. It must have been an effect of shadow, he said to himself. At any time he was likely to hear a sound of sighing, or of something moving sadly, wearily, in the other rooms. Six months after the first visitation he heard again the stir of a dress, smelt the perfume of roses, saw a dim, faceless figure in the hall, and until dawn faint sounds moved through the castle. He gave up the attempt to account for these things. He had argued that the wind was blowing about the ruin, that it brought a scent of wild roses from the edge of the wood, that rats and mice were capering in the walls, that clouds, moonlight, starlight, and the aurora had woven fantastic pictures. He could deceive himself no longer. The place was haunted. Then he gave a more believing ear to the story that had been told of the castle,—how a niece of one of the stern old governors, having been given to a man of title, for whom she cared nothing, as if she were only merchandise, was found just after the wedding, in one of the rooms, dead, in her bridal robes and jewels, and wreathed in roses. Had she killed herself in despair? Had her husband killed her when he learned that she had a lover? Had her lover killed her when he found she was not to be his wife? Had he, as one rumor had it, slain her at the altar and drowned himself directly afterward? Her lover was a poor lieutenant, her husband a prince. No one living has solved the mystery.

A FATAL RIVALRY

THE transfer of Alaska by Russia to its new owner, the United States, was denoted by the arrival of a small body of American troops to support the official dignity at Sitka. The officers were at once absorbed into the coterie that made the society of the place, and two of them, a cap-

tain and his first lieutenant, found in the change
from the fairer districts of the south no reason to
complain; for among the residents of the little
capital was a Russian girl of title, high lineage,
amiable, dreamy-eyed, and lovely. Where members of the fair sex are few and soldiers many,
jealousies are sure to occur. The young woman
apparently liked the lieutenant the better of the
two; he was younger, had more polish, and was
finer-looking than his superior, although the captain's courage had been tried on many fields, and
he made a distinguished figure in his uniform.
There was little attempt on the part of either to
conceal the fact that he was falling into a passionate
love for the young countess, and that the society
of his rival was growing irksome. Availing himself of his authority, the captain often assigned
duties to his second in command that were plainly
invented for the occasion and devised merely to
keep him at the barracks while the captain was
prosecuting a siege more difficult than any he had
before engaged in. Possibly the countess was a
bit of a flirt, and gave such slight encouragement
to the elder of her suitors as would insure his
company.

The situation was sure to lead to a rupture between the two men, and it was known that hot
words had passed; hence there was much surprise at head-quarters when both of them returned
from a walk, one afternoon, in courteous converse,

and it was understood that they were going off on a hunt together in the morning. They went up Indian River, and were not followed. At evening the captain returned, alone. He was pale and agitated. His companion had been gored by a buck deer, he said, and he had been obliged to leave the body where it lay. He called on the countess to tell her of the accident, and took a cup of tea from her hands before he left. On reaching head-quarters he found that a search-party had gone up the river trail with lanterns to seek for the body, and his commanding officer, intimating in pretty plain terms his belief that a duel had been fought, advised him to retire to his chambers, which he did. Toward the middle of the night the soldiers came back, bringing the dead man on a stretcher. There was a hole in his chest, but it had been made by a bullet, and his own rifle had been found close by. The captain's arrest was ordered at once. A sergeant and a squad went to his rooms and knocked. There was no answer. The door was forced. The captain lay propped in bed, staring in horror, his jaw fallen, his face colorless, his hands clinched in agony. He had been dead an hour. In the official reports it was said that he had died of heart disease and the lieutenant had accidentally shot himself; but the common belief was that the Russian woman had put poison in his tea, and that in his last moments he believed that his victim was standing at his bedside.

Beyond Our Borders

BAD BOYS OF NA-AS RIVER

SOME mischievous boys who lived beside the Na-as River of southern Alaska were amusing themselves by catching the young salmon in that stream. They first lifted them from the water to see them flop and wriggle, flashing their bright scales in the sunshine; but, that sport growing too tame, they took sharp stones and scratched and cut the poor creatures. Finally they made wounds in their backs and put pebbles into them, as though to find if laden in this manner they would sink to the bottom and stay there. They laughed gleefully as the fish twisted about under the water in the attempt to get rid of the burden, or floated near the surface, gasping and exhausted. All this time the Great Spirit was watching them with stern displeasure. Like children who are not so savage, the youngsters found the sport flagging as their victims weakened, and they prodded the unhappy fish with sticks, and turned them this way and that as they floated seaward. At last the wrath of the Great Spectator could no longer be kept in bounds. From his seat on a mountain he arose. He lifted the cover from the peak, and the bubbling lava within flowed down the side and into the bed of the Na-as. The fish rushed away to sea, but the wicked boys were caught in the flow, their feet were burned off, they were suffocated in hot ashes, the river itself was turned to steam. After bellowing and belching rebukes for a time, a calm fell once more; but it was on a region of bereavement, and the Indians will at this day show you the bones of the bad children in the distorted lava forms beside the Na-as.

THE BAFFLED ICE GOD

THIRTY or forty miles up the Stickeen River, in Alaska, is a glacier twenty-five miles long and five miles wide, a stupendous ice mass, that is a part of a bridge once flung across the river. A god of this region, who had most power in winter, closing the smaller streams, covering the mountains with white, stripping foliage from the trees, and cumbering the inlets with floes, was angry at the spirit of the Stickeen for its refusal to submit to the power of the frost. As the long winter came on, brooding and threatening, the god shook his spear of icicle in triumph, and began bawling his orders in a north-wind voice that roared and echoed from the cliffs and shook all the loose snow out of the passing clouds. The Stickeen went dancing and frolicking to the ocean, without any notice of the god, until, filled with wrath that one child of nature should disobey him, he gathered from the mountain-side great masses of ice and snow and flung them across the stream. He could not close it, but he bridged it and shut it from the air and sunlight, and the people who had gone to

it daily for fish were frightened, and asked its spirit
what could be done to make it free again. Crushed
and shamed, the spirit made no answer, but the god
cried in his stormiest voice that he must have two
lives to pay for this disobedience, and must have
them soon, or he would visit his wrath on all the
men who dwelt along the river.

An old chief asked who among the company
would make the sacrifice,—make it by that most
dreaded death of drowning. His people shrank
away, and there fell a silence. But presently a
young woman arose and in faltering tones announced
that she would die to save her people. At this a
young warrior of the tribe sprang up and cried,
proudly, that he would be the other to make this
gift of life. A canoe was brought to the shore,
sadly decked with flowers and carvings for the last
voyage of the two, and they were bound so that
they might not attempt an escape when the boat
was swept against the ice bridge and sucked into
the deeps below. Tearful farewells were said, and
the boat was pushed into the stream. As it neared
the low arch of ice the people turned aside, that
they might not see the tragedy. But there was no
tragedy. Pleased and touched by the willingness
of these innocent ones to give their lives for his
selfish whim, the god stamped on his new-made
bridge, and a part of it fell into the water, leaving
a space through which the boat was carried by the
river manitou in safety. Then it swung to the

shore and grounded. Loud were the cries of praise and quick the release of the willing captives, who were led back to their camp in triumph. And the god desisted from his battling from that hour.

Mexico

M EXICO and the adjacent country enjoyed a
civilization that must have seemed to its
people something better than the substitute offered
by the pale-faced strangers who came among them
carrying tubes of metal that uttered lightnings and
thunders and slew by hundreds, and who stabbed
and cursed and tortured and imprisoned when they
could not have their way, and pillaged whether
they had it or not. The shameful treatment of
the owners of the western continent began in the
day of Columbus, and has continued ever since.
Long before any permanent settlement of white
people on our continent, before even the visits of
the Norsemen, a great, strong, religious race, the
Mound-Builders, had disappeared, leaving not even
a name. Whether they had crossed the Atlantic
or the Pacific, or had sprung from native stock, is
conjectural. There are Chinese who have built
mounds, though none on such a scale as those of
the central States or the great heap of Cholula, and
none so splendidly adorned as those of Koh. It
was at about the dawn of the Christian era that
the Nahuas entered Mexico and built houses, while
the Toltecs, who followed them, erected temples,
and these the Aztecs decorated with sculpture.

The Toltecs said that they came from Atlan, or Aztlan, which some believe to have been Atlantis. The Mound-Builders may have been earlier than all of these, and they have left the records of their march, or their retreat, from Manitoba to the domain of Montezuma. As the kingdom of peace had not then come upon the earth, it is likely that this great family, the Aryans of the western world, the people of arts and gentle living, met their end among the deserts and snows beyond the Rio Grande.

But, great as the destruction of the red race may have been in its intestine wars, it was not doomed until the white men landed. On the island of Cozumel, which the Spaniards took in the middle of the sixteenth century, it is reported that they found a population of one hundred thousand, and half as many others from adjacent lands yearly visited the shrines of the sun-god. Now but a few hundred remain.

As among the Canadian tribes, so among the Mexicans, we have tokens of an early teaching of at least the forms of Christianity. The cross appears in Aztec sculpture, though not needfully as a Christian symbol. The Lower California Pericues tell of Kwahayipe, son of the lord of heaven, and his wife, who lived in the Acaragui Mountains and brought men into being, pulling them out of the earth. Men killed him, put a crown of thorns upon him, and in a remote place he lies to this day, dripping fresh blood and uncorrupted. And the second coming of a Messiah was so confidently looked for that Montezuma believed that the great white god had returned when Cortez landed. Cortez, forsooth! This god, or demi-god, was Quetzalcoatl, "the plumed serpent," the son of a virgin in Tula, he whose symbol was the morning star, bringer of light, and who was worshipped in Cholula. He came from the east to help the human race. He was in many ways like Hayowentha, or Hiawatha, albeit a large, bearded man, wearing white garments and a mitre, and red crosses were painted on his feet. He was a celibate, hated war and sacrifice, delighted in fruits and flowers and things of natural beauty, and was constantly preaching and working for purity and peace. When, through the wiles of his dark enemy, Tezcatlipoca, he was driven away in exile, sailing eastward in his snake-skin boat, yet glad to meet the sun, he promised to return; so, when Cortez arrived the Mexicans hailed the strangers as brothers of the plumed serpent. Heartless was the violation of this trust.

Another indication of early visits of white men to this land is found in a legend told among the Indians of Colombia, to the effect that Bohica, a bearded white man, appeared to the Mozcas on the Bogota plains and taught them farming, building, draining, and civil government before he retired to a hermitage for two thousand years. Like him was Manco Capac, who with his sister, Mama

Oello, gave laws and arts to the Peruvians before returning to the Sun, his father; like him were Kukulkan of Yucatan, and Bochica of the Muyscas.

When the Spaniards invested Bogota they guarded the roads, so as to cut off the chance of escape and intercept any approach of reinforcements. The savage men-at-arms soon had the city in their power, the natives having been awed by the thunder and murder of their guns into the belief that the Spaniards were invincible. The invaders as they entered found the people either attempting flight or extended along the streets in supplication; but, paying little attention to them, save when it was necessary to beat back a threatening band, they pressed on toward the centre of the town, from which a great smoke was rising, for here they knew was the temple, and here they hoped to find treasure. The sound of a solemn chant arose within, and as they came clattering and shouting to the door, the people, in a frenzy at their intended sacrilege, made one last and vain attempt to stay them. Benalcazar and his men rushed in. Before the statue of a grim god a funeral pyre had been reared, and the flames were snapping over it. Gums and spices had been thrown upon the logs, and the smoke was choking in its fragrance. Vessels of gold had been heaped in a corner, ready to carry out or to hide, and the eyes of the Spaniards fastened on them greedily; but as the smoke swung aside the leader saw what made him pause. Three white men, not Spaniards, nor like them, stepped upon the brands, still chanting, their look turned skyward, their hands raised high. Long beards flowed upon their breasts, and their rich gowns were heavy with gems and gold. Without look or word for the intruders, these men of a race unknown went calmly to their death.

THE WHITE GOD

WHOEVER he was, whatever he was, or whatever it was, the white god of Mexico made possible the conquest of the Aztecs. Nothing but a belief that Cortez might be this Messiah admitted his little army into the heart of a land of haughty, suspicious, if not hostile people who outnumbered his force a thousand to one. Much is due to the craft and diplomacy of the invader, much to his downright courage, much to the awe created by his horses and his thundering arms ; but these alone did not conquer the subjects of Montezuma. The Aztecs were victims of false hopes.

In the year 1121 Bishop Eric left Iceland for America, which Leif the Lucky had found over a hundred years before, and never was Eric heard of afterward. May it not be that, repelled by the desolate aspect of the northern lands, or driven by lasting winds, or misled by vague reports as to the new continent, or lured along by the increasing

warmth and fertility as his vessel coasted southward, Eric reached Mexico, and, finding its people
tractable and intelligent, began teaching the doc-
trines in whose earnest promulgation he had found
his life-work and won his bishopric? One myth
sets forth that a white man with a hooded robe and
long beard, carrying a cross, landed at Tehuantepec,
on the Pacific side of Mexico, and urged the Indians to perform penance for their sins, make confession, and take vows of chastity. In another
version he carries a sickle, condemns all sacrifices
except of fruit and flowers, teaches arts, including
gem-cutting and metal-casting, invents letters and
a calendar, and when there is talk of war puts
his fingers into his ears. The Christian faith, or
something like it, was taught to these people long
before the arrival of the Spaniards, and some of
their arts may have had their rise in the instructions
of the Norsemen. For the southern tribes were
expert in many ways. They had phonogrammic
writing, as well as pictographs, they knew the
metals, they made splendid cloaks of feathers, they
adorned their helmets with precious stones, they
wove cotton and dyed it gorgeously, quilting it,
too, for armor. Something like a mail and express
service was furnished by a corps of royal mes-
sengers, who carried picture-writings and goods,
running at top speed along the fair roads, and relieving each other of messages and burdens at post-
houses. By this means the emperor kept in touch

with all parts of his kingdom, and enjoyed many luxuries that we are used to think of as modern. He ate fish at his dinners that twenty-four hours before had been swimming in the Gulf of Mexico. Many of the arts and benefits of Aztec civilization were the probable inventions of the people, however. They did not know the use of steel, which Eric would have taught them, but employed obsidian, or volcanic glass, for their knives, weapons, and utensils. It is said by the Indians of the Andes that they once had the art of softening gold by steeping it in some liquid, so that they were able to work it into any desired form, after which it would harden ; and, curiously, among the gold ornaments found in graves and ruins some bear finger-prints. More of the metal was, wrought with hammers and chisels, and the great golden shield, worth two hundred and fifty thousand dollars, that Montezuma sent to Cortez,—a shield like a cart-wheel,—was richly ornamented with carvings. Precious metals were abundant. The skeleton of an Inca found in Chili in 1854 was wrapped in a sheet of gold. Much that might have been learned of this strange people is hopelessly lost, for nearly all the picture-manuscripts of their schools were destroyed by the Spaniards, who believed that they were compacts with the devil and would work magic.

Thinking how long a time elapsed between the voyages of Eric and Cortez, it appears likely that many of the arts and beliefs which may have been taught by the former suffered a change, and that his personality should have been merged in that of Quetzalcoatl, the god of the air, one of the thirteen principal gods of the nation. There were over two hundred others. In his temple at Cholula were two elders, one wearing for his totem a tiger, the other an eagle, and here also was a monastery, the inmates being bound to the duty of praying before the statue of this god for rain, health, and peace. The novices wore black capes for four years, then one of black and red for other four, then for the same term a black one with red border, again the black and red, then black, and in their age, red. They were allowed to visit their wives until midnight, when they were summoned to return by blasts of a trumpet. The same instrument sounded for prayers at daybreak and at sunset.

Before leaving the country to which he had brought prosperity, this god, who was white, bearded, and unlike an Aztec, promised to return with his children. He had incurred the anger of a brother god, and Mexico was no longer a pleasant land to him; so he walked to the sea, carving crosses on the rocks as he went, entered his magic boat of snake-skin, and floated away to his own cool country of Tlapalan, leaving his people mournful. Some of them reported that he had died, that his ashes had been carried to heaven by brilliant birds, and that his heart became the morning star. This luminary descended into hell for four days, then reappeared, more brilliant than ever, as the seat of the departed god. The Aztecs soon forgot his gentler teachings, at all events, for they restored human sacrifice, even at his altar, cutting out the heart of their victim, holding it to the sun, then throwing it before the image of the god or spirit that was the tutelary genius of the temple. After this they ate the corpse. At the dedication of the temple of Huitzilopochtli in 1486 about seventy thousand captives were slain to appease the deities. Is it any wonder that the consciences of the people were troubled? that they asked one another if the white god would praise them, when he came back, for turning their temples into shambles? Signs and wonders made them doubt afresh at the beginning of the sixteenth century. Eight years before the arrival of Cortez the lake arose, without rain or earthquake, flooding the city of Mexico, sweeping away houses and drowning many people. Next year a tower of the temple took fire, without visible cause, and none could put it out. Three comets were seen, and a vast pyramid of light stood in the east. Voices were heard grieving and whining in the air. A royal princess died, and came out of her grave to prophesy ruin. An Indian was snatched from his field work by an eagle, and carried to a cave where a spirit told him of coming doom, after which the bird flew back with him and delivered him safely to the earth where the church of San Hipolito now stands. The king of Tezcuco, who was an astrologer, was asked to give comfort, but could find no promise of it in the stars. No wonder, then, that when Cortez landed, in panoply and with ceremony, the people kissed the boats that brought him, believing that the white god was come again ; while others thought upon the prophecies, and feared that here was a white devil.

According to Father Sahagun, the white king-god had of old a temple in Tula, and his image was placed there, lying extended under blankets. His worshippers were expert mechanics and masons : they carved the green stone chalchiuite, and had foundries for metals. In his honor they built houses of silver, chalchiuite, turquoise, sea-shells, and wood, and covered them with feathers. On the mount of Tzatzitepetl the god spoke to his people through a stentorian prophet whose voice was heard three hundred miles away in Anahuac. He never spoke save wisely, and by obeying him the people thrived. They had maize in abundance, an ear of it being all that a man could carry, pumpkins were two feet thick, cotton-bolls opened in a dozen colors, and the birds repaid kind treatment by filling Tula's streets with color and music. Still, Quetzalcoatl had his bad hours, and he did penance for his weaknesses by drawing blood from his legs with maguey spines. Once, when he was ill, the evil god Tezcatlipoca presented himself as an elderly man who had a cure for his pain of body and heaviness of spirit, a water of eternal life, and, tasting the mixture, Quetzalcoatl was so pleased that he drained it all, and thereupon became drunk, for this cure was wine that stole the sense and weakened the will, so that in the end the mischief-lover gained his wish. Quetzalcoatl quickly grew old, and set off for Tlapalan, weeping bitterly, after burying or destroying his treasures. His people followed him, playing on flutes, till within six miles of the site of Mexico city, where he rested on a stone, leaving hand-prints and tear-marks on it that may still be seen. He threw his jewels into the fountain of Coaapan, and rested from the persecution of his enemies for twenty years at Cholula. In crossing the mountains on his way to the sea his dwarfed and hump-backed servants died of cold, but four lads of noble birth followed him to Coatzacoalco, where he parted with them, after making his prophecy of the coming of the new race, and sailed for Tlapalan.

The wondrous success of Cortez's march to the capital made it seem to the subject tribes more certain that it was the god who had returned. He sent his soldiers into the temples and to the tops of the pyramids, to throw down. the statues of the gods that stood there, and this he did, they argued, because those gods had wronged him before he went away. As the great figures came tumbling down the slopes and stairs the people fell and cried in fear, lest the wrath of the deities who looked out of the clouds and saw this insult to their images should be visited on the multitude. Cortez placed wooden virgins and saints on the pedestals thus vacated, and the Indians never entreated these new divinities so rudely. At Tlascala the people refused to destroy their idols, as they were called, but were willing to add those of the Christians to their number. A cross was erected in one of their squares, where the invaders were allowed to celebrate mass without interference, and all night a cloud hovered over this cross, shedding light upon it,—a phenomenon that decided the Indians to be converted. At last, in Mexico, Montezuma, once the splendid emperor, now the stricken captive, affected to believe that the men who had repaid his thousand favors with imprisonment, pillage, and indignity were children of the white god, and he asked his people to befriend them. As Cortez sat beneath the Tree of Dismal Night and wept in the time of his besetment, did he think it worth while to pose longer as a god? And when they picked their way among the gory corpses of their friends and children, did the Mexicans believe that any god could be like Cortez?

SPIRITUAL GUIDANCE

IN no part of the world has the Church ruled more absolutely than in Mexico. The ignorance and barbarism of the natives made them desirable subjects for conversion, and also made them easy to control, once they had passed under priestly sway. Long after civilized protest had put a stop to the horrors of the Spanish Inquisition it remained a power in Mexico, "the strong fort and mount of Zion," as the abomination was called, continuing until this century. In the city of Mexico its victims were roasted alive near the church of San Diego, and a monument has been raised to the renown of Morelos, its last victim, who was put to death in 1815.

In order to spread the faith and enlarge their temporal power the spiritual authorities gave currency to many tales that in other parts of the world would at once have been laughed down as mythical; but they doubtless had their uses. The defeat of American troops at Monterey, in the unjust war of conquest waged against our neighbor people, was ascribed, not to lead, steel, numbers, or generalship, but solely to Our Lady of Guadalupe, who hovered over the Mexicans during the battle, seeking out weak points in the invading army and advising the Mexican officers where and how to strike.

Every year, in October, crowds of people go to

dismal Mitla, with presents for the priests, that the good fathers may be persuaded to renew their prayers and masses for the deliverance of their ancestors who died in sin before the conquest, and whose souls are haunting the ruins. Probably a great cemetery once existed in Mitla.

Though we have a dim tradition that the Aztecs saw spirits hovering over the site of Puebla, the circumstance did not impress them, for they took no action upon it. It was not until after the conquest that Puebla came into being,—not the Puebla de Zaragosa, as it is called to-day, but the Puebla de los Angeles : city of the angels. For strategic, commercial, and other reasons a town was needed between the city of Mexico, of which the Spaniards had none too secure a tenure, and the port of Vera Cruz, which gave them touch with the other colonies and Spain. On the Bishop of Tlascala they imposed the task of fixing a site. He thereupon dreamed of a beautiful plain, edged by white-topped peaks, and as he looked two angels came into his sight who, with rod and chain, set about the work of laying off streets. So vivid was his dream that when he searched for the spot he recognized it immediately on his arrival, and there was built one of the fairest of the cities of the south ; almost the only large one not erected on Aztec ruins.

Early in the period of Spanish rule a chief near Querétaro, who had adopted Christianity, was persuaded that it was his mission to convert an adjacent tribe to the same faith. Lest the prospective converts should object, he took with him an army, copying the spiritual methods of the Spaniards in that respect, and on reaching Querétaro he commanded his neighbors to pick out their strongest men and he would fight them,—that is, an equal number of his strongest men would do so. The challenged people had no occasion to engage with him, but he insisted that they should, and told them in advance that if his side won the other side must become Christians, whereas if the pagans were the victors he would go home and leave them to their idols. The trouble was finally agreed upon, and it shows an already benign influence in the new faith that the fight was to be without weapons, the combatants agreeing to kick and pound instead of slaying each other. It was a long and bloody battle, and was waged in the space between the armies, that cheered and prayed and advised, as lookers-on will always do, even in a baseball game. We do not know what the result might have been, but there is a suspicion that the unregenerate were getting the better of it, else why did the heavens open and the blessed Saint Iago show himself there, with a red cross in his hand? In presence of this vision the converted chief became complacently triumphant, and the idolaters ran to the Spanish priests, flung themselves at their feet, and begged to be baptized and saved from the figure in the air. A stone cross was erected under the spot where Saint Iago appeared, and if anybody doubts the tale he is taken to the Church of the Holy Cross, where this relic is kept, and it is shown to him in proof.

Another appearance of this saint was during the battle that Cortez waged against one hundred and fifty thousand (!) Tabascans. To the terrific aspect of this heavenly champion, as he swooped upon the savages, mounted on a gray horse, is attributed the victory. One monkish writer insists that it was not the saint that made this charge, but "the ever-present Virgin." Cortez returned thanks to heaven, and he baptized the twenty women that the beaten tribe had given up, before turning them over to his soldiers to be fought for. One of these women, Marina, who became the mistress of Cortez, his spy and interpreter, was the first convert to Christianity on the American continent. A statue has been erected to her in Puebla.

It has been feared that in some parts of Mexico the natives are church people for revenue mainly, or that they go to church to avoid trouble and rebuke, and this is known to be the case in some of the South American states, the Indians of Peru, for instance, being pretty fair Christians while the white men are looking, though they are sun-worshippers at other times. In Yucatan the natives have been known to go to church under compulsion of the lash. In Cholula the barbarian practice of providing food, rum, and woman's milk

for the dead is continued if the vigilance of the priests can be avoided, while a rod is buried with every dead girl, that she may beat off the monsters that will assail her on the road to paradise. There are caves in the ridge between Popocatepetl and Iztaccihuatl in which are old stone statues which are still secretly worshipped, their public recognition being prohibited. One of these caves is alleged by believers to be the opening of a long passage under the sea, that leads to Rome, probably that good Indians may go there to be blessed, after death. Yet this was a home of evil spirits before Cortez came, and the people told the Spaniards that no man could reach the top of Popocatepetl and live. Diego Ordaz climbed as far as the snow-line, and Francisco Montaño reached the top and was lowered into the crater, that he might gather sulphur for powder, which was sorely needed; but the natives apparently believed that these soldiers were bragging.

Many old beliefs have disappeared, like those in the giant with long, lean arms who embraced and smothered the whole Toltec tribe; the spectre of a white child who followed him about, and from whose decaying head noxious gases spread over the country as it sat on a tall peak,—a possible myth of volcanic eruption; and the Titans who built the pyramid of Cholula; but Miquiztli, the dead man, and the crying white woman, Iztaccihuatl, walk in the villages of these Indians, while their sorcerers change themselves to animals at will, and their medicine-men practise their art almost as it was practised before the conquest. The people are more peaceable than they were, more courteous, yet more secretive.

Izamal was a city of four mounds, the largest one hundred and fifty feet high, with a temple on its top where old men preached and burned copal before the statues to make a pleasant smell. Here, every day at noon, the " fiery macaw with sun eyes" lighted the fire at the altar. It has been hinted that concave mirrors focussing their rays on the tinder kindled the flames. However that may be, the mounds and temples, having been declared sinful by the Spaniards, were ruined, and the people were forced to support the church and monastery that were presently built in the place. This they did more willingly when they found that the Virgin's statue in the church would cure diseases. The images of their old gods had done that too, but not so well; and when a new statue of the Virgin arrived from Guatemala, through the rain, the priest convinced them of heaven's blessing on it, for not a drop had fallen on the box containing the figure, nor on those who carried it. In order to gain the complete confidence of the Indians, the Spaniards had to represent that the Virgin was a brown woman who wore an Indian dress.

EAGLE, SNAKE, AND CACTUS

THE great plaza of the city of Mexico is the country's heart. It was here that in 1312 the Aztecs, who had been conducting an Israelitish pilgrimage for seven hundred years, marching southward after their birth in the Seven Caves of Chicomoztoc, saw the sign that had been revealed to their astrologers that was to show where they were to plant their capital. Here was a lake; in the lake, where now is the zocalo, was a rocky island; on the island was a cactus; on the cactus was an eagle, his great wings spread toward the sun; in his beak and talons was a snake. The sign was hailed with cries of rejoicing, and the foundation of a great city was begun, a huge teocalli, or temple, being the first structure to be erected. As it happened, the prophets were frauds. There never was a worse place to put a town upon than where Mexico stands. It is in a basin, only six feet above its lowest part; it has no natural drainage; the houses had to be built on piles; the soil is not rich; it is in danger from floods, in the seventeenth century it was not dry for five consecutive years, people went through its streets in boats, and the dampness has caused malarial disorders; but expensive public works have secured dryness and health, and in the high, cool region, in the bright sunshine, with snow-covered volcanoes heaved into sight, with modern devices for beauty and comfort, Mexico is in many ways an ideal city. If it were to be built again it would be in accordance with the plans of engineers and sanitarians, not of prophets. Still, the settlers were so well satisfied that they adopted the eagle, snake, and cactus as their totem, and they remain to-day as the coat of arms of the republic.

Mexicans will tell you that this basin was the earliest home of man in the Western world; maybe in all the world. Here were settlements of the Ulmeca early in the Christian era, if not before its beginning; then, in A.D. 635, came the Chichimecs, who were routed by the Toltecs that came over the great hill of Tulla in 648 and built a city there; and the Aztecs arrived in the year 890. Here for six centuries it has been the capital, where the cacique, or native chief, the Spanish conqueror, the viceroy, the emperor, the dictator, and the president have ruled or served the people. The Aztecs were a soldier folk, hence the name they gave to it commemorates their war-god, Mexitli. On the site of the rocky island the invader, Cortez, fought the last battle with Quauhtemotzin, and for three centuries the victory was celebrated by processions. Here occurred the famine riot of 1692, when three million dollars' worth of property was wrecked and burned; here stood the gallows, and before the viceroy's palace was a frame on which criminals' heads were placed; here functionaries took the oath of office; but now

the band plays and people take the air on the spot
where the sign of their liberties was seen.

TOLD IN YUCATAN

LONG before the Spaniards knew that there
was a Western world to conquer, a people
occupied the tropic belt of the Americas who, at
the time that the palaces and temples of Central
America were erected, were the equals of those same
Spaniards in civilization. These people were archi-
tects and sculptors, they knew the use of metal, they
embalmed and entombed their dead, they had roads;
they had, moreover, a government, a religion, a
writing, and they built the great cities whose ruins,
even where overgrown by the dense forests of the
lowlands, are not less surprising than those of
Egypt and Assyria. One enthusiastic antiquary,
who spent some years among the long lost and
newly found cities of Yucatan, believes that he has
verified much ancient history as a possession of our
own. He says that the garden of Eden is in
Mexico, the tomb of Abel in Yucatan, with in-
scriptions on it recounting the tragedy,—carved
possibly by Cain,—and that from this birthplace
of the human race the Old World was peopled.
Egypt, he says, was colonized from Yucatan, the
Egyptian mummies were carried to Africa from
America, the Sphinx was a monument to Abel,
erected by his widow, and the Greek alphabet was

an account, in Yucatan hieroglyphics, of the sinking of the continent of Atlantis. The fierce Quiches, who have inherited from their ancestors of the sixteenth century a hatred of Europeans, or "white monkeys," are thought to keep alive the language of the ancient Mayas, which is as old as the Sanskrit, if not older, and is believed to be allied to that of the ancient Egyptians, the picture-writing of the two families showing many things in common.

Yucatan is a Mayax word, meaning "first land," and the country reached from Tehuantepec to Darien. The word *maya* occurs in many Asian, African, and European tongues, where it always expresses strength and wisdom, and in certain of the relics bearded men, like Assyrians, are represented as visiting Uxmal and Chichinitza, big cities that drew to them scholars from all over the country. The story of Cain and Abel occurs in Egyptian tradition and in the Sanskrit poem Rama-yana in such a form as to assimilate it to the Maya legend that the two sons of King Kan (or King Snake) fell out on a question of prestige, and Prince Aak (The Turtle) stabbed his brother Koh (The Leopard), who was embalmed, all but his heart, which was cremated and placed in an urn, together with the stone spear-head that did the murder. Some say that the statue of the slain prince is to be seen in the national museum of Mexico, where it is labelled Chakmool, the sun god. After this untoward event the assassin, a veritable Richard III. of his day, laid a vain siege to the heart of the dead man's widow, Moo (Macaw), his own sister, by the way, the Mayax royal families, like those of Egypt, being resolved to keep their blood free from plebeian stain; and a wall-painting shows Prince Aak with his serpent totem, tempting the woman with fruit from a tree in which perches a monkey, representing wisdom.   Queen Moo raised a statue to the departed, the figure of a leopard with three stab-wounds in the back; and on going to Egypt afterward, she had the workmen of that empire raise a statue to his memory, that took the shape of the Sphinx.   To this day certain Africans wear a leopard-skin as a charm against spear-thrusts.

Another of the traditions of the Mayas was that of a flood.   All races have this legend.   The Egyptian priests, who scoffed at the Greeks for believing that the entire human race had been drowned in Deucalion's deluge, told Solon, nevertheless, twenty-five hundred years ago, that the land of Mú, in the Atlantic Ocean, had sunk in a day and night, nine thousand years before his visit. A terrific volcanic outburst had destroyed the island.   Plato told of the same disaster.   Over the door of a room in the "house of the dark writing" in Chichinitza is another account of the lost Atlantis, which has been translated to this effect: In the year 6 Kan, 11 Muluc, the month

Zac, occurred terrible earthquakes that kept steadily on until the 13th Chuen. The country of mud-hills, Mú, was destroyed. Twice it was upheaved, then suddenly disappeared in the night. When the surface gave way ten countries were torn asunder and scattered. Unable to withstand the force of the convulsions, they sank, with their sixty-four million inhabitants, eight thousand and sixty years before the making of the record. The superstition attaching to the number 13 is ascribed to the occurrence of this appalling catastrophe on the 13th Chuen, or February. The blacks that the Spaniards found in America are held to be survivors from the people of this lost continent.

We have no living elephants, yet gods and demigods with elephant-heads were carved by Mayas and Aztecs. This proves no alien origin in the artists, for the elephant lived in America, doubtless within two thousand years. The worship of serpents is alleged to have originated in the popular love for the good king Kan, whose totem, or seal, or name-sign, or coat of arms, was a snake. The cross is likewise seen in the ornaments of buildings, the ground-plan of a temple in Uxmal is cruciform, and statues found in Palenque and other ancient cities of Guatemala bear the cross on their breasts. Its use is said to be related to the appearance of the constellation of the Southern Cross, which in the month of Maya, or May, stands above the horizon in Mayax, and the people welcome it because the long, dry season then breaks up in copious rain, bringing coolness and plenty to the earth.

We know that Kopan had bound books and phonetic writing long before the conquest, as well as splendid arts. That education was encouraged in ancient Mayax is hardly true, however, since learning was surrounded with difficulties and ceremonies, though the priests and teachers doubtless allowed the children to learn a few simple facts without scaring them into as many fits. The hazing to which candidates for admission to the temples were subjected was very dismal. Still, the account of it found in the sculptures and in the sacred book of the Quiches may be allegorical, since it appears to be characteristic of primitive peoples never to say a thing plainly if there is any way to cover it with parable and set people to quarrelling about it afterward. The ancient initiation was this: First, the unhappy wretch who wanted to learn the multiplication table and other portentous knowledge had to cross a river of mud and another of blood. There are no such rivers, except in-doors. However, when he got over he had to walk on four roads, white, red, green, and black, which took him to a hall where a number of veiled priests awaited him. He had first to pick out the priest who was made of wood, because one of the party was bogus, and he was then invited to be seated. The stone bench was burning hot, and when the victim pensively arose the company said it was a lesson to him not to be familiar in presence of his superiors. Then he had to spend a night in a guarded cell holding a lighted torch in his hand and a smaller one in his mouth. These he must not put out, yet they must go out, and he must give them back in the morning, under penalty of beating and death. The next act in this useful and entertaining performance was to defend himself against the attacks of an able-bodied spearman. Then he passed a night in an ice-house,—and where did they get the ice? —and danced for ten hours to keep from freezing and catching pneumonia. Another night in a den of wild animals prepared him for nearly anything that might follow, and if he still wanted to study the multiplication table he was put into a house where fires were burning all night. After this what was left of him was thrown into the house of bats, and these pleasant creatures got into his hair and nibbled his flesh and nearly put his eyes out with their wings, while Camazotz, the bat god, who, you may be sure, was one of the priests in disguise, capered about, trying to get a chance to cut off his head. If the scholar lived through all this he was congratulated, and spent the rest of his days pining for a chance to initiate others. Such performances had their use. It was the able that survived.

Beyond Our Borders

OUR LADY OF GUADALUPE

THE hill of Guadalupe is a place of pilgrimage for Christians to-day, as it was for nature-worshippers more than a thousand years ago, when it was called Tapeyacac. Here stood a temple of the goddess of corn, sometimes named the fruit-bearer, also mother of the gods. When the Spaniards came they told the people that in praying to this principle of life they were doing an evil thing. The invaders smashed the temple into ruin and tore up the road that led to it, but the natives kept climbing to the top to give their homage, as of old, to the creative forces that were symbolized in their statues. It was not deemed advisable to keep the Mexicans virtuous by killing, maiming, robbing, and enslaving them too constantly, lest they should become restive, yet the good priests were in distress that the natives refused to put the " Christian God mother in place of the heathen mother of the gods." But all came about as they would have it, without long resort to violence, for on the 9th of January—this was in 1531—a reformed native who bore the Christian name of Juan Diego heard angels singing on this hill as he passed it on his way to mass, and a shining lady appeared to him with an order to report to the bishop what he had seen and heard, and to tell him that she wished a church to be built, in her name, on the hill where she was standing.

In no wise disturbed by this vision, for he was an
Indian, Juan Diego repaired to the functionary and
delivered the divine command. The bishop was
sinfully suspicious, or obtuse, seeming to think that
if any such order were given it should have been
to him, personally, rather than to an ignorant
Aztec, and he refused to build. Juan went back to
the hill and told the shining lady that the bishop
was sceptical. She directed Juan to climb the hill
again next day, so he went back in the morning,
which was Sunday, and she sent him to the bishop
with the same order. His excellency sent the
Indian packing again, and told him to bring proof
that what he said was true. Juan trudged back to
the hill-top, and on relating this second failure was
ordered by the shining lady to return again next
day, when she would cure the bishop of his doubts.
Juan was kept so busy with these errands for two
days that his poor uncle at home became very weak
with hunger and neglect, and on reaching his cabin
the old man bade him hurry for a priest to shrive
him, for his end was near. Early in the morning
the Indian, now weary with much travel, set off
for town, and, fearing to have more errands put
upon him, he went around the mountain, his bare
feet patting softly over the earth, but again the
shining lady arose in his path and repeated her
command that the bishop should build a church
for her. Juan begged to be allowed to pass, for
his uncle was dying. The shining one bade him

not to think of the old man, for he had already recovered his health through a divine ordinance. The messenger must pick the flowers at his feet and carry them to the bishop in his blanket. Flowers? There were no flowers in that barren spot. Why, yes! For, look: the ground was gay with them. The Aztecs loved color and perfume, and to gather these pretty blossoms was a congenial task. Juan filled his blanket and hurried to the bishop, hoping that he would be convinced at last. And he was; for it was found that the juice of the crushed flowers had painted on the blanket, which he immediately took from its owner, a beautiful portrait of the shining lady,—none other than the Holy Virgin.

This portrait was seen to be authentic, for it was the same as one in the village of Guadalupe, in Spain, and forthwith the hill of Tepeyacac became the hill of Guadalupe, and the bishop made all haste to amend for his unseemly doubts by beginning work on the church, long since replaced by one of the finest cathedrals in the Western world. The bishop and Juan together had little difficulty in proving to the Indians that the spot was henceforth sacred to the Virgin, and that heathen worship could be tolerated there no longer. The hill is now a place of yearly pilgrimage, by sanction of the pope, who set aside the 12th of December for that purpose, and confirmed the choice of the people in making Our Lady of Guadalupe protector of New Spain. She has ever been a kind patron; she has led them in their wars for liberty; from 1629 to 1634, when the city of Mexico was a Venice, Our Lady of Guadalupe lived there, in order to make the water go down.

On the hill are a stone mast and chapel that were set up by sailors whom she delivered from ship-wreck. The mast with its sail they carried on their shoulders all the way from Vera Cruz, and after planting it here they encased it in stone that it might endure forever. Near by is the spring that broke out when she angrily stamped her foot on learning of the bishop's obstinacy. The mud about this holy well is eaten by the devout for its moral and healing properties. Juan Diego, in effigy, upholds the pulpit in the chapel of the well, and his blanket, with its radiant picture, is framed in gold and silver in the great church, " the holiest shrine in Mexico."

OUR LADY OF THE REMEDIES

AS Our Lady of Guadalupe hears the prayers of those who suffer from too much rain, so Our Lady of the Remedies heeds the request of those who lack it, and sometimes the agricultural interests of the valley lead the farmers into a conflict of petitions. A dozen miles from the capital rises the hill of Totoltepec, crowned in former centuries by a temple. In the shelter of

that work, which his own men had injured, Cortez
and his army rested during the retreat of the Noche
Triste.   As a protection against the native hordes,
one of his soldiers carried an image of the Virgin
that had been brought from Spain.   It had been
set up in a public place, with Montezuma's per-
mission, but Cortez feared that the angered people
would destroy it, as he had destroyed the statues of
their gods.   Wounded and tired, the soldier for-
sook his trust and hid the figure near the temple.
In 1635 a reformed Aztec found it in a clump of
maguey, and, delighted with his discovery, was for
taking it home with him, when the image began to
work miracles to show its intention to remain on
the hill.   The priests decided that a chapel must
be built for it, and this was erected, the Virgin re-
warding her worshippers by continuing her miracles
and benefits, especially that of giving copious rains
after the dry season.   So greatly was she esteemed
that during the civil war in the early part of the
nineteenth century the royalists took the statue to
the city with them when Hidalgo drove them in,
and made it a general in their army, as Our Lady
of Guadalupe had become a leader on the other
side.   But her efforts were without avail, and when
the republicans triumphed, the people were so in-
dignant at her faithlessness in accepting a commission from their enemies that they stripped away
her jewels, valued at a million dollars, broke her
nose off, cut out one eye, and formally decreed

her banishment from the country. The latter sentence was never carried out, for she was too strongly placed in the affections of some of the people to make her removal possible, so that she is now back on the hill where Cortez's soldier left her, and there she rewards the faithful and deserving according to their prayers and needs.

SOME OTHER MIRACLES

IN Jesus of Nazareth Church, Mexico City, stands an image of great age, known as Our Lady of the Ball. It was at one time the property of a poor man in Ixtapalapan, who made a shrine for it and worshipped it constantly. It would have been better for all concerned if his religion had been more in his life and less on his lips, for on the mere suspicion that his wife had been flirting with some dusky neighbors he charged her with infidelity, refused to listen to denials and explanations, and loaded his old horse-pistol, intending to shoot her as she knelt at the foot of the Virgin. The woman begged the protection of the statue so earnestly that, just as the husband fired, the statue threw out its hand and turned the course of the bullet so that it entered the clay wall of the cabin. This intervention convinced the man that his wife was innocent, and the couple worshipped the statue so incessantly afterward that it was hardly possible to get them to work, until the priests carried it away to the capital, where they were sure that it would do good to more than two people.

In the chapel of the convent of Our Lady of the Conception, Mexico City, the Sisters were puzzled by what sounded like the ticking of a clock, although there was no clock in or near the building whose pendulum was set to so slow a swing. The chapel was inspected frequently without result, until a nun more adventurous than the rest discovered that the noise was made by drops of water falling behind the organ. The miraculous part of this occurrence is that it came from a dry ceiling, and there was no water above it. The Virgin at length revealed to one of the Sisters in a dream that so long as the water ticked off the hours the building was safe, but that when it ceased to fall the building must fall instead. And it did. It fell into the hands of prosaic reformers and real estate dealers, who partitioned it into dwellings.

From this it appears that the power of the spiritual authorities over water had declined since the time of that priest in Tacubaya who on a hot day rested beneath a tree and blessed it for shading him. The result of his blessing is seen in the constant greenness of the *arbol benito* and the continued flow of a spring that gushed into being under its root at that moment.

In 1580 an Aztec chief saw a picture of the Virgin floating about in the flood in Mexico City and rescued it. As soon as the inundation had subsided he made a chapel of adobe on the spot where it had been found, and placed the picture in it. Though the lazy people did not keep the building in repair, allowing its roof to fall and its sides to breach and crack, the Virgin always protected her picture from the rain and dirt, and at last the mysterious canvas was housed in the church of Our Lady of the Angels, which was built for it. The figure of the Virgin is now hidden behind a dress that a pious tailor made for her in 1776.

THE PICTURE AND THE STORM

THE church of Our Lady of Piety, in Mexico City, was founded by the Dominicans in 1652. Shortly before that time a member of the order went abroad on some business to the Holy City, and was directed, while there, to order a picture of the Virgin and the dead Christ from the most famous painter in Rome. This commission he fulfilled, but the artist, being of a postponing disposition, made such slow progress that when it was time for the monk to start back to America the work had been merely sketched, and not a brushful of color had been applied to it. In those times a journey of such distance was not undertaken every day, and as it might never fall to the Dominican to visit Rome again, he concluded to carry the picture with him, slight though it was. He paid the artist a small sum, jogged on muleback and trundled in carriages to Spain, and there took a vessel for Mexico, the canvas, closely rolled, forming a part of his luggage.

Not many days from port a furious storm set in, and it seemed doubtful if the ship could weather it. Sails were torn, cord·ge broken, bulwarks staved, and all on board were in terror, until, at the monk's suggestion, they vowed to build a church to the Virgin in Mexico if she would permit them to reach that land in safety. She allowed the storm to rage a little longer, the better to impress them with their peril, then the clouds were scattered, the waves stilled, the winds abated, and the ship rode serenely into harbor. The sailors were as good as their word. They spent their time ashore in collecting money, and with it the Dominicans laid the foundations of this church. After the altar had been completed the monk bethought him of the drawing he had brought from Rome. He unrolled it, and, to the astonishment and admiration of all, it was finished in color, to the last brush-stroke. It hangs above the altar, and is greatly venerated.

THE MISCHIEVOUS COCKTAIL

NEW World drinks are a grateful astonishment to visiting foreigners, and a matter of joyful pride among the natives, for the performances of our bar-tenders have been studied by French, Germans, and English without avail, the strong or sodden fluids sold over the so-called "American bars" in Europe being a reflection on American art. Among these various beverages none is more popular than the cocktail: a gulp of liquor in a cold glass, with a dash of bitters and syrup, a drop of lemon, and a garnish of fruit; and it is said to be quite pleasant. In their names our various inventions are stimulative of curiosity, though stone fence, Tom Collins, high ball, whiskey rickey, gin sling, silver fizz, whiskey skin, whiskey daisy, cobbler, smash, and royal punch are more apt to excite apprehension than thirst among the uninitiated. Cocktail, especially, is a term that has not received the amount of study that was its due among philologists and historians, though lame attempts are made to account for it on the score that physicians used to anoint the sore throats and swollen tonsils of their patients with a cock's feather that had been dipped into healing lotions, —an operation that explains the Colorado terms "throat paint" and "tonsil varnish" as applied to whiskey, but that brings us no nearer to the origin of cocktail, it being a mere and obvious guess that gargles succeeded the feather applications, that doses succeeded the gargles, and that drinks succeeded the doses. Another ineffective tradition is that in the sixties sprigs of mint, used in the preparation of mint-juleps, were called cocktails, because they had not the slightest resemblance to any kind of tails, and are not used in cocktails anyhow.

No: the true tale of the cocktail antedates Columbus. It has to do with the Toltecs in the eleventh century. In Mexico the common drink is pulque, a poor beer made from the sap of the maguey plant. The exhilarating possibilities of this juice were discovered by a native of Tula, who was either a nobleman at the time or was ennobled for his service to the race. Finding pulque to be a good thing, from the Mexican point of taste, he sent his daughter, The Flower of Tula, to the emperor with samples. His majesty having consumed a couple of quarts of the beverage was vastly comforted, and, being in a mood to do good, he offered to let the nobleman's daughter be one of his wives. His offer having been suddenly accepted, for royal offers of this kind are never refused, he declared that the drink was fine enough to perpetuate in its name the beauties and graces of the demoiselle who had been his Hebe, and he called it, after her, Xochitl. Moreover, he started an inebriate asylum of his own, and kept his imperial skin well filled with the mysterious juice, thus offering an example to other kings, who are frequently in debt for their cheer.

The head wife of the king, who regarded this new-comer in the harem with sharp disfavor, was reminded that she had never invented a drink, and that silence was becoming to women. In time the inheritor of the kingdom was to be declared, and the choice fell, not on the son of the older wife,

but on that of Xochitl. The family disturbance
that began then led to faction fighting and the final
disruption and downfall of the Toltec dynasty,
though the Aztecs continued the brewing industry,
and they keep on making pulque and the worse
mescal in Tula to this day. People in Mexico
and on the edge thereof worried along with the
name of Xochitl for the insidious destroyer for
years and years, for they had not gumption enough
even to use an easy word, unless somebody showed
them how. Somebody did. It was the United
States army. It went to Mexico, conquered it,
found it warm work, acquired a thirst, was served
with xochitl, couldn't say it, though it could drink
it, called it cocktail, and there you are.

THE COUNCILLORS OF LAGOS

SOME of the things that they tell about the
Dutch aldermen in New Amsterdam, in the
days of Peter the wooden-legged and iron-headed,
are strangely like some other things that have happened in this strange land of the sun. Lagos, a
thriving city of twenty thousand people, was for a
long time the butt of light wits from other towns,
and its councillors seem to have been chosen
with especial reference to unfitness for their places,
wherein they differ from all other statesmen. They
have a bridge in that city which for some time was
allowed to bear this inscription :

Beyond Our Borders

This bridge was built in Lagos.
To walk under, and not over.

Needless to add that some joker had painted on the last half of the sentence. There were twelve of the famous law-givers in Lagos, and they were accustomed on assembling in their hall to occupy a long wooden bench. One day six of them arrived in advance of the others and sat down, each with his hat beside him,—the big sombrero that takes as much seat-space as a man. Presently came the other six, who looked at the bench in astonishment.

"Santa Maria!" exclaimed one of them. "The dry season is here, and it shrinks the bench."

"True," said another; "but perhaps if we all pull hard we can stretch it out as long as it used to be."

Up arose the six, put on their hats like the rest, and all pulled. Then the twelve sat down with their hats on, and, lo! there was room for all.

At another time the people were much troubled by a hole that had been left on the plaza in consequence of some public work. Our wise men ordered it to be filled. The dirt to fill it was dug about fifty feet away, and that left another hole. Children were continually tumbling into it, nearsighted and elderly citizens had narrow escapes every day, graceless beings who had looked upon the fire-water when it was inflammable fell into it head first and went to sleep. This second hole was worse than the first, because the people had not grown used to it. So the councillors held another meeting and resolved to fill this second pit. The contractor took the earth from a place some yards away, and this left a third hole. In time this, too, was filled, and the holes thus proceeded in a slow and orderly fashion until they had been chased to the edge of the town, where the last one was left for time and the dumpings from neighboring residences to abate its dangers. Lagos may have been the original place where it was decided to build a new jail in this fashion: " Resolved, that we build a new jail. Resolved, that we build it out of the materials of the old one. Resolved, that we use the old one until the new one is built."

The next time that the minds of the councillors were disturbed was when it was found that grass was growing on the roof of one of its public buildings. How could it be shorn? Various costly expedients were suggested, but the most wakeful intellect in the company conceived this remedy, and his plan was adopted: a road was built from the street to the top of the house, a cow was driven up this road to the roof, the cow ate the grass, was driven down again, the road was carted away, and the council slumbered.

THE HUMPBACK OF COLIMA

IN Colima, which stands in the shadow of peaks that spire to a height of sixteen thousand feet above the sea, lived a wood-chopper, hump-backed, poor, but merry and kind, beloved by all the children, ready to share their games and make toys for them. Juan worked hard, lived hard, but sang all day long. For neighbor he and his wife had Emilio Romero, who had also been a peon, but was now rich, and people said he had gained his money in a devious fashion, if he had not actually robbed men in the highway. With money Romero took on a "nasty" pride that made him snub his old companion; yet he put on none of the decencies of life to support his state, for he would get drunk, beat his wife, and was an uncomfortable citizen. It was while chopping a· tree in the wood one afternoon that Juan suffered what he thought was a misfortune, so soon as he was in any state to think, for he was stunned by a falling limb, and did not regain his senses until the rise of the moon. Propping himself on his elbow, he rubbed his noddle and looked curiously about him, for he had heard voices, and presently he could see in the dusk a crowd of elves dancing about the glade. They were singing the Spanish words for "Monday, Tuesday, Wednesday—three," over and over again.

"Why don't you sing the rest?" asked Juan.

"We don't know it," piped the little creatures.

253

"It's like this: Thursday, Friday, Saturday—six."

The elves leaped and tumbled about in delight at being able to learn the rest of the song, and they chorused it with zest. After a little one of them said, "We ought to pay Juan for his goodness. Let's take off his hump."

How they did it he never knew, and the neighbors said it was the falling tree that did it, anyway; but Juan arose from the earth a straight, sound man. Ah, but he went home with a hump on his back none the less,—a hump nearly as big as the old one, only it was made of gold, and carried in a bag. With many good-byes and kind wishes the elves took leave of Juan, and in the moonlight he tramped away to his home, where he astonished his wife by showing the quantity of treasure that the fairies had given to him. Juan immediately bought a house and set up a shop with his money, and this led Romero to wonder whom he could have robbed, to grow so suddenly wealthy; for it never occurred to him that honesty could have its rewards no less than industry. By persistent questioning of Juan's wife the envious fellow learned the story, and at first he disbelieved it. "Dwarfs!" quoth he. "There are no such creatures in Mexico. Yet, I do remember it was a savage dwarf that built the Soothsayer's House, in Uxmal, in a night. Perhaps it is so, and if I see them, I, too, shall win my share of elfin gold."

It irked him to think that his once poor neighbor was richer now than he. So he went to the wood and pretended to sleep, and presently the little people came out, sure enough, and danced about, singing, as before,—

Lunes, Martes, Miércoles—tres;
Jueves, Viernes, Sabado—seis.

" Why don't you end it ?" asked Romero, suddenly sitting up.

" How ?" they cried.

" Domingo—siete." (Sunday—seven.)

They tried it, then shrieked, " Why, it doesn't rhyme. It spoils it all." And they fell upon the intruder, pulled his hair and cuffed him soundly. Then they recognized him as a proud, mean man and a robber, and they put Juan's old hump on his back, which he wore ever after. That is why people who interrupt, or make needless and foolish remarks in company, are quieted by saying, " Domingo—siete."

WHY CHOLULA PYRAMID WAS BUILT

IN the land of Anahuac and elsewhere were many giants. The Tlascalans who showed their bones—real bones, taller than a man—could not be persuaded that such things might have belonged to lizards and elephants, for there are no such animals about here now. The Tlascalan people were so annoyed by the misbehavior of the giants, many centuries ago, that they were forced to kill them or drive them into the wilderness, to perish of starvation. Nevertheless, so many were left that the lives of the people were in constant peril, and around Cholula the monsters became so wicked that the gods decided to destroy them, even though they incidentally had to drown or change the innocent also, and they poured a mighty deluge upon the earth. All the people were overcome by the sea and turned into fishes, except seven, who succeeded in gaining a cave, where they stayed until the waters were withdrawn, either into the sky or under the earth, when they came forth and peopled the world again. It appears that these folk learned little from having been drowned, for they acquired new sins, and, in order to get the better of the gods in the event of another deluge, they decided to rear a pyramid whose top should reach the heavens. They might have climbed any of the great volcanoes, but perhaps those peaks were in eruption; and they began to build on Cholula plain. Bricks were shaped and sun-dried at a distance from this spot, were passed along from hand to hand by a file of men extending for miles across the country, and after being put in place were plastered with bitumen or some other sticky substance. The work was not to proceed far, because this monument of presumption angered the gods anew, and according to one report they bent down from the heavens and blew off its top, their breath striking the earth as a tornado, while another account says that they hurled down fire.   Reasons for this latter version are strengthened by the fact that a great meteorite was preserved in the sun-god's temple on the summit of the pyramid, where it probably fell, and was greatly venerated.   This meteor, the priests said, was the thunderbolt of the gods.   On the destruction of the mound, which some say was merely defensive in its purpose, the people were further punished by being unable to understand one another.   Aztec historians said that Cholula pyramid was built, not by giants or wicked people, but by the fair god, or prophet, Quetzalcoatl; for he lived there, taking refuge from his enemies (Cholula means "place of the fugitive"), and teaching useful arts and forms of worship to the inhabitants.   A relic of his father, a quantity of blond human hair, was shown to the Spaniards when they came, but the god himself had long been gone to happier climes.

THE ARK ON COLHUACAN

OUR Aboriginal deluge legends resemble the Bible narrative of the flood more closely than do those of any other people.   The fertile-minded Ignatius Donnelly says that it is because they came direct from the continent of Atlantis, the sinking whereof in earthquake throes gave rise to the story of a destruction of all the earth's people, save a handful of the wiser. In the cosmogony of the Mexicans the world has passed through four ages: an age of giants, who were killed by famine; a succeeding age that ended in an enormous fire; an age of monkeys; and the age of "the sun of water," that ends in a deluge. The man, Coxcox, and the woman, Xochiquetzal, who survived floated about in a boat or raft hewn from a cypress trunk. This tale is variously told in different parts of the country, the Mechoacaneses relating that the man, with his wife and children, made a big vessel, drove animals into it, and also laid in a stock of grain, with which to replenish the earth when the seas should subside. After floating for one hundred and four years on the shoreless ocean, Coxcox freed a vulture. It never went back. Possibly it fell into the sea; mayhap it found some lonely peak rising from the flood and stayed there to feed on the drowned creatures. Then some other birds were set at liberty, and at last the humming-bird, the only one of them all to return, appeared to Coxcox with green leaves in its beak. The subsidence had begun. Presently the ark found shore at Antlan, wherever that may be, but it kept on to Chapultepec, and finally settled upon Mount Colhuacan, to which they gave the name of Antlan, after the first landing-place. Looking forth, the weary ones could see that the hills grew green as fast as the waters dropped away. They left their boat where it had found land, and went down into the comfortable valleys.

MAKING THE SUN

THERE was a time of darkness on the young earth, when the air was thick and damp and winds blew keen, when deep waters covered the valleys and strange creatures wallowed in the ocean slime, when faint forms of light appeared in the sky, though men could see little by them, when men were hungry, chilled, and sad. Wearying of this state, the earth gods built a temple on a tall place and called on the higher gods for light, begging also that the waters might be drawn off a little, so as to leave more foot-room. They prayed long, they offered sacrifices, they expressed humility, and sought commiseration by cutting themselves with stone knives. In time the waters drew away and there was light. Then came a hurricane that swept off trees, mounds, houses, and those people who had not hidden from its violence in caves, and the darkness brooded once more. No lamp had shone in heaven for many years, and the gods gathered at last at Teotihuacan, less than twenty miles from Mexico, and made a great fire, while they debated what should be done to make the land more happy. At last they told the people who had fallen prostrate about them that if any one would cast himself into the fire he should receive worship and honor, and win a place in the sky, as a sun.

One of the men, Nanahuatzin, advanced with reverences, and begged that he might be light-bearer for the world. His request was granted. With a cry of farewell to his people he plunged into the blazing mass. The flames eddied about him, vast showers of sparks went up, and the heavens were overcast more blackly than before. Now the people turned their backs to the fire and began to peer this way and that, curiously, eagerly, for in the long time of darkness they had forgotten where the east and the west lay, and even what the sun was like. At last came a bright star, heralding the dawn, and then all voices cried, "There!" It was in the east. Then the people implored the god whose sign is the snake to make an end of the fogs and coldness, and change Nanahuatzin, according to the promise. Soon a green light appeared, edging the horizon against the sky; it heightened and cleared, and in a joy the people danced, with faces toward the east, holding high their pans of smoking incense, and presently they dropped forward, for the sun was up. At first he gave little heat, for the mist hung about him, the earth dried slowly, and the people sang a hymn lamenting all who had died in the dark. "We, indeed, have seen the sun, but now that his light appears, what has become of them?" At each rising the sun grew warmer, the ice left the ponds, the plains dried and became green, birds sang and animals gambolled in delight; and, always keeping their faces toward the sun, the people forgot their other gods. When, at length, they turned to Teotihuacan, lo! those other gods were figures of stone. The sun had petrified the beings from whom he had gained his power, and, forgetting their dead divinities, the people gave all their worship to the new one, the source of life.

THE POPUL VUH

THE Popul Vuh, the book of the Quiches, of Guatemala, was translated into Spanish in 1721 by Francisco Ximinez, a Dominican priest in a small Indian town in that state. Most of his manuscripts were destroyed, on account of the revelations he had made of the sly and brutal measures to which the Spaniards resorted in their hope of gain and conquest, and this work was hidden in a convent for over a century. The book says that the heaven was made by him who was creator, father, mother, and cherisher, the wise and excellent one. Nothing was, but the sky and sea: utterly still. And the lesser gods brooded. All through immensity nothing moved nor made a sound. When the silence was broken the creator spoke to the sea, crying, "Earth!" and instantly it arose through the waters, the mountains leaping like fish, with torrents streaming down their sides, and trees appeared. The lesser gods were filled with wonder and delight, crying, "Blessed, O Heart of Heaven, Hurakan, Thunderbolt!" In the sign Tochtli was the earth created ; in Acatl, the lights ; in Tecpatl, the beasts. On the seventh day man was built out of dust and made alive. But first the animals were told to hail the gods, worship them, and speak their names adoringly. The creatures tried, but could only grunt and chirp and croak, and the gods said, "As you cannot praise us, you shall be broken with teeth, and eaten." The first man, of clay, could speak, but could not turn his head, and had no mind, so he was thrown into the sea, a failure. Next a man and a woman were made of soft wood, and they peopled the world with little wooden men, but they had no blood, they dried in the sun, and they did not know how to pacify their makers' greed for praise, so the heavens rained gum on them, their houses fell, the trees shook them out of their branches, the caves shut themselves against them, and, being unsheltered, they went mad. Beasts and birds were sent to tear their flesh, pull out their eyes, and crush their bones, and the few that escaped became apes, the parents of the monkey tribe.

Again the gods made men, this time of maize, and this time perfect. Large, bold, strong, four fathers of the race to be, they stood ˅under the single light of the morning star and with one voice began to repeat thanks to the gods. After their hunger for worship had waned, the gods once more fell into doubt. The men were too perfect, too nearly like themselves; they saw too far; their attention must be taken in some other way than by the gods. So four women were made while the men slept, and when they awoke they were delighted, and looked, not on the gods, but on their wives. They travelled to the west, and soon the earth was peopled, men living peacefully in the twilight, still wondering at times why they had been made, but resuming again their praise for being placed on earth, and hoping for a sun. Certain gods came down to Tulanzuiva, or the Seven Caves, and lived among them, that they might be applauded more constantly, and also to supply them with fire, for it was raw and dark, and there was much rain. The rain put out the flames, but Tohil, the fire-god, roused them again by stamping with his sandal. In this land of Tulan the speech of the four fathers was changed, so that they could no longer understand one another, and under Tohil they set off to look for another home. They suffered much, and at one time had nothing nearer to food than the smell of raw wood. Mountains they crossed, and seas, though the waters parted to make a dry road for them.

Finally they reached Mount Hakavitz, named thus for one of their gods, and at last the sun arose that they had so long awaited. The men fell upon their faces and sent up cries of thankfulness, while

the beasts gambolled in delight. The old gods
were turned to stone, yet still the men knelt and
praised them, and cut themselves and held the blood
to them in cups, and offered freshly slain animals.
A city was founded, and the people of it spent a
part of their time every day in telling the gods how
great they were. Incessant praise being not enough,
their gods now demanded human victims, and these
the priests began to steal from outlying villages,
purposely covering and confusing the trails by which
they regained the mountain, and trying to spread
the belief that wild animals had destroyed the missing men. Finally the villagers arose against the
Quiches, but none can defeat the gods, and in the
end the rebels submitted and became a tributary
people. Then came the summons to the four
fathers to quit the earth, for their work was done.
Calling their wives and children to them, they said
farewell, cautioning them to praise their memories,
and instantly they vanished. In the place where
they had been was a great bundle without a seam.
This was called The Enveloped Majesty, and the
people long burned incense before it.

FATHERS OF THE MIZTECS

FAR back, in the time before light, when the
earth was covered with water and slime, a god
and a goddess appeared. They knew their power,
and they practised it in building a palace for them-

selves that should be worthy of the occupancy of gods. It was vast in size, splendid in appointments, a true Walhalla, and on its roof was a copper axe, edge upmost, on which the heavens rested. The rock on which this palace stood was near Apoala, in Mizteca Alta, and was called The Place of Heaven. Two sons were born to these deities, the elder amusing himself as an eagle by long flights through the air, and the other turning himself into a winged snake, in which form he could pass through rocks. Such were the roaring and clashing in their wild rushes that the mountains rang with echoes. These sons made a temple in a flowering and fruiting meadow, where they burned incense in clay vessels and made sacrifices to their father and mother, praising them greatly and begging for a better light. Their garden was the only dry place, except the Place of Heaven, and they prayed that the waters might be drawn off so as to leave other spots to stand on. In order to please the parents more, the sons lacerated themselves, cutting their ears and tongues with stones and throwing the blood over the garden, with willow twigs. Thus they gained light and other favors. Afterward came the human race, and being wicked it was drowned from off the face of the earth, all save the ruling family, for this did not owe its origin to the gods, but to two great trees that stood at the gate of Apoala gorge, bending in a constant gale. Each of these trees begat a boy, and the braver of the two, finding the sun mischievous in its glare and heat, shot at it with arrows until he had much wounded it and forced it to hide behind the mountains. To our own day the Miztec coat of arms remains,—a chief with bow, arrows, and shield, with the sun setting behind clouds in the distance.

THE WILLING CAPTIVE

CORTEZ hurried his departure for Mexico not merely because he was greedy for gain and power and feared the intervention of a jealous Cuban governor, but because it had been rumored that four Spaniards who had been wrecked on the mainland a few years before were held in slavery by the natives and compelled to suffer at the hands of their dusky masters. As soon as the conquerors had secured an interpreter and had gained the confidence of the districts they intended to pillage, inquiries were set afoot respecting the white castaways, and rewards of trinkets and friendship were offered for their safe conduct to Vera Cruz. Their captors, a tribe living southward from this port, wanted the trinkets, and presently appeared, bringing with them the four adventurers, who were well and hearty, in no wise the worse for their experience. Cortez distributed a few beads and bits of metal to the natives, and cordially welcomed his countrymen, promising ample gains to them if they would follow him, and hinting at punishment of the people with whom they had been living; but this latter offer was refused by the " slaves," who declared that the Indians had done no injury to them. When the time came for the return of the native company to their villages, one of the four men, who had been growing thoughtful and reserved, arose and prepared to go back with them. " How's this?" asked Cortez. " Have you left something with these people, Alvarez ?"

" Yes," answered the man. " My heart."

A shout of incredulous laughter went up from the troop at this.

" I beg you, captain and gentlemen, forgive me if I have something lost the fashion of nice speech in my five or six years with the natives, but let me tell you that you misprise some of the noblest attributes in human nature when you set down these men as savages. As you may know, sir captain, I was a bit of a scholar in Spain, and I came here full of contempt for these untaught sons of nature. But I soon had to own, with humility, that all knowledge is not in books, that all courage is not the soldier's courage, best of all, that happiness and content are not in the far future. I have shaped my way of life to that of this race, my people henceforth; not masters, but brothers. Warlike and passionate they are when dealing with enemies, but peaceful and loving at home. How is it with you? They live up to their laws at all times. How is it with you? They are free from all greed of possession and pride of place. How is it with you? You say they are heathen. Behind the symbols of their faith they see the same truths you affect to worship, and they do not make converts with cannon, sword, and rack. They use signs and images? Yes, but what do I see in the hands and on the girdles of your priests? You ask me to follow you, to share in the gold you intend to get, I can guess how. What will gold do for me? It will make toys for my children: nothing more. For I have taken a wife from among this people, and with them I cast my lot. You will risk life, health, some of you will risk honor, for the treasure of the Aztecs. I will keep life, health, and honor, for my treasure is won. Adieu." And, with a bow to Cortez, Alvarez beckoned to his Indians and strode away into the forest.

THE DEATH-DANCE OF TEZCATLI-POCA

TEZCATLIPOCA, the Mephistopheles and Hercules of Mexican mythology, wanted to gain power over the Toltecs, or, if he failed in that, to destroy them, and to this end he sought an alliance with the daughter of Vemac, their king. He put on his best appearance, and not much else, for though he could change his form he chose to enter Tula as a naked boor from the hills, peddling green peppers. Looking over the market-place, the girl saw the fellow, and in spite of his low trade and apparent poverty her heart went out to him, for he was tall and strong and handsome. King Vemac noticed presently that the girl had grown sickly and silent, and he asked her maids what ailed her. They were obliged to tell him that she suffered for love of a peddler who called himself Toveyo, and was like to die if he refused her love. At that the king sent a crier to the echoing mount of Tzatzitepec, calling on Toveyo to show himself at the palace. Days passed, and the people sought eagerly in every part of the province, for the life of the princess was in peril, so sick was she for love. They had no success, and great was the surprise of all when the man appeared in the market-place with a fresh lot of peppers for sale. The king sought him at once. "Where do you belong?" he asked.

"I am a foreigner," quoth the peddler.

"Why do you come here without a blanket, and with not even breeches to cover you?"

"Such things are not the custom in my land."

"Then come with me and you shall be clothed, for my daughter perishes of love for you, and you must cure her."

"I am not worthy to meet the daughter of a king, nor even to hear your words. Let me rather die, for I am humble and poor."

But he was bidden to have no fear; and so they took the scamp to the palace, and after he had bathed, had his hair cut, and dyed his body handsomely, he was richly dressed and led into the presence of the princess, who could not conceal her joy, as women commonly think it meet to do in the like event, but was quickly won and wedded; and seeing how good a figure was made by this new son-in-law, the king was half inclined toward him, even though he had been a peddler. But the people grumbled, "Was there not among us all a Toltec who could have wedded this princess? Could the king find no husband for her but an alien and a huckster who had not even riches enough to go in rags?"

These things came to the ears of the king and made him fear an estrangement from his people; nor was he truly proud of this Toveyo, who had sold peppers under his windows. The Toltecs about this time were having one of their usual wars with Cacatepec and Coatepec, and the king secretly urged his generals to take Toveyo to the front with them and lose him. A brigade of dwarfs and cripples was organized for Toveyo, and on arriving on the field he was placed in an advanced post of danger, with instructions to hold it while the trained troops led the attack in another quarter. After a feint at a charge the Toltecs pretended to be driven back in panic, leaving Toveyo and his invalids to get away as they might, for nobody waited to see whether they were saved or slaughtered. Arrived once more in Tula, the generals told the king how they had betrayed his son-in-law to presumptive death, and all except the princess rejoiced greatly. Presently a cripple came hobbling from the front with news. Toveyo had beaten the men of Cacatepec and Coatepec, and would be back before dark. A good face must be put upon the matter. The troops who had run away must honor the troops who stayed, and this they did with better will than they had felt in going to war, for the fellow had courage, though he was a vender. So the peddler of green peppers and his army of knock-knees and hunchbacks marched into Tula to the music of flute bands, the dancing of maidens, and a brave show of arms, shields, and feather dresses. Every man of the victorious troop was painted yellow, with his face red, and plumes in his hair, for these were the signs of success, and the king said to Toveyo, " Son-in-law, the Toltecs greet you, for you have proved brave in the fight and quick in leadership. You are worthy to be of us. Therefore enter the palace and be at ease." Toveyo saluted and kept silence, but he laughed in his heart.

Soon after he sent a crier to Mount Tzatzitepec to call all the people to Tula, to a great dance and feast, and they came, a countless throng. Standing among them on the plain of Texcalapa, he led the dance, marking the time on a drum. Unknown to the others, this was a magic drum, and so long as he played all must dance. Hour after hour its thump sounded above the song, but faster and faster. The sweat poured from the leaping company, their breath grew thick and short, yet they could not stop. Toveyo artfully moved toward the ravine of the Texcaltlauco, and the multitude followed, blind, bewitched. He broke the stone bridge as he crossed it, and, jumping to the opposite bank, beat his drum still more quickly and fiercely. On came the mob, singing, still stepping in time to the drum, and he roared in delight as they went over the edge into the cañon and became stones on the ledges below.

OTHER WILES OF THE EVIL GOD

TEZCATLIPOCA was not satisfied with the mischief he had wrought at Texcalapa. He knew the reverence of the people for his enemy, the white god, and summoned them all to work in the flower-garden which belonged to that kind deity, using the disguise of one of their respected soldiers when he called them together. While the people were bent at their work he passed down the line knocking them on the head with a stout wooden hoe, and in this he exhibited such a fury that all ran away who could, and many were trodden and killed in the panic. He lighted the peak of Zacatepec, and the Toltecs nearly died in their terror. He threw stones upon them in showers, and the sight of one great meteor was so appalling that many of them went mad and ran to the blistering hot stone, after it had fallen, as to an altar, and were there killed. He turned all provisions sour, so they could not eat them; then, disguised as an old woman, he roasted maize and threw the scent of it to every quarter, until the people became delirious with appetite and ran to the house in the white god's garden, whence the odor came, to beg or buy the food. As each one reached the door Tezcatlipoca struck him dead. At another time this god sat in the market-place of Tula with a dancing manikin in his hand, and the gaping multitude so pressed about him to see miracles that many had their breath squeezed out, while others fell and were crushed. Then Tezcatlipoca cried, in derision, "You fools! Don't you see that you are deceived? You kill each other instead of killing us!" This angered the company. They gathered stones out of the street and killed the sorcerer and his manikin. The corpse lay so long in the public place that the air was tainted by it and the people were sickened, yet none could move it. The corpse itself demanded to be cast out of the town, and the crier summoned all the people to bear a hand. A long rope was tied to the neck of the carcass, and the men bent back with a will. Snap went the rope, and down went the men, who, striking on their heads on the

stones, became as soundly dead as Tezcatlipoca was
not. Again they hauled, again the rope broke,
and again several were killed. Then said the
corpse, " You need a song. Sing after me." And
he intoned a verse, which the Toltecs sang in
unison, pulling together at certain words, just as
sailors do at the heaviest part of a lift; and so the
body was taken out, though not till more lives had
been lost in the moving. When the survivors
returned to their homes they could remember
nothing of all this, for it was as if they had been
drunk.

THE AZTEC TANNHÄUSER

THE Venus of Mexico was Tlazoleotl, a goddess of lustrous beauty, who lived in the
ninth heaven in a garden of many delights, attended
by little, misshapen people and clowns who danced
and sang for her and ran with messages. Nowhere else were such sparkling waters, nowhere
else such glorious flowers, nowhere else such luring
eyes as hers. She was bold in her amours and
made others love on whom she cast her spell, for
if one but touched a blossom in her garden of
Xochiquetzal he would love constantly. Weaving
and spinning a gorgeous fabric, she looked earth-
ward, and on the lonely pillar of rock called
Tehuehuetl she saw a naked, wasted man. This
devotee, Yappan, had separated himself from the

world, the flesh, and the eighty-seven devils, and retired to this lonely pinnacle to pray and purify himself. The gods set his enemy, Yaotl, to spy upon him, to see that he kept his place and his intention, and, indeed, he would not look on the women whom the gods sent down from time to time to tempt him. He began to rise in the estimation of the watchers in the sky, and they debated as to how soon he might be translated and become as one of them. But Tlazoleotl, angry that love and beauty should be spurned, though in the desert, cried to the other gods, "Do not suppose that your hero can resist my charm. He cannot come to heaven yet. His vow is worthless." She descended to the rock, unveiled her shining form, and said, "Brother, I am Tlazoleotl. I come to comfort you after your weary vigils in this place, for I admire your constancy and am sorry for your pains." Then the watchful spy was glad, for the goddess had conquered, and her lover and victim lay on the rock whence she had vanished, imploring mercy and beating his breast in self-contempt. Yaotl stole upon Yappan, and with a slash of his stone axe struck his head from his shoulders. The gods turned Yappan into a scorpion, whose forearms are often lifted, praying, and he crawled under the stone where he had dwelt, while Yaotl hurried away to the village where the pious man's wife lived, led her to the rock on which Yappan had perished, told her the story of his failure, sin, and death, and while she wept smote off her head too. She also became a scorpion and joined her husband, and from these two have come all the scorpions that hide beneath stones in shame and fear. But Yaotl had been too eager in his enmity to the fallen saint, and he had no excuse for slaying his wife, so the gods turned him into a locust,—a food for scorpions.

HUITZILOPOCHTLI

AMONG the many gods of the ancients in Mexico none had higher estimation than Huitzilopochtli, or Vitziliputzli, god of the air and god of war. He was born in the city of Tula after a miraculous conception. His mother, Coatilcue, renowned for the uprightness of her life, was walking in the temple court when a ball of gay feathers fell from the sunlit sky. She caught it in her hand and put it into her bosom, intending to decorate the altar with it, but at the end of her walk it had disappeared, and she discovered, to her astonishment, that she was about to become a mother. She already had many children, who said that she was dishonored, and they planned to kill her; but the unborn god cried to her not to fear, that he would avert the danger and bring renown upon her. And with a war-whoop that rang through the city he leaped into being, full-grown, plumed and painted for battle, a spear and shield in his hands. He fell upon his brothers and slew them for their meditated cruelty, and took the name of Tezahuitl, the Terror. Like Moses, he led his people through the wilderness for many years, to find the best land for their homes. He introduced dress and other comforts, made laws, invented ceremonies, and conferred on his people the gift of fire. Gigantic statues of him were set up in his temple, and to him were offered more sacrifices than to any other of the deities. It was believed in after-years that the devil spoke through his skull—his bones were canonized in Tenochtitlan—and ordered these cruelties. Around his temple in the city of Mexico were rows of trees joined by rods, rank on rank of them. From the feet of the trees nearly to their tops these rods were hung with the heads of prisoners who had been slain on his altars. When they fell to fragments others were put in their places. He himself showed in what way he preferred his sacrifices, for his priests having offended him, he fell upon them in the night, cut them open, pulled their hearts out, and this abominable method prevailed until the arrival of the Spaniards, who did that much of good, at all events: they stopped religious murder, their own murders being merely those of policy and conquest. Images of the war-god were made of dough kneaded by the priests with the blood of children, and to such images the people thronged with offerings, and deemed themselves blessed if they could touch the object, even as others struggle to kiss and touch holy relics in Italy and New York in our own day. In some places an image of this god, made of bread, was broken and eaten by the populace every year, the women alone being forbidden to eat of it. Slaves were bought and fattened for his altars, and it is said that human sacrifice began in his temples, the first one occurring in the thirteenth or fourteenth century. Others say that the first sacrifices were made by the Aztecs while they were captives of the Culhuas. They did not dare to attack their masters, but they showed their willingness to shed blood, and revealed a dangerous power by falling upon and slaying four captives, ripping out their hearts and throwing them into the lap of a stone statue of Huitzilopochtli. This frightened the Culhuas, and they let them start on their long migration. While most of the sacrifices were of captives, some were of young men who were solemnly slain, after a month or so of liberty and feasting, that they might bear messages, complaints, compliments, and prayers to the gods. But happiest was the soldier who died in battle defending his country, for he was caught up from the field by the wife of Huitzilopochtli and taken to the sun-house that stood in the eastern heavens amid gardens of fruit and honey-yielding flowers, and wide pastures where game abounded. Every morning when the sun left his home the translated warriors marched before him, flourishing their spears, that seemed like light-rays, and singing their proud songs of battle.

THE WAR-GOD TAKES A BRIDE

IT is said that Huitzilopochtli wearied of mere punishment sacrifices—the offering of beaten armies on his altars—and longed for a fairer gift. He was lonely : he wished for a sister, a companion, a wife. So he afflicted the earth for a time, as a sign of his displeasure and his need, that the oracles might tell the inquiring people what to do. It may have been a long rain, a drouth, a plague, a series of hurricanes ; whatever it was, the populace groaned and asked the priests how they might avert its continuance, and the priests, inspired by the god, bade the Aztec emperor send a princess to him. A messenger was despatched to the king of the Culhuacans, to beg that he would honor his favorite daughter by making her the bride of the war-god and sharer of his throne. Flattered and frightened, for he had reason to hold the Aztecs, as well as the god, in fear, realizing, too, that unless he brought the affliction of the people to a quick end they would not be slow to avenge the selfishness of his love with the destruction of himself and his family, the king took a tearful farewell of his daughter, who in gorgeous robes and flowers was escorted to the altar. The pomps having been observed and the murder committed, a ceremony followed which consisted in the flaying of the victim and a public wearing of the skin by the priest who had taken the life. With good intention, doubtless, but with a refinement of cruelty, the Aztec emperor asked the king to attend his girl's deification. He entered the temple after the killing, for that he could not bear, and was groping his way forward in the darkness, when a copal torch flashed up and he saw the priest beside Huitzilopochtli's statue, receiving the homage of the multitude and dressed in the freshly stripped skin, that still bore a ghastly suggestion of the victim. The king shuddered and moaned in grief and horror and rushed from the place to vent his sorrow beneath the stars. The stars? Yes, there was comfort. Was not one of them now his daughter? If only he could know the one!

EL DORADO

EL DORADO (the Gilded) has come to be a term signifying a wealthy place, a wealthy land, a paying enterprise. It means nothing of the kind, however. It relates to a gilded youth, and here again tradition justifies a common phrase. He was a Chibcha chief, who anointed his body with fragrant gums, and over whom his priests twice a day blew gold-dust, through a bamboo. In 1536 three expeditions set out for the conquest of the present republic of Colombia : Fredemann's troop, from Venezuela ; Quesada's, which ascended the Magdalena River; and Pizarro's, that went up from Peru in charge of Benalcazar. Oddly enough, they reached the plain of Bogota almost together, Fredemann's company arrayed in skins, Quesada's dressed like the natives, and Benalcazar's in glittering armor, with banners. Quesada had divided two hundred and fifty thousand dollars in gold and two thousand emeralds among his men before he met the others, but none of them had seen El Dorado, from whose coffers they expected to plunder gold and gems far in excess of this, and the wealth alleged to have been stored in the temple of Suamoz was never taken out of its ruins. Its priest fired it on the approach of the Spaniards and was crushed by the tumbling walls, with him perishing " the traditions of a people and the history of a nation." Gold was picked up in other temples, and to this day is found in ancient graves. Ornaments and images of the metal have been discovered in the sabana, the lagoons of which are thought to have been held sacred. Their sanctity may have arisen from some tradition of the tremendous cataclysm by which the great lake that once filled this valley was drained through the gorge of the Tequendama. With the lowering of the waters were revealed the gold-bearing ledges and gravels that furnished to the Indians a wealth abundant and unprized.

Myths and Legends

El Dorado ruled in Manoa, a city that may have been some other than the predecessor of Bogota. On state occasions he showed himself to his people all shining with gold, and threw metals, emeralds, and such gifts into a sacred lake, where he bathed presently. In addition to the three expeditions named, others essayed the mountain country in various directions, and, while El Dorado eluded them, considerable geography was added to the world's meagre store of that science. Orellana declared that he found El Dorado in a voyage down the Amazon in 1540, but he didn't. He may not have been a wilful liar, however, because the practice alleged of the Colombian natives may have been followed elsewhere, and may, indeed, be the source of the El Dorado story. It was that of anointing and gilding a chief on a certain festival, the gilded one personifying the sun. It is a wee bit unlikely that any man could endure to be gummed and gold-plated for any length of time. The clogging of his skin-pores would at least injure his complexion. It is related of a boy who was gilded and carried in a religious procession, to represent the infant Christ effulgent, that he died in a few hours, because he could not perspire. The Spaniards never thought upon these matters. They were willing to perspire, some, themselves if they could only get the gold that had been won by the sweat of other people.

THE DWARF'S HOUSE

UXMAL has three famous ruins, the palace of Las Monjas, the Governor's House, and the Dwarf's House, which are monuments of an extinct civilization, and remarkable for the soundness of the masonry and the richness of their decoration. The Dwarf's House crowns a steep mound a hundred feet high. It contains three rooms decorated with masonic symbols, with an elephant's head above the entrance. A curtain formerly concealed the rites and tragedies enacted within. Its story is this: The son of a famous witch was a favorite among the people, although he was a mere dwarf in size. They courted him, because they feared his mother. The gifts and flattery lavished on this little creature excited the jealousy of the king, who, pretending kindness, took him into his family and by gradually increasing honors that involved the doing of much work he hoped to exhaust the boy and bring him into contempt for disobedience, that he might punish him with death. But with the help of his mother the boy always managed to do what was required of him. At last the king ordered him to build a mound and a house on its top in a single night. He ran home, crying, " Mother, I am dead. This task is beyond me." And he told her what he had been commanded to do.

" Do not be troubled," answered the sorceress. " All will be well in the morning."

Sure enough, there stood the mound and the house at sunrise. Though secretly enraged, the king thanked the dwarf and expressed his pleasure in the work. "And now," said he, "I give you my daughter in marriage. Only, it will be a condition that I first break six cocoyoles on your head."

"But I don't wish to marry, and I am not so vain or ambitious as to expect to wed into the family of a king. As to the nuts, I know that cocoyoles are very hard, and while my skull is as thick as some others, I doubt if it will stand the thumping."

"Pah! A mere ceremony. Surely a princess is worth a twinge."

The dwarf ran back to his mother. "He will surely kill me now," he said; and he told of his fresh misfortune.

"Go back and tell the king that you will let him break the nuts against your head if, afterward, he will let you break the same number against his."

The dwarf asked if this agreement would please his majesty, and the king laughed his willingness. He intended to kill the dwarf at the first blow. But the witch had rubbed a magic ointment on her son's head, so that it was like iron, and though the king broke all six of the cocoyoles over his head, the youth did not even wink. Greatly disappointed and much astonished, the king pretended to congratulate the dwarf on his courage and the firmness of his bones. Then, with some misgivings, he placed his own head on the earth, to undergo the same test. He did not survive it. The first blow smashed the cocoyol, but also cracked the monarch's pate. The test had been fair. The dwarf had proved himself the stouter of the two. So the populace buried the king and placed the dwarf on his throne, while his marriage to the princess was celebrated with great splendor.

WHY VALDEZ BOUGHT PRAYERS

BEFORE the railroad days Juan Valdez was the engineer of a mule-train that plied between Monterey and Guadalajara. It was rough travel, with steep grades, and, with to-morrow always ahead of one, why should a freighter expect to cover more than four or five miles in a day? Coming o' this easy fashion to Saltillo, on one journey, Valdez went to the cathedral to give thanks that he had, so far, been preserved from brigands and broken harness, and perhaps to pray in secret that he might have a few worthy temptations thrown in his way during the next week. Returning toward his wagons in the light of a young moon, he passed an old adobe house, large, though a single story high, whose ruin was so particularly mournful that he paused before it and waited to hear a night-bird's call, as if he were sure it would come out of the rank trees that had grown up in the patio and leaned over the skeleton roof. There was no hurry, so he loitered about the place, held by a sort of fascination, and finally entered the court, stirring dust out of the rotting timbers that he kicked, evolving melancholy smells of decay, and bringing at last the startling quaver that he had expected from the trees,—a bird's protest. Over an old well in the middle of the patio dangled a rope, swinging in the breeze. Pshaw! It was too saddening. He would go up to the plaza where all the people were, and hear the band play. Yet—look! He is not alone.

In a little space of light, so phosphorescent that he seems to carry it, stands a child, looking from the door of the hall. It is a poor, misshapen little thing, hump-backed, hollow-chested, with one short leg, and it holds its hands out to feel its way, as though its eyes were poor. Great, sad eyes they are, and the face is that of a being who has never known love or tenderness. Valdez's heart goes out to it. With a simple gesture the boy beckons to the teamster and limps through a gap in what had been the stable, as if expecting the man to follow. This he does, for his curiosity is now keen, though he stops to mutter an *ave* when the boy swings open a rickety door and descends into a cellar,—an unusual adjunct of a Mexican house. But it is not a cellar: it is a vault, through which flows the water that supplies the well. Where the light comes from now Valdez does not know; yet there is light in the place, at least enough to see that two other figures have come down the stair behind him. He can hear his own heart going like a hammer. Why has he been lured down here? The two others have not seen him, and he stands breathless. The boy is looking into the water and has not seen them either. Heaven! What creatures! One is a man with a purple face and a neck marked by a rope. His head swings loosely on his shoulders, as if he could not raise it. The other is a woman with streaks of blue in her flesh. Corruption has set in. Both look with hate at the child, then smile meaningly. They steal forward. The woman clutches the boy. The man pulls out a knife. Once—twice—it falls. A splash is heard. The two exchange a look, half fright, half joy. Then it is very dark. Nearly crazed with terror, Valdez stumbles up the stairs, rips and crashes through the weeds and rotting beams, and regains the quiet street. Pistol in hand, he waits to see if he is followed. No: it is all still in there. He goes back to the cathedral, rouses a sleepy priest, and counts a dozen silver reals into his hand. " Pray out of purgatory," he says, " the soul of a little cripple who has been murdered by his parents."

" In this city ?"

" In this city."

" When ?"

" Alas, father, I cannot tell. Perhaps it was years ago. But I saw the murder done—to-night."

FATHER JOSÉ'S LOVE

FIERCE troubles came upon New Spain as the seventeenth century was drawing to its end, and the stout old soldier, Diego de Vargas, was hurried north to crush the Pueblos in their strongholds. As lieutenant he took his son, José, despite the setting of the march for the very day whereon the young man was to have married Doña Ana de Orñate. The sadness of the parting was softened, so much as might be, by assurances that the troops would soon return, and who knew but they might bring some of the wealth of Cibola with them? In that event the Doña Ana should be jewelled like a queen, should live in the fairest hacienda in Mexico, should have slaves and servants, and a gilded carriage; yes, if she chose, she should live in old Spain and ruffle it with the proudest of the old families. And so, watched through tear-dimmed eyes, the troop set off.

The Indians were not so easily put down. They were fighting for their homes, their religion, their lives, and they fought well. Nearly two years passed before the army went back to Mexico City, worn, broken, sadly less in numbers. They had beaten the red men, but it had cost many lives and two human hearts to do it, for on a report that José had been killed in battle Ana had withdrawn to a convent; and finding that he was thus deserted, José cursed the church and its priests who had robbed him of his treasure. In a cooler hour he repented this frenzy. He begged and received comfort from the blessed Saint Francis, who appeared to him in a dream, promising forgiveness if he, too, would live the religious life. The world held nothing for him longer: he became a monk, asking only that the bishop would send him away from a city where the sight of familiar objects kept memory alive to torture him. So he was ordered to the Franciscan monastery in Monterey, there to enlighten and gospel the heathen, to care for the sick, to teach useful arts, and all this he did, softened by a sincerity of repentance for his blasphemy and thankfulness that it had been forgiven. Though he had been a soldier and had tasted wild, free life, his bent was toward books and gentle things, and—he could not deny it—toward the memory of that fairest of beings, the Doña Ana. He could pray her image out of his mind in chapel, but in his dreams he was not his own master, and neither prayers, fasts, nor penances could prevent the rising of that vision, pale, appealing, yes, seductive, at his bedside.

Returning on a hot day toward the monastery from the chapel of Our Lady of Guadalupe, where he had just said mass for a company of stolid Indians, Father José—he kept his worldly name—drooped to the ground in the shade of the palms that grow below the chapel, and thought and suffered. Before him lay a tiny palm that some wayfarer had carelessly plucked up and tossed upon the ground, and as carelessly he took it up and switched the dusty earth with it; yet, somehow, his compassion was moved for its thwarted life: it recalled his own; he would befriend it. Plunging it into an irrigating canal that flowed lazily and turbidly past him, he washed it free of dust and felt something of life stir in the wilted leaves and stem. Then, packing it in moss, he walked to the town more hurriedly than usual, and planted the little thing in the garden, where he could see it from his cell. He tended it as palms are seldom tended in that country, loosening the earth at its roots when it became hard, freeing it from scale and insects, picking off dead leaves, watering it in the dry season, and shortly it dawned upon him that the love he could not give to a woman he was bestowing on a tree. Perhaps in its grace, its beauty, its uncertainty, it reminded him of a woman, and he felt that as it owed its life and strength to his care, it had a love for him. It grew prodigiously and was most fair to look on,— as you may see, when you visit Monterey,—and sitting in its shadow, his arm about the trunk, he was nearer to content.

As the tree gained in beauty he increased in age. His face was sad and pale, and lines were cutting themselves upon it. Then came the fever, the dreaded typhus, and townsmen, monks, soldiers, Indians, were struck down as in a battle. He attended them constantly, ministering to the sick, praying for the dying. Every house was a hospital, and for the first time the Capuchina nuns were released, and went into the town to give comfort to the tortured and the perishing,—a breach of vow for which they readily gained absolution from Rome. Worn with his work, José caught the fever too, and at its height he had dragged himself to his cell to die. Knowing that his end was near, he begged the brothers to carry him to his palm-tree and so leave him. He leaned against it and watched the great peaks in the west, toward which the sun was sinking as fast as his own life ebbed; but it was sweet to end the world like that; to fade like the day; to see beauty to the last. He started. His pulse leaped wildly. A woman was coming up the path, a Capuchina. Their eyes met. With a little sob and cry the woman sank to her knees and wet his hand with her tears. It was Doña Ana. For an hour they were together, calm, after the first agitation had passed, their hands clasped, his voice growing fainter, her face more saintly resigned. Now the sun was down. A wan smile struggled over the man's lips; a breeze shook the palm-leaves overhead, and he raised his eyes to the golden glory in the sky. Palm-leaves? They used to betoken victory. The Angelus rang out, musical and silvery, and a star trembled like a tear on the brow of Mitra. It was an hour of peace. Father José's long unhappiness was over.

THE DEVIL IN PRISON

TO Ojinaja, on the Rio Grande, came a Spanish priest in some forgotten year of the eighteenth century, and set up his abode there among the Indians. He taught Christianity, which the people were slow to accept, and he sensibly avoided any attempt to force his religion on them, preferring to show in his own life the advantages that enlightened people enjoyed over savages. In time his good offices had so won their confidence that he gained a sort of chieftaincy among them, yet they clung to their old beliefs and secretly wearied him with their unreasonable superstitions. At length a visitor arrived in Ojinaja who completely changed the aspect of affairs in that village, and converted every Indian to the true faith overnight. That visitor was the devil.

The good father had left his house and gone up the valley for his evening meditations, and had been absent for a couple of hours, when he came running back to the Indians, crying that he had seen the devil, had chased him up the side of a mountain, and had shut him up in a cave on the summit. He had chanced to look up, he told them, and was astonished to see that the valley had been spanned by an immense chain, hung from one mountain to its opposite, and that a fierce-looking creature was seated in the sag of it, swinging in a way to make one's head swim, for he flew a mile back and forth at every rise and fall. Realizing that this could be none other than the devil, the priest plucked his cross from a fold of his robe and held it toward the evil one ; for there is nothing that so affrights the fiend as the holy cross. And, truly, no sooner had he seen it than, with a howl of dismay, he ceased his sport and scrambled along the chain to one of its holds, tugged at it until the ends gave way, and fled up the height, dragging the two or three hundred tons of iron after him with a prodigious rattling.

The priest was close upon him, still holding the cross on high, when the devil, in a final effort at escape, rushed into the cave, still drawing his chain. As it was disappearing the pursuer touched it with his cross and the last link fell off. Then, with a cry of joy that he had so easily overcome the fiend, he planted the cross at the cave's mouth, thus making him prisoner, if not forever, at least so long as the emblem should be kept whole, and replaced when it decayed. Yet, to make more sure, he would have the people build a chapel there, and he asked them to follow him to the mountain-top, that they might know his story to be true. Keeping close together, with some fondness for being in the rear, the Ojinajans made the ascent, and were struck into a great trepidation when they heard the undoubted clank of metal within the cave. The priest bade them be of courage, to embrace the faith immediately, and help him to erect a shrine before the cavern that should secure them against further evil. This they did, and the chapel still stands on the peak of Ojinaja. The missing link from the devil's chain is preserved there among its relics, and every year, on the night of January 25, the natives climb to the little church, give thanks to God for their preservation, and feed bonfires on both sides of the valley, to express their joy in this escape.

THE ALLIGATOR-TREE

WHAT the English call the alligator-tree, that grows on the Tehuantepec isthmus, is known to the natives as the "alligator's tail." It affords a wood that promises to be of value in the building arts, and its rough, thorny bark suggests the skin of the lizard whose name it takes. In days of old the alligator was more respected than now, but for a different reason. It was because he was wise. He was represented in stone, clay, and wood, was painted on walls, and princes bowed before him. He became vastly proud of this distinction, and began to put on airs about it. Among the beliefs in his family was that of its need to live among the rivers. Salt water and cold water meant death. But the younger members of the tribe were discontented. They sniffed at the axioms of the fathers, and scorned the notion that they were to stay in one country forever.

They would travel and learn. They had heard men talking of the land beyond the mountains, where great cities were, of a sea that spread to the world's edge, of alligators larger and wiser than those of the Gulf side; so they held a meeting in the deepest and darkest forest on the Coatzacoalcos River and derided their elders for superstitious old fossils, and resolved to be at least as free as men were. "Those queer little creatures, with only two legs, thin skins, and no teeth to speak of, who cannot stay a minute under water, nor go for two days without food—they travel where they like, and why, therefore, should not we? Their gods are surely their betters, and the whole earth should be ours."

This speech, by one of the party, was instantly approved, and soon after a crowd of young alligators, several hundred in number, began the passage of the mountains. They ascended the Coatzacoalcos through the night, coming into an open country near the hills just as the sun was rising. Great was the surprise of all to find that the river was coming to an end, for they had supposed that they could cross to the Pacific without walking on dry ground. What excited their alarm, also, was the chill. The water grew so cold as they ascended that they could finally bear it no longer, but climbed upon the bank, where the sun fell warm upon them, and fell asleep. At nightfall came a god of the hills. "What are these monsters doing in my country?" he cried. "Have I not warned all creatures of the coast to keep to their own kingdom? Up with you, spirits of the springs, and help me to punish these fellows."

Then came the water elves capering down the hill-sides, curling and fawning about his feet, making a gurgling laughter as they thought of the surprise in store for the alligators. They whirled about and about until each had bored a hole two or three feet deep in the earth; then they seized the sleeping reptiles, and plunged them, head first, into the holes, with their tails in the air, and there they are, at the edge of the *tierra templada*, to this day. One alligator, who had hidden in the wood when the water sprites came down, escaped and swam down the river to his old home, where he told the sorrowing parents of the fate that had come upon the youngsters in punishment of their rashness, and the elders mourned, but vainly. Never since then have the alligators tried their fortunes out of the warm coast lands and waters.

EVIL SPIRITS IN THE SPRINGS

ATZCAPOTZALCO, near Mexico City, is renowned for two springs and somewhat feared because of them. The first, near the ruined Zancopinca aqueduct, is an innocent-looking pond of sweet water; but beware, especially if you hear singing; for down beneath it is the palace of

rock-crystal where the dreaded Malinche lives
during a half of each day. During the other half
she is in her spring at Chapultepec. Forbidding,
even fiendish, in her disposition in Atzcapotzalco,
she is angelic in Chapultepec. This is probably
because she adheres to the old gods of the nation
that linger about the battle hill, while the nearness
of Christian shrines and blessings in the other
home arouses every fell instinct in her nature.
She spends her days in Chapultepec and her nights
in the Zancopinca pool. At early morning and
in the evening she sings, and her voice bubbles
through the cool, clear flood in wondrous melody.
Christian, if you are one, be careful as you approach the edge. Down there the moving reflections of the sky resolve themselves into a lovely
form, a face with star eyes, hair like the finest
water moss. Put your hands upon your ears, hurry
off and say your prayers; for if you stay the song
will dull your sense like wine, a languor will en-
chain you and delude you with dreams. You will
bend over farther and farther, the face will smile
up at you, the graceful arms invite you, the buried
treasure of Guatamotzin, that Cortez could not
win, though he put its owner on the rack, will
glitter behind the figure, and it is all yours, nymph,
palace, treasure, all. You plunge forward. The
arms enfold you, and it grows dark. Christian intruder in the Aztec land, have you won joy, or
death?

In another direction you come upon a grove of large ahuehuetes surrounding a space where a fount once brimmed its basin,—brimmed, and never overflowed. It was so cool and pure, that spring, that in the warmth of mid-day the stranger coming upon it was moved to fall to his knees, bury his face below the surface and cool his dry throat with a long draught. Hapless mortal if he did so, for this spot, too, was inhabited by a spirit as dangerous as the Malinche, and at the first sip the drinker disappeared, nor ever again returned to the air in the sight of men. One day a procession of priests emerged from the church, not far away, carrying the Virgin's image and chanting solemnly. They walked up the road as far as the spring, set up an altar for the statue beside it, one of their number mounted its step and preached against the wickedness of the water sprite, then all threw in stones and earth until the basin was filled, and a chapel was presently built above it to keep the water down. In time the chapel crumbled away, and the spring may yet be free again ; for, if you listen, you may hear it, deep down, laughing softly to itself. It is as much alive as ever, and who knows—— ?

DEVILS AND DOUBLOONS

DEVILS and doubloons have been perplexingly associated for more than two centuries among the West Indies and neighboring coasts. Often the devils guarded the doubloons out of fondness for the pirates who had hidden them, and sometimes the pirates were pretty good imitations of devils themselves. Wherever there is wealth sin is not far. The love of money is a root of several evils. How many shaggy creatures have been marooned on the sand keys from the Carolinas southward, how many have been killed there in wrangles over the division of treasure, and how much treasure was unearthed during the absence of its winners in distant ports, can never be guessed, but the memory of these crimes and burials haunts thousands of miles of shore. Very likely it was the discovery of so strange a race as the Indians that forced the first explorers into a belief that the New World was filled with devils, yet even remote and lonely places, without mortal inhabitants, were so peopled. The Bermudas, for example, were regarded as inaccessible, darkened by terrors, and were known as the Devils' Islands. They belonged to Ferdinand Camelo, a Portuguese, who merely put his initials on a cliff, together with a cross, the one to keep the English off, the other to frighten away the imps. He may have succeeded with the imps, but an English ship went ashore on one of Camelo's islands, and—well, pretty soon the English owned them all.

To our own day strange things inhabit the tropical belt of the Western world. Jamaica has its "duppies" and "rolling calves," that prank around in the night, pestering poor negroes. Porto Rico was one of the islands on which the prophecy was given, before the coming of Columbus, of "ruin and desolation by the arrival of strangers, completely clad, and armed with the lightning of heaven." Days were set for solemn dances and lamentations, in a hope of deferring the dreadful time, and these ceremonies lasted into the years of white ownership, for other devils than the white ones had also been discovered. Mugeres Island, off British Honduras, has had its devils in the flesh and out of it, for it has a typical buried-treasure story : Pirates went ashore there in the last century with the sack of a coast town, including coin, communion cups, and bishop's jewels, which they had sealed in large lead boxes. These chests were lowered into a pit at the north end of the island, sixty steps from water, and covered with tarpaulin. The captain asked for volunteers to guard them, and two negroes of the crew stepped forward, thinking to live there pleasantly, without work, and perchance to rob the robbers as soon as the ship was out of sight. Mistaken fellows ! They did not know the traditions of their trade. The captain pulled out his pistols and shot them dead. Their bodies were thrown upon the tarpaulin, then covered with sand, the captain saying that they would care for the treasure better dead than alive, for their ghosts would drive away intruders, and, beside, any one finding bones would dig no farther. This treasure can be taken up only by the one for whom fate intends it. The watchful, jealous people of the island, who still hope to find it themselves, say they will kill any other. Do you wish to try your luck?

INCIDENTS OF WAR

IN reading the history of South America it seems as if its normal state for three centuries had been that of war. Originally the people were lovers of peace. Such were the thirty million Inca Indians to whom Manco Capac, son of the Sun, preached gentleness and justice on the bank of Lake Titicaca, for whom he built roads like those of the Romans, one of them extending from Cuzco to Quito, almost two thousand miles, and for whom he erected a temple of the sun with its roof of seven hundred gold plates, each of them a burden for four men. Among these people—the first successful communists—Pizarro and his Spaniards wrought havoc. Though teaching Christianity and promising rewards after death for an intolerable patience in this life, the invaders were false to every tenet of their own faith, for they robbed, enslaved, tortured, and slew the natives, and showed them easy ways to self-destruction through sins and vices. Greatest of these vices was war. Uneducated, priest-ridden, swindled, and oppressed, the people arose from time to time, yet never won a real or lasting liberty. The arts found meagre expression, industries never became important, road-building lapsed into a forgotten art, and caste, implanted by the Spaniards, was inherited by the republics. Revolutions were not accomplished by votes, but by the sword. The idol of one decade was in the next the prisoner, the fugitive, the suicide. Victories were celebrated by pillage and massacre. The policy toward the purely Indian tribes was destructive. When Mendoza marched against the Araucanians—those fierce soldiers, who took nightly courage from the heavens, for they believed that the stars were their dead but still conquering brothers—he defeated, but could never subdue them. He gathered a large company of these Indians into his fort by making them believe his men to be asleep and at their mercy; then, closing his gates, he fell upon and killed them every one. Their chief, Caupolican, being captured alive, was solemnly and benignantly baptized, then flung upon sharp spikes and there allowed·to die.

Barbarous, inexcusable as many of these wars have been, they seem to have tended toward a higher liberty and a sounder, if more boastful, national strength. They have developed heroes and heroic attributes, and they have abolished crowns from the Western hemisphere. Among the incidents of battle that one contemplates with a more admiring disposition than is inspired by the usual savagery is the exploit of General Pringle at Chancai. The war for Peruvian liberation was desperately waged, and no fighters were more stern than the troops from the Argentine, some of them of English descent, who had climbed over the Andes and come up from the Chilian cities in ships to engage the Spaniards. At Chancai, where the rebel army was outnumbered ten to one, the defeat was total, yet the battle was fought so stoutly that of all the Argentines but three were left uncaptured and unhurt. One of these was Pringle, who, crying to his companions, "We will not be taken; follow me!" rode along the sea-wall until he reached deep water, then leaped in, heading the horses toward a beach. The click of locks sounded along the Spanish line, and fifty muskets covered them; but before trigger could be drawn, the Spanish general, Alvarado, cried to his men, "Stop! Not another shot! These men are soldiers worthy the name. Their courage shall be respected." Then, calling to the horsemen, he told them they might return in safety and leave the field unchallenged. The Argentines gained a landing-place, and, with a salute and a cheer on either side, they dashed away. They had gained a victory in defeat.

GAMBLING AWAY THE SUN

THE disk of solid gold that represented the sun in the temple of Cuzco fell to one of Pizarro's scallawags, Mancio Sierra Lejesama, in a division of Peruvian spoil. It could be melted into doubloons enough to keep the wight in wine and bad company for ten years, if he could prevent his throat from being slit that long, and for a while he seriously thought of cutting away from his ruffling associates and returning to Spain to enjoy life as a guzzling libertine, and possibly to wear a title. But his old ways were too strong upon him. He had been a gambler, and a gambler he was still. Could he play but one more winning game and get some of his comrades' cups and rings away from them, there was no doubt that he would be able to live without work for the rest of his life. " Come, gentlemen," he cried, " I am going to give you the greatest chance you ever had. This time it is no beggarly handful of yellow boys we'll toss the cards for, but the great sun of Peru itself. We will play for the biggest stake in history." The game was long and earnest. Lejesama lost. He arose from the table silent, crushed, convinced as never before of his own folly. The gold was gone, but he brought out of his meditations what was better, a chastened spirit. He abandoned stealing and gaming, took an Inca's daughter to wife, worked for the welfare of the people he had

injured, and left behind him, as a token of his re-
form, a history of and tribute to the Peruvians.
One of his sayings lives in Spain to this day. It
is, " He plays the sun away before it rises." This
means that a person is an incurable spendthrift.

HUASCAR'S PROPHECY

YEARS had gone by since Huanya Capac, last
of the Incas, had donned the jewelled sash
and lifted the rainbow banner of kingship. The
festivities attending his enthronement lasted for
many days, and included many dances in the Garden
of Delights at Yucay, a dozen miles from Cuzco,
where sacred birds were kept among flowers of
gold and silver plate and leaves of emerald, where
nobles bathed in tubs of gold, and where dancing-
girls went before the Inca, strewing fresh blossoms for his sandalled feet. Peace and plenty were
in the land, but their end was near, for Pizarro
and his prayer-pattering rapscallions were on their
way toward the new world. Huanya Capac had
marched to Quito,—the city where the invading
Caras, descending the River of the Emeralds in
the year 1000, had built great temples to the sun
and moon, the one with its disk of gold flashing
reflections on the priests, the other with its plaque
of silver that repeated the beams of the rising
moon. Here the last of the Incas worshipped, and
here the people worshipped him. At the end of

his reign he left the empire, not to the true heir, Huascar, but to him jointly with his brother, Atahualpa. It was soon evident that no throne is large enough for two. The brothers quarrelled, and Atahualpa, being the stronger and more ambitious, soon gained the ascendency over Huascar, who was a man of gentle nature. Then came the Spaniards, who robbed the Incas of everything except their title, which they would allow only one of them to wear. The wicked brother saw that the kingship was slipping from his grasp. He resolved to hold it at the cost of crime. His retainers seized Huascar and drowned him in the Andamarca. Before he was cast into the river Huascar cried to his tyrant brother, who stood scowling on the bank, "What you do to me the white man will do to you. He will soon avenge me."

Not long afterward Pizarro had imprisoned Atahualpa, in spite of his many friendly services. "Let me go," begged the king, "and I will cover the floor of this cell with gold."

Pizarro shook his head.

"Let me go, and I will fill this cell with golden vessels, as high as I can reach."

"That is well. You shall have your liberty when your people have brought the gold."

It took a long time to collect such a quantity of treasure. Pizarro took it as fast as it came in; then, alleging that his prisoner had plotted against him, he condemned him to die at the stake in the square of Caxamalca. As a concession to morality, the victim was urged to become a Christian, and as a reward for changing his faith was told that he might enjoy a death by strangling instead of burning. The Inca allowed himself to be baptized, and after passing from the hands of the priests to those of the garroter he became a public show in death. Then a requiem mass was sung for him. During the service the people rushed into the church, that they might be killed at his side by the Spaniards, and so reach the sun in his company. But death was waiting for a third one of the actors in this tragedy, and it came swiftly. Jealous of the master thief, some of his followers broke into the house of Pizarro, and although he mortally wounded one, he had his own quietus at the instant. With finger dipped in his own blood the bravo wrote the word "Jesus" on the floor, and died as he tried to kiss it. Not one human being remained in that house to mourn.

THE MEDAL AND THE ORCHID

THOSE who have lived among the natives of South America say that they are a finer people, morally and mentally, than their northern cousins. Their life is under less stress, therefore less heroic, than that of the Sioux and others who obtain their subsistence by the hunt on the wide, cold plains, and they come from a stock that was more than half civilized, enjoying, therefore, a heritage of refinement and intelligence. When Europe awoke to the beauty of the orchid, seekers for this strange plant of the air began to invade the forests of the Amazon, for rare strains of it commanded little fortunes from rich amateurs. Among these hunters was a French botanist, Pierre de Vert, a young man who had given his life to study. He was retiring, sensitive, and religious, as those are apt to be who spend their years in the company of woods and mountains, and to him an orchid was not merely a flower: it was a problem, a mystery, a symbol.

A Paris nobleman had offered a prize for the most beautiful flower that could be found for the Easter festival, and knowing Pierre's love for orchids he gave him money for a trip to Guiana, together with a medal which the Pope had blessed and which in case of a pecuniary strait would assure his return to France, for its gold value was five hundred francs. Landing in Cayenne, Pierre set off at once for Mount Roraima, of which fabulous tales had reached his ears, and, careless of malaria, of tormenting insects, of wild beasts, of loathsome snakes, he reached the highlands where he hoped to find the largest and most striking of the orchids. During his search he stumbled on the habitations of a rude hill tribe of savages. They were unable to understand why he had come among them;

they had suffered from the treachery and misconduct of the whites; they disbelieved him when he said that he had travelled all the way from the farther shore of the great water to seek flowers, because flowers could be had in any place: so they took him prisoner, and the unrestrained clamored to have him roasted. They searched his pockets and took his money. They had seen enough of white men to know how many vices could be indulged with gold. "Is this all?" asked the chief, holding the coins before him.

Pierre was about to answer, "Yes," but as he placed his hand on his heart he felt the medal there. He could not lie.

"All?" repeated the Indian.

Pierre bit his lip and looked into the sky. It was hard to be robbed of every coin, and have to give up his medal also.

"All?" demanded the chief again.

Pierre shook his head, parted his clothing at the throat, and revealed the medal.

"The lad will not lie, yet he is white!" exclaimed one of his captors, in astonishment.

"It is his soul that is white," declared another.

The people would not touch the medal. Pierre had won them. They made a bed of fragrant leaves for him, and he slept unguarded until the call of birds aroused him in the morning. When the Indians had shared their meal with him they gave back the money they had taken. "You are good," they said. "You do not deceive. Keep your coins and rest, and we will help you."

The people dispersed, and did not return until night. When they came back they were laden with the strangest and most exquisite blossoms, whose heavy perfume was almost overpowering. One of these was of remarkable size and color, and that one, Pierre knew, would win the prize. He detached the plant from the tree to which it had fastened, and some weeks afterward it bloomed in Notre Dame. The wonder and admiration of the people were almost reward enough for his toil and hardship. With the money he received as a prize he returned to Guiana and taught the gospel to the Indians.

THE HONEST MULETEERS

ROUGH and ignorant as are some of the mountain men, honesty is no rare virtue. Old José of Coquimbo had been guide, freighter, and messenger across the Cordilleras since boyhood, and the priest was not more surely trusted than he. The mines had been worked as never before one summer, and there were many laborers up there in the mountains awaiting their pay. "It will be a heavy bag for you to carry this time, friend José," said the superintendent. "I am putting two hundred gold doubloons in your charge."

"They shall be safe with me, señor."

"I know it, José. To hide it the better we will put half the weight at one end of the bag and half at the other, for we can tie the mouth of it secure. Now, put it across your mule's back, under the saddle and the blanket, so it shall not be seen, then wear your longest poncho, and I'll warrant there'll be no danger."

Three thousand dollars in gold is not so great a burden, yet it is not a thing to exhibit to the covetous and lawless; so the best place for it was under the saddle, no doubt. José rode away toward the snowy peaks; he reached the desert at the rise of the moon and rode on, enjoying the vastness, the silence, and the stars until his mule began to go heavily. "Anita, girl, we're not so light on this trip as usual, eh? Come, then. We'll rest. There's no forage for you but this handful of oats, and no water till we reach the hills, but you shall sleep. Only, you must wear the saddle this time, for there's something under it—aha!—something to make the eyes of the peons sparkle when they shall see it." He put his hand under the saddle. Yes, the doubloons on the right side were safe. He went around to the other side, reached up, and— the money was gone! The string had untied, and the gold had been spilt among the desert sands. Lost! And his good name! Would they not believe him to be a thief? Or, if they thought him honest, would they ever trust money to him again? His heart sank until he felt a sickness.

Nothing could be done until day, and he would spend the rest of the night praying that he might find the missing gold. With the rise of the sun he started back afoot, leading his mule and examining every foot of the way. He had gone only two or three miles when a cloud of dust appeared away out on the plain. It drew nearer. It was a pack-train with ten drivers. He knew them all, for they had been his pupils in the business,—true-hearted lads every one. They were laughing and calling. "They would not laugh if they knew how ashamed and miserable I am," he said.

"Ho, friend José," called the first, as he galloped up to the old man, "why are you pulling so long a face?"

"I have lost half a bag of doubloons, and my reputation, and my peace of mind."

"I cannot return the peace of mind, but here are ten of the doubloons. I found them in the sand."

"Thanks to God. My sorrow is by so much the less."

Then came the second muleteer. "Father José," he cried, "what is lacking with you?"

"Ninety doubloons," said José.

"Tut! It is only eighty, for here are ten."

Then followed Domingo and Carlos and the rest, each with his question and his ten coins, until the last, who had but nine,—for so they had divided the treasure. The missing piece had been trodden into the sand and lost. Between them all they made up the hundredth doubloon. José went to his knees, and with wet eyes raised toward the sky he thanked God that his prayer had been heard, that neither the treasure nor his honor had been lost. The bag was now so tied and sewed and twisted that its contents could not possibly be spilled again; then, with lightened heart, José rode on at the head of the train, singing. "Boys," he said, after a time, "I taught you to ride, to swim, to ford, to pack, to make camp, to splice and hitch, and all the rest of it; but I've got my reward now when I find that all of you are honest."

AIGUERRE'S FIRE

IN the times when Indians lived in villages built on stilts in Lake Maracaibo, thus gaining for their province the name of Venezuela (Little Venice), there was a *farol* that hung about the southern end of that sheet of water. This "lantern" appeared to shine through a pale mist and often affrighted the people. It has been seen in our own day, and ascribed to malignant spirits. But the water flames are less malignant than the land fire. If any fortune sets you down on the Venezuelan plains, beware the ghost of Aiguerre. Bitterly has he suffered whose purgatory is the pampas, but he tries to make others suffer not less bitterly. Lope de Aiguerre, who discovered the upper Amazon, was, like too many of the explorers from his country and of his day, a harsh oppressor, a greedy seeker after others' wealth. On his appointment as governor of this southern country he bent all public interests to his own advantage, tyrannizing over the whites as savagely as over the Indians. He had the hate of nearly all men, and of heaven, too, for after his death in these wilds his soul was compelled to haunt the plains, appearing to the lonely cattlemen as the will-o'-the-wisp, or Aiguerre's fire, and if you draw near you will see, with horror, that in the centre of the flame the entrails of the wretch are burning. No native in his sober senses will go near. He knows the danger. For no sooner is such a follower beyond call and sight of his companions than he falls under the enchantment of the light. He forgets time and space, he is hypnotized, if you prefer, and rides on and on, until presently he finds himself at the brink of a ravine or a morass with the light dancing before his face, red, confusing, mocking. Lucky indeed is it for him if he can pull up his horse or bring himself to a stop. Too commonly he pitches into the abyss, or sinks into the marsh's black embrace, and if his body is ever found it is buried hastily, for the people who do that service are quick to get away from a spot that has been cursed by another of the tragedies of Aiguerre.

THE AMAZONS

CERTAIN women of the tribes living along
the Amazon wear beads of a green stone,
possibly jade or jadeite, possibly that more showy
if less valuable mineral, Amazon stone, a variety of
feldspar. When Cortez landed in Mexico, these
stones, which were from hearsay thought to be
emeralds, were worn by the Aztecs, who carved
them in strange and symbolical forms, such as fish
and parrots' heads. These ornaments were held
in great esteem by the natives, who valued them
more than gold. Their use probably spread from
Mexico through Peru and so to the Brazils, for the
women who now wear them say that they had
them from the first owners by direct inheritance,
and that they are amulets which preserve them from
many ills. Orellana, who first ascended the Amazon, was also the first to tell of the existence of a
tribe of female warriors in the great wilderness along
its banks. Certain of the Tupinambas women had
sworn an oath of chastity, agreeing among themselves to suffer death if they broke the compact.
They disdained the employments of other women,
rode horseback astride, after horses had been introduced into their country, and lived by the hunt,
like men. They were expert with bow and spear,
and they had servants to cook and make clothing
for them. So like were they to the women de-
scribed by Herodotus as living in Scythia and Libya

that it was natural to call them Amazons: hence the river along which they fished and hunted took that name. There are scholars, it is true, who declare that the name is Amassona, an Indian word meaning boat-destroyer, and applied to the terrible bore, or tide avalanche, that is encountered at full moon on the lower river. The fierce creatures of the Tupinambas shared the toil and peril of war with the men of their tribe, but they also fought by themselves, battling against male soldiers of the enemy with entire fearlessness.

BOLIVAR AT CARACAS

NATURE did not share in the dulness of Lent. On the contrary, she was full of promise for Easter joys. Flowers blazed on the lower slopes of the Andes, and bright birds flashed through the air. Holy Week of 1812 was nearly over; the people of Caracas were preparing to decorate their altars; their gatherers were out on the hills, collecting orchids and cactus blooms, and all was tranquil and beautiful. Two men walked apart at the city's edge, one of them tall, dark, garbed as a civilian, the other short, slight, strong-faced, suggesting, in his uniform, both Jackson and Napoleon. They were speaking of the progress made by the people in the fight against a foreign and monarchical government. Said the tall man, " Yet, Simon Bolivar, there are times when I fear.

Of late we often have smoke and dust in the air, and I have fancied that I heard faint rumblings and felt an ague in the earth. Suppose the masses should be told by some fanatic that these were signs of the divine wrath against our cause!"

"It would be sad. The people are credulous. They remember, too, that Caracas has already suffered from the anger of heaven, as some of them phrase it. We are walking at this moment in the basin of a lake that disappeared in a night. This city may be swallowed up in as short a time. But I believe that the just cause wins. Whatever happens, liberty will be ours."

The two men kept for some time in earnest talk, not noticing that the sky was becoming overcast and smoky, that the sun had grown red, that the day had lost its freshness and the very birds were uneasy. A portent seemed to be in the air. The mountains were fading. The silence and breathlessness had become intense. Sharing in the vague apprehension that began to possess all living things, General Bolivar and his companion started back toward the centre of the town. As he was recognized, the people cried, "The liberator! The liberator!" His strengthening presence gave comfort to them. In the churches the Lenten music was low and mournful, and in the dim light of their candles they were cavernous and full of mystery. Hark! From some unguessed place, in the sky or in the bowels of the earth, came a rumbling, as of thunder. Then, silence, in which creation held its breath to listen. Some of the people left the churches, unable to endure the oppression and suspense. Bolivar had paused at the cathedral door, when, with groan and crash and grinding of masonry, the earthquake came. Peaks toppled, cliffs broke and slid to their bases, the sea battered the coast in stupendous breakers, the air darkened to twilight, towers and houses fell, flames began to rise among their wrecks, the earth cracked and gaped and swallowed people, two volcanoes burst their seal of centuries and belched lava, while roarings and boomings added to the terror. The city melted like wax in the heat. It was soon over. Death and desolation are quickly wrought. Twelve thousand people were killed. Bolivar's heart sank as he looked about him on the panic-stricken survivors. In a sort of childlike helplessness they turned to him, standing on an eminence of ruin, and called again, "Liberator! Liberator!" He clambered down to them and urged on the work of rescue, with his own hands dragging blocks and beams from groaning victims, wiping dust and mortar from eyes that stared at the dusky heavens, restoring children to parents and binding the hurts of the wounded. "It is the wrath of heaven," cried one white-faced man. "God is against us."

"Silence!" commanded Bolivar. "To say that God sides with the tyrant is blasphemy. Our city is destroyed, but not our freedom. Neither men nor nature can avail against the right. Cities, governments, may fall, but justice, brotherhood,— nothing can shake them."

" It is true," cried another. " Our priests are dead, but God has spared our leader, Bolivar, to march with us to victory."

A wan gleam of the sun, piercing the dreadful canopy, lighted the face of the Liberator with a halo.

THE END

www.ingramcontent.com/pod-product-compliance
Lightning Source LLC
Chambersburg PA
CBHW020807060726

47498CB00017B/912